Piper Mejia is an advocate for New Zealand writers and literature. Her short fiction has been published in a range of magazines and anthologies, including *Room Enough for Two,* which appeared in the Sir Julius Vogel Award-winning anthology *Te Korero Ahi Ka* (2018). A collection of her original short stories, *The Better Sister,* was published by Breach in 2020. In addition to writing, Piper is a founding member of Young NZ Writers – a non-profit organisation dedicated to providing writing and publishing opportunities for young writers. As a child, Piper stayed up late laughing at horror films. As an adult she has never lost her love for science fiction and horror, two genres that continues to ask the question *"What if…"*

DISPOSSESSED

By Piper Mejia

This is a work of fiction. The events and characters portrayed herein are imaginary and are not intended to refer to specific places, events, or living persons. The opinions expressed in this manuscript are solely the opinions of the author and do not necessarily represent the opinions of the publisher.

Dispossessed

All Rights Reserved

ISBN-13: 978-1-925956-84-9

Copyright ©2021 Piper Mejia
V1.0

This book may not be reproduced, transmitted, or stored in whole or in part by any means, including graphic, electronic, or mechanical without the express written consent of the publisher except in the case of brief quotations embodied in critical articles and reviews.

Printed in Palatino Linotype and Aracnoide.

IFWG Publishing International
Gold Coast

www.ifwgpublishing.com

For my children - there's a little piece of each of you in every monster I imagine.

Acknowledgements

This novel would never have been completed without the support of my amazingly talented friends: Lee Murray, Jean Gilbert, Chad Dick, Lauren Haddock, Deryn Pittar, and Jan Morrison. Special shout out to Tauranga Writers and SPEC Fic NZ who have been a rock in supporting, promoting and publishing emerging NZ writers.

CHAPTER ONE

Even before the final bell rings, students stream across the school grounds, eager to celebrate their release for summer. Yearbooks flutter from hand to hand, the pages filling with optimistic messages that read like greeting cards. There's air-kissing and photobombing. Animated conversation.

Slate treads across the field, avoiding a collision with a group of energetic cheerleaders performing backflips and summersaults on the lawn.

"Creep." The fit and nimble debs are joined by their masculine counterparts, all flicking scorn in his direction. "Freak."

Slate cringes. His stranger-danger reputation is too well known by experiences too recent and too many to be forgotten with a little bright light and blue sky.

July again. Can it have been six years?

There are no summer diversions on Slate's mind, only a creeping dread of how to fill the empty time until he's forced to return to high school in September.

Two more years until I'm eighteen. Might as well be twenty.

Alone, with nowhere to go and no one to meet, Slate turns his back on the students and drags his feet along the pavement away from the school.

Caught in a recurring nightmare, too soon he's standing on the pavement in front of the house. He can't bring himself to call it home. The building is typical of the houses in purpose-built communities found all over California: sandy-coloured stucco exterior walls, with a two-car garage, a tiny front yard and a kidney-shaped swimming pool out the back. When he'd first arrived, it'd taken him a month to tell it apart from the other houses on the street without checking the number on the mailbox. Even the garden is filled with an identical arrangement of water-loving plants, as unsuited to the desert environment as Slate is to living with the Hosts.

Justin and Grace Host, his foster parents, have made a life of being exactly like everyone else. Being different is social suicide, and that includes not only their home, but also their physical appearance. On the day he arrived on their doorstep, he didn't need to see their faces drop to know wouldn't fit in with their Ken and Barbie lifestyle, their soccer mom carpool fantasy crushed at the sight of his mottled skin.

While his father had lovingly teased him about the uneven dark and light splotches, calling it a unique parental blend, the Hosts find his appearance an embarrassment. Despite the undesired accentuation of his thuggish qualities, they expect him to keep his deformity covered up in long-sleeved hoodies and jeans, only escalating his self-loathing. However, each morning it becomes more difficult to re-dress in the clothes of the day before as he continues to grow thicker, denser; becoming coarser with each new layer of skin. As a child, he'd wondered if his genetic code couldn't make up its mind about which race he should belong to; the Hosts make him wonder if he belongs to any race at all.

But it isn't just the way he looks that causes them to keep their distance; they're afraid of him, as if they sense that at any moment he might rip out of his quiet repose and burn everything, and everyone, to the ground. Slate isn't sure they're wrong. Resisting the desire to run—even if only to be caught and caged again—Slate heads inside.

"Oh, um, you're...early." The Hosts stop in mid-conversation as they emerge from the kitchen, their plastic faces frozen in artificial smiles.

"We didn't expect you so soon." In a protective remnant from his youth, Justin steps in front of his wife, whose hands are fluttering nervously from mouth to hair.

"I can tell." Slate takes a meaningful glance at his bags, leaning neatly against the wall. The Hosts make no attempt at an excuse. "So, when does my ride get here?" His mind stampedes through disbelief, anger, and finally acceptance. He doesn't need them; he doesn't care that they don't want him. This was never his home, they were never his family.

"She'll be here at four." Justin Host checks both his wristwatch and the clock on the wall. "About five minutes." Satisfied that the second hand is still ticking, he adds, "Look Piedra, we're sorry it hasn't worked out. But Social Services have..." Justin stops, unsure how to continue. He looks around the room, as if to catch sight of where the next part of his thought has flown. "Hey, this is a good opportunity for you. A new start with...a new home in..."

Slate tilts his head as he tries to make sense of Justin's incorrect sentences and the eerie vision of Grace, poised like a clockwork doll wound down after expelling its mechanised energy. Justin has never called him anything other than bud or sport, so the use of his last name just adds to their unusual behaviour. He's dismissing the idea of a drug overdose or a gas leak when he's caught off-guard by a sharp rap on the front door. The shortened hairs of his recent bad-boy haircut bristle and he turns his back on the Hosts to open the door.

Cold, almond-shaped eyes, metallic blue scales, claws...

Reanimated by the intrusion, Justin pushes Slate aside, blocking the visitor from Slate's line of sight and jarring him out of his trance.

"You're right on time. He's packed and ready to go." Justin

sounds far away, like an ill-remembered conversation. "It was no problem at all."

Shaking the image of those claws out of his head, Slate focuses on the stranger. Wearing a dark blue business suit over a white blouse, she's everything you'd expect a social worker to look like, except for the long, thick braid of blue-black hair hanging heavily down her back like a whip winding up to strike.

"Thank you. I appreciate your cooperation." She brushes aside Justin's proffered hand and turns her attention to Slate. "I'm Malice Apata from Social Services. Sorry, we're on a bit of a tight schedule. It was tricky finding your house. They all look alike, you know." She looks directly at Slate. "Ready, Slate? It's time to go." There's urgency in her eyes. Slate has seen that look before.

"He's all packed... *Alice,* was it?" Justin pushes Slate towards his luggage, miming an offer to assist in carrying them out of the house. "You heard the lady. Time to go. Mustn't keep her waiting."

A compulsion to touch the social worker distracts Slate from becoming angry at Justin's eagerness to see him gone. *What's going on here?*

Ducking under Justin's artificial attempt at a hug, Slate shifts his school bag higher on his shoulders and grips his entire life off the floor, a bag in each hand. Outside, the trunk of the social worker's car stands open, already half filled with a couple of well-used, mismatched suitcases. Slate shoves his bags inside and slams the lid closed. Not as good as hitting someone, but it will do.

Justin joins his wife in front of the social worker, both unblinking as their heads bob and shake in unison.

"Yeah, unwanted purchase to be returned, a little worse for wear but what can you expect? We tried the boy out but he didn't match the furniture," Slate mocks from the passenger's seat, the perspective allowing him to crush the distant figures between his fingertips.

Finally, with the nodding and shaking over, the driver's door opens and the social worker slithers into her seat. Without a word, she manoeuvres the car smoothly away from the house, and the remorseless turned backs of the Hosts—then floors the accelerator.

"So, *Malice*. Not Alice?" He raises an eyebrow.

"Yes, Malice. Is that okay with you, *Slate*?" She mimics his scorn, tone and pitch perfect.

"Yep. All good with me." No time like the first time to make a good impression. "Anyway, Anthony and Cleopatra—I mean my foster parents, Justin and Grace—were a little thin on the details about where I'm going. Will I have to change schools?"

"I can tell from the reports from your foster parents—and, may I add, a record number from teachers, doctors and, my favourite, concerned neighbours—that you are fitting seamlessly into your stable suburban environment."

Slate can't help feeling apprehensive at the social worker's sarcasm. Maybe things are going to get worse. He hadn't thought it possible. For a moment, he wonders if unadjusted foster kids go to juvy. Shaking off the idea, he looks at Malice, waiting for her to explain.

"Your grandfather asked me to bring you home."

If she'd had bared fangs, Slate couldn't have been more stunned.

"It's not that I'm disappointed leaving the Hosts. They are…*were*…getting cagey, but I'm pretty sure I have no extended family. Why else would they put me into the foster system. There must be some sort of mistake." His voice cracks, and the compulsion to touch her is making him increasingly uncomfortable: an itch that he worries will expose more than a bug bite.

"Your father was…estranged. But you do have a very lively grandfather, and others who would claim you as kin, in Aotearoa. I've been asked to bring you home." She pauses, making a quick lane change to merge with the thickening traffic.

"So, you're sending me there?" he asks. "Wait, you can't send me! I don't even speak—well, whatever it is they speak there."

"You'll find English will do, unless you speak the old language or Māori." Turning her gaze back to the road, Malice makes a series of random and occasionally dangerous turns, without the use of indicators. Concerned that any more questions will cause a car crash, Slate decides to wait for a moment when he's regained control of his emotions.

The buildings blur, reminding him of being lulled to sleep as a child by the sight of passing houses and trees. Everything he experienced before the accident was interspersed with travelling. His first memory was of being removed from his bed, warm and still half asleep, wrapped in a lime green, satin-edged woollen blanket. His parents whispering to one another while they bundled him into the back seat, before setting off into the night. They never stayed anywhere longer than a year, often less than a few months. They would get the "feeling" and, between heartbeats, they'd be on their way to a new job in a new place. Once, when he'd woken with fear squeezing the air from his lungs, he caught sight of his mother twisted around in her seat. She was looking at him like she was both afraid for him and *of* him.

"Go back to sleep, dream sweet dreams, and when you wake you'll see a whole new world," she reassured him, pulling the blanket up. Until now, he'd forgotten how her hand had trembled, stroking his cheek until he fell back to sleep. But he caught fleeting glimpses of that look for years after: love filled with fear.

"Why weren't they more careful?" Slate's words float away on his breath, briefly steaming up the passenger window.

"Who?" Malice asks, her question lingering in the air like the end of an alarm.

"No one," Slate says.

Everyone, he thinks.

They hurtle past an overhanging sign stating *LAX—5 miles,* which pulls Slate out of his reverie. "I'm leaving today? For Aotearoa? I don't know even know where it is. It could be full of cannibals and cannabis."

Malice slants her eyes towards him. "One: it's *we,* not *you*. Two: Aotearoa, is an island in the Pacific. And three: as for being full of cannibals and cannabis, that's a matter of opinion." Horns blare and Malice returns her attention to the oncoming traffic, swerving back into the correct lane.

"Are you crazy? You almost killed us," Slate yells, unclenching his grip on the seatbelt.

"Not even close. I'm an excellent driver."

Malice makes her way to the rental parking lot, where she chooses an isolated area to stop, turns off the ignition and unclips her seat belt.

"Ready, Slate?" she asks for the second time. "It's time to go."

For a moment Slate considers being defiant, shouting that he's never been ready, but his anger is cold. Reaching instead to undo his seatbelt, he feels Malice's approval. No doubt she expected worse. She probably has pages of documentation stating just how much worse he can be.

Malice returns the car keys to the rental drop box, leaving Slate to grab a trolley. His jeans already tighter than they'd been this morning, means it's a tight squeeze to force his hand into his pocket for change to release a trolley from the bay. With a sudden jerk, he spills a handful of coins across the floor, sending them spinning in all directions.

"Shit." He bounds from one to the next, slapping them flat underfoot before they roll beyond his reach.

"What kind of money is this?" Pinched between a thumb and forefinger, a small boy holds out a coin he's retrieved from the fallen stash.

"Sorry?" Slate's face blanches in recognition. "Thanks. I don't know. I found it."

"You should take better care of it, like wear it or something. It has a hole." The boy looks up expectantly. "Do I get a reward?"

"Yeah. Sure. Here." Slate hands over the few coins he's collected so far, his focus on the one in his hand. He hadn't lied to the boy; when he woke in the hospital he'd found the coin lodged between the tongue and laces of one of his shoes. Everything else he owned had been lost in the fiery wreck. So, though he'd never seen the coin before, he'd kept it as his only tangible connection to his parents.

"Where's that trolley?" Malice calls across the empty bus bay, motioning urgently to the pile of bags at her feet.

"Coming." Exchanging the coin for another, Slate releases the imprisoned trolley and is soon pushing their bags towards the departure entrance.

"Hurry, we're late." Malice drags the front of the trolley through the crowds of travellers towards the check-in counters.

Her recklessness reminds Slate of her driving. After almost falling over a briefcase and bumping into a tearful couple entwined in a desperate embrace, Slate is tempted to ask why the rush, but her actions remind him too much of his parents' paranoia, and it's strangely comforting. Instinctively, he knows he'd receive the same answer: *to be on the safe side.*

"Final check-in for Air New Zealand flight NZ705, LAX to Auckland."

"That's us. Just in time," Malice says.

Slate leans against the counter while she hands over their passports and tickets.

Boy, the Hosts must have been planning my departure for ages to have arranged a passport for me.

Reading his mind, Malice collects their documents from

the steward and says, "No, the Hosts were only told this morning. I thought it best. This was all me. I like to be prepared."

Unsure of how to respond and still clutching his school bag, Slate lets her hurry him along to the boarding gate.

Heading down the ramp, fear grips him, making his heart thud so hard he can feel his ribs move, cracking like river ice at the start of a spring thaw. With the desperation of a drowning man, Slate grabs hold of Malice's hand. Her smooth, warm touch acts like a slow leak in an overfilled tyre.

"Don't make me get on the plane. I can't get on a plane."

Coolly, Malice prises Slate's fingers from their desperate grip and takes hold of his chin; her sharp nails dig crescent moons into his flesh.

It's going to be fine, Slate," she says calmly as his eyes, the eyes of a frightened animal looking for an escape, dart back up the ramp.

All that's preventing him from throwing up and running is her touch. Breathing raggedly, the pressure building again, he barely hears her take a container of pills from an inside pocket of her jacket.

"Here, you better take two…and don't look at me like that. They'll help you relax, that's all. You don't think I want to take a corpse with me on the flight, do you? Look, I was going to take a couple, too. I don't like flying either. None of us do. We prefer to navigate by sea and stars." She shakes the white pills into the palm of her hand, taking two and holding the other two towards Slate.

"Sorry. I'm okay now." He takes the pills and swallows them.

"Good." She bobs lower, forcing him to look at her. "I want you to know that you're safe with me."

Still caught in her phantom grip, Slate muses over her words while he follows her onto the plane.

What does safe *even mean?*

He lets her place his bag in the overhead compartment and settles into the window seat. Feeling more tired than calm, he turns to see her eyes closing.

"Trust me," she says. "It's better this way. See you in thirteen hours."

Slate watches her relax into her seat, as if she has no bones for her flesh to cushion. He doesn't have time to argue, the sound of her soft hissing dragging him to sleep.

CHAPTER TWO

Leaving their dark grey sedan parked in the empty suburban street, Jude Lively and Terrance Trapp move with mechanical ease towards the non-descript house. Lively stops to check the number against a crumpled piece of paper, then takes the lead up the garden path. Her double tap on the front door reverberates around the house, while she turns to give Trapp a uniform check. Every detail is perfect, from the hair under their caps to the shine of their highly polished shoes; even the stiffly ironed creases of their regulation white shirts and black pants emphasise their powerful posturing. With eyes hidden behind twin mirror sunglasses, their humourless expressions complete the desired impression: *This is no social call.*

Hurried footsteps respond to a second knock. The door opens and there's a slight pause.

"Oh hello, officers," exclaims Grace. "Justin, the police are here." Her raised voice betrays no hint of concern and is matched by the casual entrance of her husband into the hallway. Folding his newspaper in half, he lays it on a side table and joins his wife at the door, one arm draped possessively around her waist.

"How can we help you, officers?" He holds out the other hand in greeting.

"Jus' a routine visit, sir," Lively replies, gripping his hand tightly. Justin is the first to let go. "Can we come in?"

"Sure, sure." Justin motions towards the living room with his elbow and rubs the feeling back into his fingers. "What's this all about?"

Trapp and Lively follow his lead, taking note of the don't-touch-anything feel of the décor: the pale carpet, and even paler furniture adorned with glass vases of white lilies and arty black-and-white photos of the couple in a series of contrived poses. Why would they choose to open their home to a foster child? Kids are messier than animals.

"Would you like something to drink? Tea? Coffee?" Easing into the corner of a beige two-seater, Justin signals Grace to be ready for their requests.

"No thank ye. We're here to speak to your foster boy…" The two officers stand on either side of the entrance, their glances covering all the exits.

"Slate?" Grace smiles vaguely before crossing the floor to cosy up to her husband. "Um…that's strange, he should be home from school by now."

"Is he often late?" Lively takes a step closer, but ignores the seats left vacant. The light through the windows casts cold shadows across the room. Grace shudders and slides next to her husband.

"No, he's a strange boy. No friends. Just goes to school, like he should, and then spends the rest of his time in his room…drawing." Justin's mouth turns into a twisted sneer with obvious distaste at his foster son's choice of occupation.

"Um, so when was the last time you saw the boy…Slate?" Lively continues.

"Hmmm, I'm not sure. Must have been at breakfast." Grace turns her head and lifts her chin, giving her husband command of the discussion. "Honey?"

"Yes, breakfast," he confirms shortly. "Boy eats like an animal. It's hard to forget."

"Did he mention meeting anyone new, or did you see him

with someone you don't know?" Leaning forward, Lively studies Justin's eyes, but all she sees is the hostility of someone who feels accused of the one crime they have not committed.

"No, no one. Like I told you, that boy's a loner. Doesn't know anyone and doesn't want to, either. Plain weird," Justin answers dismissively.

Nodding, as though the answers are what they expect, Lively continues the questioning. "Have you received any unexpected phone calls?"

"No." The Hosts laugh together at their doubled response. There is no room in their world for anyone else.

"Seen any cars that don't belong to your neighbours?" The questions are routine.

"No. Look, Officer, what's this all about? Has he done something?" Justin stands defensively, knocking the glass coffee table out of its perfect alignment as he pulls his wife alongside him. "It's not easy being responsible for a kid with issues, but we've done our best."

"I'm sure you have, sir." Trapp closes his notebook, tucking it into his shirt pocket, and nods his head towards Lively. They have all the information they need.

"He should've been home by now," Grace repeats, her voice fading with an edge of concern: less for the boy, more for appearance.

"Will that be all, officers?" Justin Host moves to show them the way out.

"Just one more thing… How tall is the boy?" Trapp unsnaps his non-regulation sidearm and spins the silencer into place. "Sir?"

"I'm not sure… A little shorter than me, I guess." Justin's eyes never leave the gun. He steps in front of his wife.

"Well, you know kids these days; it's always the quiet ones." Trapp bends his knees, raises his weapon and fires.

As the bloody stain grows towards her shoes, Lively takes a step back. "What do you think? Found?"

"No doubt. Those puppets were manipulated into letting him leave. Memories wiped, too."

Splayed across his wife's body, Justin Host's corpse is beginning to grey, matching the décor perfectly.

Lively opens the door, her gloved hand slipping against the metal knob. "We'll have to make a call."

They turn into the parking lot of a local strip mall. Released from the constraints of school, hordes of young shoppers revel in the freedom of early learner permits and part-time job funds. The stop-and-go parade of cars, emptying and filling the parking spaces, causes Lively to grind her teeth before spotting a couple of satisfied shoppers returning to their car. She hovers territorially, waiting for them to leave before roaring into their spot. She leaves the engine idling: they're not staying long.

Pulling a phone out of her pocket, Lively taps a number from memory. A single ring. *Was the person waiting for her call?* Not a good sign.

"He's gone," she says. "…No, *persuaded*… Yes… Now?… Of course." She hands the phone to Trapp.

Her partner wipes the call log clean, hops out of the car and walks towards a group of kids waiting at the bus stop. Lively watches the pantomime of Trapp's earnest attempt to return a lost phone. One of the kids, a skinny boy with a haircut she wouldn't give a poodle, flashes an actor-of-the-year smile of recognition and eagerly accepts the return of his "lost" property. The easiest way to cover your tracks is a teenager with too much time on their hands.

Trapp waits until Lively has driven out of the parking lot and onto the main road before breaking the silence.

"So?" He lets the question lie between them, a weapon

either could choose to use. This was meant to be an easy snatch-and-grab.

"She's not pleased," Lively answers. "We're to track him to the Hill if we want to keep our contracts active."

"The righteous path is never safe," replies Trapp. "But it can be profitable."

CHAPTER THREE

Dr Noel Ledger strolls across the room, from door to window and back again. He re-reads the patient file a third time, but the words don't make any more sense. He closes the thin brown folder, secures it with a thick rubber band, and places it back in the centre of his desk: the place he reserves for tasks needing ongoing attention. Besides the folder, a framed photograph of a sleeping girl is the only other object on the regulation desk of black steel and faux wood: the sole personal touch in an otherwise sterile office.

Though considered young for his profession, Noel's recent step into run-of-the-mill middle management means he has fewer opportunities to be in the trenches, working in patient care. This slide into anonymity is complemented by his attire: his tired blue jeans, cowboy shirts and hiking boots mean he's sometimes mistaken for a gardener or caretaker.

His mind awhirl with possibilities, Noel peers out his window. The calming sight of well-kept lawns, beautifully appointed gardens, fields of sheep and the large stand of native trees designates the area of free movement for the patients: a therapy that can't be quantified. As such, he isn't surprised that the only disruption to the pastoral scene is the subject of the file now sitting on his desk. Warnner Williams is pacing the bricked courtyard like a wind-up toy precariously patrolling the interior of a tabletop. Intrigued, Noel rests both hands firmly on the window frame and leans out to take a better look. The boy is systematically working his way from north to south and from west to east in a grid formation, stopping at each turn to sniff the air.

"What is he up to now?" Noel asks the empty room. He pulls his head inside, missing Warnner's glance at the now-empty window frame. He checks the time and decides it's one of many oddities that'll have to be put off for another day. Instead, he heads off to his morning briefing at Hearth-Thorn Centre for Maladjusted Youth.

Noel strides down the corridor to the main conference room and makes his way to his usual seat at the large oval table. He sits close to the coffee and cookies, with a view of the distant mountain range, but far enough away from the head of the Centre, who has a bad habit of spitting when he talks.

"…that kid Warnner."

Choking on his coffee, Noel swivels to see Dr Charity Heart swaying towards him. She sits heavily in the chair left vacant next to him, her chins coming to rest soon after, and helps herself to a cup of coffee.

"I give up." She stacks a handful of cookies in her palm, unworried about leaving any for the rest of the staff. Nibbling one around its edge, she blows the crumbs across the tabletop with each laboured breath. "I used to be naïve enough to believe that everyone has potential. That there's always a way to connect with them. But I can't reach this kid. He doesn't respond to anything, and I know it's not the meds. He doesn't even take the mildest of anti-depressants. Says it interferes with his senses. Can you believe that—*his senses?*" She licks the tips of her fingers and starts on a second cookie. "If he reacted to anything—another patient, a therapy…or *do* something, even break something…then I'd have a place to start. But when I'm feeling useless, it's as if he uses the opportunity to analyse *me*. Like I'm the one who needs help for being in this place. I can't stand it anymore. I'd rather have a hopeless client than a client that isn't a client at all." Her emotional dump completed, Charity brushes the accumulation of crumbs from her ample chest and spins to give her full attention to the meeting getting under way.

Sometimes therapists just need someone to talk to, and Noel knows you should never underestimate what you hear. The simplest slip-up could lead to the greatest discovery and, contrary to her intent, Charity's outburst only heightens Noel's interest in the boy. Unable to give his attention to the meeting's topics of staffing, supplies and supplication, he thinks instead about the enigma that is Client 4877832/11. Since Noel was hired to review client therapies and staff practices three months before, the name Warnner has kept popping up. It isn't that his case history is strikingly unusual. He'd been in and out of care since early childhood, a common occurrence for clients at Hearth-Thorn. His inability to form any type of attachment to family or staff is also nothing out of the ordinary. It's hard to define what bothers him about Warnner, but something isn't quite right. Staff members in contact with the boy have nothing exceptional to say about him. In fact, their reports lack even the most basic observations. Even more unusual, when Noel has brought this to their attention, not one is able to explain why their notes are so brief. Warnner makes no impression, positive or negative, on any staff member…other than Charity. After being in his vicinity for a while, people simply forget he's there.

Warnner's personal file, while hinting at intriguing irregularities, gives few clues to why he should cause such reactions in people. His birth took his mother by surprise. She claimed not to know that she was pregnant, and denied Warnner was her child. Drug or alcohol abuse was suspected, but never proven, due in part to his abandonment. Shortly after being discharged, she simply walked out of the hospital and out of his life, destination unknown.

Put in the care of his father—or at least his mother's husband—his welfare had become a concern for authorities when he was discovered unattended in the back seat of the family's car.

Mr Williams had gone shopping with his two older boys, and all three said that they'd just forgotten Warnner was in the car. That was the first time Warnner was taken into care. His father's selective pattern of neglect had continued for several years. After the boy was found abandoned in parks, school playgrounds and unsupervised at home, Warnner was admitted to various foster homes and temporary care facilities. But each time, it wasn't long before he returned home for another round. In the end, with no other family offering to take him, Warnner had been taken into permanent care at Hearth-Thorn Centre, where he was destined to stay until he could legally look after himself.

Which is exactly what he'd been doing all along.

The rustling of papers and scraping of chair legs drag the doctor back to the present. The meeting is over. Before Charity can rush off, Noel puts a hand on her arm to hold her in place.

"Hey, if Warnner gives you any more trouble, send him to me... That's if you feel you need a break." Noel keeps his offer low key, more empathetic than eager.

"Oh, I don't know. I just needed to unload, but thanks. I'll keep it in mind." Charity wiggles her chubby fingers in farewell before disappearing beyond the conference room doors.

Noel doesn't think Charity will take him up on his offer, but a couple of days later there's a light tap at his door.

Without waiting for Noel's response, it swings open to reveal a long and lanky teenager, complete with dishevelled dirty blond hair and untied shoes. The boy gives the impression of needing both a good bath and a lot of sunlight. Noel motions him forward, holding out his hand for the proffered white envelope Warnner waves in his direction.

"Why don't you take a seat? I'll just be a sec." Noel gestures towards a pair of padded leatherette chairs angled away from his desk in order to avoid distraction and cultivate camaraderie.

The note is scrawled with Charity's defeat: *I don't know why I'm doing this. He's yours—if you want him.*

Noel folds the note back into the envelope and slips it into Warnner's folder, not the official one kept in the Centre's secure file room but the unofficial one he reads when the past keeps him awake at night.

Noel takes his time tidying his desk while Warnner wordlessly arranges himself in his chosen chair, legs straight and crossed at the ankles, fingers picking at the loose seams at the end of the chair's arms, head twisted at an unnatural angle to peer through the window over his shoulder. Every movement appears planned: a predator attempting to dispel the fear in his prey.

"Is that the best you can do?" Warnner sounds exasperated, his gaze still fixed on the view outside.

"Pardon?"

The first time in proximity to his subject, Noel is surprised by his rapid desensitisation, his mind wandering, his tongue thick and his eyes losing focus.

"You've gone to such effort to get me here and you're just going to stand behind your desk and watch me?" Warnner lowers his head, eyes peering through long lashes and unbrushed hair, the word *lame* forming on his lips.

Lame? Warnner is not the first client to attempt intimidation, yet the scientist in him yearns to record the attack on his senses. Despite Warnner's contempt, there are observations to be made. "Are there things I should know?"

Warnner shrugs and holds out his right hand to count off his life on his fingers. He extends the thumb. "My mother was a psycho." Pointing at his index finger: "She suffered from post-natal depression." Middle finger: "My father didn't know how to look after babies and never felt comfortable having me around—." The fourth finger curls out from his hand – "so he got rid of me and took up breeding show dogs." He finishes on his pinkie: "I'm gone. No big deal."

"So, you've never wondered why?" The question rushes out before Noel forgets his train of thought. *It's like I'm being drugged.* He concentrates on pulling himself back into control, pushing his intellect to divide its focus: one part on Warnner, the other on Warnner's effect. "Why you and not your brothers?" *What are you?*

Warnner stares at the lines creasing his knuckles as if the answers are written beneath the skin. "Don't know, don't care. I'm just here to kill time."

"Killing time? Ah yes, you've got a birthday coming up." Noel feels himself losing his grip on reality, floating away from his words. *How is he causing this?* "Turning 17… You could apply for emancipation and leave."

"Leave?" Warnner leans back and stares at the ceiling, the antagonism gone from his voice. "Why would I do that when I'm having so much fun here?"

"I can tell." Noel yearns to shake off the creeping lethargy and bounces to his feet. "Perhaps what you need is a distraction." He crosses the room in three long strides, opens the top drawer of his desk and rummages through a pile of papers, plucking out a brightly coloured brochure.

Warnner shrugs; sitting up straighter, he takes the brochure and leans forward. A shaft of sunlight flickers across his features, and for a moment Noel imagines he sees a creature far different from the boy in front of him.

"An art festival?" Warnner frowns, then draws the brochure closer to give it a more detailed inspection.

"It's a *living* art festival. I'm a great fan of live entertainment, and they even have a traditional gypsy carnival. I was planning to go this weekend. How about coming with me? My treat." Noel hopes his voice doesn't sound desperate; he wants the boy distracted, so he can observe him under less contrived conditions.

"What do I have to do in return?" Warnner runs his fingers over the paper, perhaps searching for a hidden message in some unseen indentations.

Gotcha!

"Don't read more into it than what it is—a break from this place. I notice that you never go on any of the other trips offered. You're not supposed to be cut off from the world here," Noel says.

"Fine. I'll go, but I don't see how that will help you with…whatever this is." Warnner hands back the brochure, his fingers reluctantly releasing their grip.

"This is therapy. Getting you to reflect on your life and make plans for your future is our job here." Returning to his seat, Noel steeples his fingers under his chin. "You can't stay here forever. Surely you have some aspirations, something that inspires you, something you want to do while you *kill* time?"

Unsure of what to expect, but certain it won't be the usual "nothing" or "don't know", Noel is still caught off guard when Warnner, once again lounging back in his seat, replies, "A mercenary. One of those people hired to steal secrets and assassinate targets."

"What?"

"You know, slipping into someone's life just to betray their trust. I think I'd like to do that." Warnner flicks his gaze back towards the window, missing their physical impact of his words.

"Like for the military?" Noel voice squeaks. He coughs and clears his throat.

"No, nothing so formal." Warnner replies. "Tell me Doctor, what your opinion on psychopaths? Do you think they are they responsible for their actions?"

"You mean responsible for killing people?" The possibility is there in Warnner's personality profile. Despite Charity's assertions that Warnner appeared to care about her frustrations, he could have just as easily been playing with her. If Warnner could control the effect he had on people, he *could* get away with murder. The idea chills and excites Noel. Child sociopaths are always an interesting study, but Warnner is something new.

"Warnner, I think you're…" He catches Warnner observing him carefully, and stops what he's going to say. "We all have a dark side. But we shouldn't act on it. Think of the chaos the world would be in if we did. If you want to destroy, then smash things that are worthless, things that *need* to be destroyed, ripped apart and ruined. There's no coming back from killing…not for anyone."

"I'm surprised. Isn't being against violence unpatriotic for an American?" Warnner seems amused by Noel's response, but the boy is tiring from the effort of staying hidden. "It's been fun, Doc, but I've got to take a piss."

Noel waits until the door closes before dashing to his desk and jotting down his observations in detail. The overwhelming effect of the boy's presence has left a lingering fog that threatens to overcome him. He doesn't know what Warnner has done to him, but this is the reason he came all this way…to know more.

"So, how did it go yesterday?" Charity asks. "Hope you don't think I was overreacting. I was getting exhausted breathing the same air as that boy. It's like he lives by sucking the energy out of every molecule in the atmosphere."

Joining Noel at the conference table, Charity helps herself to her usual cup of coffee and handful of cookies, living up to her mantra that nothing tastes better than free food.

"It wasn't easy, but if we wanted an easy life we wouldn't do what we do, would we? I doubt I'll have any luck with him but I'm glad to give you a break, and I enjoy the chance to keep my hand in. For a while now I've been feeling more like an administrator than a doctor," he says, stirring his coffee more than it needs. His colleague's sizable girth is matched by her intellect, which could explain why she can still be articulate about the boy when others cannot.

"Hah! You're not fooling me one bit, Noel. You're caught, aren't you? Well, let me express my condolences for your future sleepless nights. To be perfectly honest, I should caution you. He doesn't want us to help. I'm not even sure he *needs* help." She adds more sugar to her coffee and dunks her first sacrificial cookie.

"Well, then at least it'll keep us both out of trouble," Noel agrees. *And the boy will be a help.*

Back in his office, Noel waits for Warnner to appear. After staring at the clock for 15 minutes, he gives up and goes in search. He plans his approach: not too stern and not too accommodating—wild animals respect "alphas". Rather than heading for the residential dorms, he exits the building and crosses the courtyard away from the ornamental gardens and towards the less controlled aspects of the grounds. Noel follows a dirt track fading in the direction of a thick stand of native bush.

Approaching the first rimu, Noel congratulates himself on his instinct. Warnner is sitting on a rock, his bare feet trailing in a small stream that winds its way around the edge of the trees, past the fields and towards the main road.

"What's up, Doc? Don't have any real work to do?" Not bothering to look up, Warnner tosses pieces of shredded leaf into the water, creating a trail that only sprites could follow. With the last of his leaf given a watery grave, Warnner draws a deep breath, as if tasting the crisp winter air, and shuffles off the rock to relax against the bank.

This time Warnner's presence makes no impact on Noel's senses, despite a confirmation that there's something physically unusual about the boy's appearance: a shifting look, not-quite-right proportions.

What makes you so different?

"Do you want to go back to your office for a chat, or can we stay here so I can work on my tan?"

Noticing how his own white skin seems dark in comparison to Warnner's almost translucent shade, Noel removes his shoes. Joining the boy on the bank he tips his toes in the freezing stream and, closes his eyes. He puts his hands behind his head and lies back on the grass, letting the sun's warmth blanket him, the weather making a liar of the forecast for a chilly, grey winter day. A breeze blows through the trees, making them creak and sigh, as birds converse in chirps and clicks.

Almost dozing, Noel picks up a sound blending with the wind and water. He cracks open an eye. Warnner, his right arm propped on one knee, is playing a reed flute. Noel closes his eyes again and lets the music take him, to the point of physical pain, when it stops.

"Wow! Where did you learn to play like that?" The brightness in his question rings false in his ears, and a moment of panic washes over him.

"Music therapy," comes the dry reply.

"Music therapy, eh? I'm impressed. Can you play other instruments?" It's not the question he wants to ask, but where would this boy have learnt persuasive hypnotherapy?

"Yep. I can play them all, but it's difficult to carry a piano in your pocket," Warnner answers, amusement lifting the corners of his mouth.

"I'm no expert, but you've a real skill." Thoughts trip on Noel's tongue, urging him to let them free. The realisation comes just in time for Noel to send them back behind his teeth before he reveals too much. "Sorry to cut this short but I've got another patient waiting for me. See you tomorrow for our trip."

Hurrying to his office, Noel resist the urge to glance back at the boy, no longer sure that Warnner is just an aberration of humanity. No longer sure he's even a boy.

What is this creature?

CHAPTER FOUR

Wheels squeal against the tarmac, bouncing Slate from dreamless sleep. He stretches his arms above his head and his legs as far out as the seat allows, pushing away the last hold of lethargy, to the annoyance of the passengers in front. Cracking his neck from side to side, he finalises his waking routine by rubbing his eyes with the heel of his palms. Pointed looks greet him from between the seats in front. He scowls, but stops moving. Only Malice is amused by their frightened reaction, making no effort to hide her laughter as the passengers shrink their bodies into the protection of their seats.

"We missed the food? I'm starved."

"At least two meals," Malice says, offering him a piece of hard candy, "but there's time for a quick stop to eat once we land."

"Good. I'd hate to get any hungrier; who knows what I might decide to eat." He raises his voice as if to make the point a real possibility.

The plane rolls down the runway before pulling up in front of the terminal, giving Slate a clear view of flat fields of grass bordered by muddy, mangrove-studded inlets. Further out, car parks and industrial buildings give way to homes tucked behind thick stands of trees. The muted green and grey landscape feels far from home. "So, this is Aotearoa."

"Yep. Not a bad place if you need somewhere to hide."

At the ping of the seatbelt sign being turned off, Malice pops up from her seat and unloads their bags from the overhead locker.

Hide? He shrugs off her use of the word; after all, hiding is second nature when you look like a missing species.

Slate takes his bag and follows Malice down the aisle, impatient to be free.

Collecting their luggage at the carousel, they head towards Customs to present their passports and papers for approval. The lines are long, and most passengers keep their conversations short and quiet, whereas Malice chuckles loudly over the section on importation of plants and animal products as she fills in their immigration forms.

"What's so funny? You're not trying to sneak in anything, are you?"

What if she's a drug mule, using him as a cover?

"Sneak? No, not sneak," she replies, causing Slate to wonder what she's *not* sneaking in her luggage. A border patrol officer leads a dog, in matching uniform, down the queue and over their baggage. It pauses for a moment, drawing the curiosity of its handler towards them, but an almost inaudible hiss sends the dog to the next person in line, the next pile of luggage.

Malice returns Slate's questioning look with a benign shrug and a bemused smirk. In the end, they pass through Customs without dogs baying or people chasing them, but that doesn't alleviate his apprehension.

Outside the airport, a chill strikes Slate in the face, before slipping down the neck of his hoodie. He pulls the hood lower over his forehead and zips the collar over his mouth and nose. Already he misses the dry heat of the Californian drought.

"Nice car! Pretty racy for a social worker, don't you think?" he says dryly when they stop in front of another plain, four-door sedan. The rental key jangles in Malice's outstretched hand and she beeps away the security locks.

"No one notices a car like this," Malice says, indicating that Slate should heave their luggage into the trunk. "Plus, there's enough room if we need to hide a body."

"I'm going to believe you're joking," Slate says, but her expression gives nothing away.

"You can't leave that there." She sends the trolley rolling and hops into the driver's seat.

"No worries. I'm fine. You go ahead and get warm," he mumbles, catching the handle before it crashes into an oncoming car, and sending it sliding into the trolley bay. The sound of one trolley shunting another echoes across the emptying parking lot, blending into the rising sounds of horns beeping politely to keep the traffic moving. He hadn't noticed how quickly he's become alone: alone with a woman he doesn't know, in a country he doesn't know, on the way to a place and people he doesn't know. The chill that spreads across his skin isn't caused by the weather this time, but the instinct to fight or flee traps him in indecision.

"Anything else, ma'am?" Slate mocks, jumping into the passenger seat, the suspension creaking as his weight lowers it closer to the ground.

"Can you grab the map out of the glove box? Look for a place called Waimaunganui." Malice starts the engine and switches the heater on to demist the windows. It takes a moment for the frosty glass to clear before she can see well enough to pull out of the parking space.

"Sure. It's not like I've got anything better to do." He opens the glove compartment and pulls out a spiral bound A-Z road map, relatively new but well used. "Why do you need a map? Don't you know where we're going?"

"Yes and no. I don't usually travel by car, and I've been gone for a while. Long enough for them to build new roads, quicker routes." At the exit barrier, she merges with the morning traffic, moving slowly towards State Highway 1, and clicks her tongue in disgust.

"Well, that's one explanation for your driving skills. I almost felt bad for thinking it was because you were a girl," he says.

Malice cuts in front of a truck onto a single lane on-ramp, its brakes squealing in protest. "I've never been a girl and there's nothing wrong with my driving." She accelerates forward, kissing the bumper ahead as she switches lanes.

Clutching the door handle with white knuckles, Slate asks, "You know what happened when I lost my parents, right?"

Easing off the accelerator, Malice gives a brief nod. "Yes, sorry, I wasn't thinking."

"Thanks. It took me a long time to get back in a car." He lets go of the door and begins to flick through the map book. "So, where are we going again?"

"Waimaunganui. W-A-I-M-A-U-N-G-A-N-U-I." She spells the word slowly, her mouth taking the shape of each letter as it falls from her lips.

As he thumbs the index page, Slate's eyes follow his finger. He reads out the names, tasting the poetry of their pronunciation on his tongue. "Waitomo, Waitiki, Waipu, Waipapakauri. Crazy names. You're going to have to tell me what they mean sometime." He continues with his search in response to her non-committal grunt. "Here it is. Waimaunganui. On page 42, AA13. Looks like you take State Highway 1 south for…"—he closes his eyes to calculate the distance—"…I would say four or five hours, depending on how often we stop, how good the roads are, and how legal your driving is. Then, we head off on minor roads. It's a long way." He looks again at the map to confirm his estimate. "But it says Waimaunganui Caves. That doesn't sound like a town."

"No. We live out of town, far enough away to avoid unwanted attention." Malice replies, then adds softly, "Well, it used to be."

"Like on a farm?"

"Sure, like on a farm."

"So, what else haven't you told me?" They've been travelling for some time, the lengthening silence begging to be filled. "You're not really a social worker, are you?" His voice catches. "It doesn't matter to me if you're not. It's not like I've had better offers recently. But why didn't my grandfather"—the word feels wrong, like he's claiming something that belongs to someone else—"come and get me sooner? It's been years. Why did he leave me alone for so long among people who hate me?"

"That's my fault. I messed up." Malice takes one hand off the steering wheel and lays it reassuringly on his arm. The gesture frightens him. In his foster homes, school, even in public places, he has come to rely on isolation. When anonymity isn't possible, he is treated like an unpredictable, dangerous animal, as if a simple brush of skin on skin might send him into a murderous rage. He's never understood what danger others see in him, something that no matter how long he looks in the mirror he can't decipher. Slate has learned to protect himself by not forcing his existence onto anyone: he's stopped answering questions in class, stopped trying to make friends, and stopped looking for ways to be accepted. He has stopped hoping that someone will come along and explain to him why he is different, and that it's okay. But it feels wrong that Malice could be that person.

"Well now, this is unexpected luck," says Malice.

Studying the sign that's caught her eye, Slate sees nothing to get excited about: just a Gypsy fair. He'd been to countless fairs with his parents. They, too, were easily excited by a bunch of deluded hippies living a fantasy of a time that never existed, while selling crap no one wanted when they got home. "Let's pull over here and get something to eat while we talk."

The fairgrounds are situated close to the highway. Barely open, the few paying patrons are outnumbered by the stall owners preparing for the day, hanging out their signs and arranging their wares.

"What a dump," Slate comments while waiting for his order. Without the bustle of crowds and the distraction of music and performance, it's too easy to notice the rust beneath the paint, the worn wood through the varnish, and the hard lines beneath the smiles.

"You'll fit right in, then." Malice motions him towards a group of picnic tables set out around a colourful, painted rubbish bin. "Besides, I like a little atmosphere while I eat."

Finishing first, Malice pushes away her empty plate and holds her coffee between her hands. Even though he asked, Slate's not sure that he's ready to hear whatever she's going to say.

"If your parents never told you about your grandfather, how can you be so certain that they told him about *you*?"

Slate wants to argue, but he'd never known his parents to make contact with anyone who wasn't work-related. Even then, they were such technophobes, he would've noticed. They never left him alone, never let him out of their sight.

"Sorry. That's not fair. Look, I never thought I'd be the one having 'the talk' with anyone, let alone the son of a good friend." She lets out a sigh. "About six years ago, your grandfather sent me to the States to find your parents. He hadn't heard from them for a long time, and he was worried."

"I never met you," Slate accuses, stuffing the breakfast burrito in his mouth, unable to eat fast enough to overcome his hunger. "I would've remembered."

"Obviously," she says. "Our people are great travellers and we're good at not being found when we don't want to be."

"But you found us?" The food lies heavily in his stomach, like rocks anchoring him in place.

"Not soon enough. By the time I found you, you were recovering in the ICU and your parents were gone." She pauses, spreading her hands helplessly across the tabletop. "It was meant to be a catch-up with an old friend, not a kidnapping and certainly not a funeral."

"They didn't let me go to the funeral." Slate cried out, he pulls his hands inside the sleeves of his hoodie, gripping the cuffs close. "Why didn't you come for me when I was better?"

"I wasn't sure how much you knew about us. I wasn't sure you were like us—I never got a clear look at you. I had to wait and see if you needed me." She takes a deep breath and pulls her braid over her shoulder, stroking it comfortingly. "But I was never far away, though it wasn't easy keeping up with you, you moved so often…"

Slate throws her a defiant look. *She blames me*?

Malice cocks her head sideways in response. "…and social workers are lousy sources of information, terrible with paperwork. You kept slipping away with clerical errors as simple as a misspelt street name. Every time I thought I'd caught up with you, I'd turn up to discover you'd been moved on and I had to start my search again. But I never gave up. I only found you again a few days ago, and just in time by the look of it, the way you're growing."

Slate tugs his hoodie lower, covering the horizontal stripes of blending skin across his face.

"Anyway, since you have a history of behaving strangely, the Hosts didn't question the rush of a harried social worker. Didn't even ask for identification. Besides, I told them that you hadn't returned from school, so they shouldn't worry."

"Hadn't returned from school? The Hosts knew I was there. They saw me leave with you. They packed my bags and *gave* me to you." It dawns on him that he'd never questioned Malice's authority either, and that both the Hosts had acted vaguely towards him when he'd arrived home from school, not even watching as he was driven away.

"Well, *told* is the wrong word. More like *persuaded*. They have really weak minds: so focused on looking good and fitting in that it was easy to convince them of a different experience."

"Did you know my parents well?" He doesn't know what else to say; his mind is about to implode unravelling the implications of everything she says.

"Just your father. Our families often travelled together. When he decided to leave, it broke my heart. I told him he was exchanging one prison for another, but he was in love and if there's one bond we rely on, it's love. When he left we didn't realise we'd never see him again." Her eyes glaze over. She crumples her cup and tosses it into the bin.

If she thinks she's explaining anything, she's crazy. Our people? What does she mean? Afraid his questions would stop Malice from saying more, Slate keeps his lips firmly shut.

"Ten years was too long. When I discovered he'd risked having a child, it was like I'd lost him all over again… To take such a risk so far from home… He was my best friend, and I miss him terribly." Slate is caught by surprise at the intensity of her tone. This sounds like the whole truth.

"I miss him, too. I miss them both," he says slowly "When I think of them I think of the accident, of what happened. It was late. It was raining. My dad was driving too fast. Like he was scared of being caught. He hit something, or the tyre blew. I don't know. I don't even know how I got out uninjured; my clothes were burnt, but I was fine. All I remember is how quickly the emergency crews got there. My mother was screaming my father's name; he was trapped in the burning car, and I just let them take me away." It's the first time Slate has talked to anyone about the accident. "Afterwards, they wouldn't let me see them. Said Dad's injuries were too bad. Said to let Mum get well enough to come and get me. It was a lie. I never got the chance to see either one again."

Malice reaches across the table, slipping her fingers into his sleeves to hold his hands. Once again, he's surprised by the calming effect of her touch, her ability to take his pain into herself. "I'm sorry I took so long to find you, but you're safe now; you're home."

"It doesn't feel like that to me." He wants to believe her, but he finds it too uncomfortable to match her gaze. He's afraid she's looking for someone else in his eyes.

"Do me a favour, eh? Give us a chance." Squeezing his hands, Malice lets go and stands up. "Now eat up. I need to make a pit stop to the ladies' before we get going."

As she walks away, ducking behind a row of carnival games, Slate entertains a stray thought: What would she do if he left? Would she track him down again, or would she let him go? He's not sure which ending he would want.

I can always leave tomorrow, he promises himself, as he returns his attention to his food.

"Finished? It's a long way yet. We need to be going if we're to make it home by dark."

Stuffing the last few chips in his mouth, Slate rubs his hands clean on his jeans and leans back to toss his rubbish into the bin. He smiles at his perfect throw. The other patrons are staring. Probably admiring Malice's *don't-you-hate-that-you-don't-look-like-me* good looks. He dips his head to avoid comparison, his skin rushing red and destroying his attempt at camouflage.

"You know, they can never see the real you." Malice gestures for him to lift his chin with a flicker of something fierce in her face. "Their brains aren't evolved enough."

Back in the car, Slate avoids thinking about his parents, himself, or even Malice and his grandfather. Thinking leads to wanting a life he can't have, wanting to be someone he can't be. The sun drops behind the mountains, leaving the sky a dazzling shade of pink. Slate's eyelids lower and his head becomes heavy. He shifts to find a more comfortable position, ignoring Malice's distant request: "Don't go to sleep. I need you to keep an eye out for the turn-off." But it's too late, and soon he's snoring peacefully in the passenger seat.

"This is a bad habit. Wake up, Slate. You're drooling."

This time, the short sleep brought demented dreams that have left him apprehensive. "Is Malice someone you can trust?" echoes like a half-heard warning in his mother's voice.

"The turn-off should be around here somewhere," Malice mutters, rolling down the window to combat the condensation obscuring her view, the demisters having given up somewhere along the drive.

Slate checks his watch. It's still set for LA time.

"It's 7pm tomorrow, if you're wondering. At least this part of your journey is nearly over," she informs him, smiling at his attempt to work out the time difference on his fingers.

"I'm used to travelling," Slate replies, turning the mechanism to the correct time. Like the coin, the watch is a connection to his parents. His father had had a similar one that needed constant attention as they traversed the time zones of the United States. It was a ritual for his mother to announce their time travel, and for his father to slip the watch off and hand it over his shoulder to Slate in the back seat. With one hand on the wheel, his father would wait while Slate carefully twisted the hands to align with the past or the present, depending on their journey's direction, before refastening it to his father's wrist.

"We all are," Malice counters, unwilling to be left out of the conversation.

"Can you stop talking? Everything you say confuses me. You're as cryptic as my dad and I'm tired of feeling like a fugitive." He snaps the watch back into place, pinching a piece of skin in the clasp.

"Sorry, I forget you know nothing about us," she concedes, giving his knee a gentle pat.

Dismissing her less-than-authentic apology, Slate licks the blood from his wrist, then reaches into his school bag and rummages around until he locates his sketchpad. Scrunched in the corner of his seat in silent protest, Slate draws Malice. He's adding a few sweeping lines to frame her serpent-like facial features, wide-set nostrils under luminous dragon eyes, when they pull onto a gravel road.

"There's nothing here." The car's high beams light up the empty car park, bouncing off the reflector strips along a low log fence and the eyes of unidentifiable creatures peering from their lofty positions in the trees. "Are you sure this is the right place?"

"Give it a minute." She flicks the lights twice against the darkened bush and then wipes the windscreen with her sleeve as if to summon a night spirit. "He'll be here soon."

"What's he like?" Slate taps the top of his drawing pad with his pencil, wondering if his grandfather will look like his father: dark to his mother's light, tame to her wild.

"Barnabas? You're lucky, you know. He's managed to keep us together, shielded and safe from the outside world, for a long time. Not every community has been as fortunate as us." She snatches a sneaky peek at his drawing; Slate is strangely relieved at her bright eyes and hint-of-a-smile response.

"What does he do? How many are there of you? Why do you need to be safe? Are you guys some weird cult that my father escaped from?" Slate can't help himself: the more he hears, the less he understands.

"No, not a cult. We're the dispossessed, relics of the past, whispers from dark stories." Peering back into the black, she pauses. "Sit tight for a bit. He's here." Malice opens her door and glides out into the moonlit night.

Slate puts away his sketchpad and watches the two figures, gesturing like puppets without their ventriloquist. Their body language tells him their exchange isn't a friendly catch-up. Eventually, Malice beckons him to join them, opening his door for him despite his reluctance. Accepting his lack of options, Slate gets out, clasping his school bag tightly to his chest.

"So, you're Slate," the baritone-voiced giant greets him. "You're a welcome surprise."

Unsure if it's a handshake or a wave that's required, Slate is unprepared for the bone-breaking hug, followed by his grandfather squeezing his face and looming close enough that their noses touch. "You smell like your father."

Malice returns from the car with Slate's bags, handing them to Barnabas. The old man hoists the duffle bag onto his back and grabs the other one under one arm, holding them hostage and halting any protest. "Time to go."

"What about Malice?" Slate is torn between staying with the person he knows only slightly, or going with the one he knows even less.

"I've got a couple of things to do. Don't worry. I'll be back soon. Remember, don't freak out. We're sensitive." She kisses his forehead with ungranted familiarity before sliding back into the driver's seat and slamming her foot on the accelerator.

The car's spinning wheels send a spray of gravel against

his lower legs, the tail-lights dwindling. Still reluctant to leave the empty car park, Slate tilts his head upward to take in the milky night sky.

"That's Matariki." His grandfather points to a group of unfamiliar stars. "The Seven Sisters."

"It doesn't look like the sky at home." Slate gazes for a while longer. "I've forgotten how a night full of stars makes you feel so small. You can't see them in the city."

"You've come at a fortunate time. It's the beginning of the Māori New Year: a time when the stars show lost souls the way home." Without checking to see if Slate follows, Barnabas moves like the world is too small and too slow, melting into the bush-line out of sight. Taking a last look in case Malice has changed her mind about leaving, Slate hurries to catch up.

The unfamiliar bush forces him to concentrate on avoiding vines pressing in from both sides and roots trapping his feet. The evening is cold, but the unexpected exercise and his own predisposition warm him, alleviating some of his anxiety. He'd have liked to ask about the animal cries and the scuffling in the undergrowth, but his grandfather is moving too fast, creating a rhythm that matches the sounds of nocturnal life that would normally be disturbed by human voices.

It isn't until much later that Slate realises that his grandfather isn't using a torch to guide them through the darkness.

He must be a relative.

Seeing in the dark was one of the unwelcome surprises Slate's first set of foster parents had chosen to ignore. Early in his brief stay, they'd found him reading in bed with the lights off and it hadn't taken him long to perceive that this wasn't only *unnatural* to them, but a cause for concern, requiring the notification of the first of a series of social workers. They'd claimed he was still shocked by the accident, so much so that he *thought* he had the night vision of a cat. He could have proved them wrong, but he was too frightened: a little boy alone in a world he didn't understand. And though they didn't completely believe his contrition, he never let his guard down again, constantly modifying his behaviour to blend in. However, no matter how hard he tried, his changing looks prevented him from ever staying hidden from notice.

"Here we are," Barnabas proclaims. They step out of the bush and into a large clearing. "Not many have arrived yet, but this whole area will be full in time for the Welcoming." Spreading his arms wide, Barnabas points to a small group of house-trucks and caravans on the far side, barely discernible beneath low-hanging tree limbs.

You've got to be kidding me! I've been kidnapped by hippies.

Unamused, it takes Slate a while to gather that the clearing is larger than he first assumed. The edge undulates like waves breaking along a beach, creating private eddies for intimate groupings of semi-permanent and completely mobile homes. In places, the memory of past occupation is scored into the ground, and the areas are connected by meandering and overgrown tracks. There is no clear line of sight, as if each new settler had been struck by the same strain of madness that compelled them to hide their existence from even their closest neighbour.

Approaching the nearest truck, Slate's not surprised to see it's similar to those at the Gypsy fair. The cab is a high step off the ground, the body wide, with room for at least four to sit side by side behind the split windscreen. What would have once been a metal container to transport goods across the country, has been replaced by a hand-built wooden house, which grows out of the trailer and over the roof of the cab. Slate catches movement behind a curtain, but the observers are careful not to expose themselves to his scrutiny.

"You'll be staying here." Barnabas taps him on the shoulder

and points to a smaller oval caravan parked a few metres away from the others. Even in the dark, it's richly decorated in bold colours and Slate notices that the windows are made of stained glass. The intricate designs compel him to reach out and caress the details, following the flowing lines with his fingertips. The cool metal burns his skin, reminding him that he's never been fond of the cold.

Opening the door to the caravan, Barnabas pulls down a set of wooden steps and squeezes his body through the narrow entryway. Once inside, he motions to Slate to follow. "Your bedroom's back there."

Unlike the outside, which has retained its original form under a non-traditional paint job, the inside has been transformed from a weekend getaway to an artist's haven. Near the ceiling, a loft no more than a human-sized shelf is hidden behind a dirty red curtain, complete with grimy golden tassels. Below the loft, two mismatched, torn and tired armchairs are surrounded by bookcases on three sides. The shelves are stuffed with books, bits of clothing and knickknacks, as if someone had rushed to tidy up but didn't know where anything went. The less-than-lived-in feel is emphasised by the smell of long-untouched dust and a slight dampness.

"How do I get up there…climb the walls or fly?" Slate asks, gesturing towards the loft.

"Not fly, unless there's something I don't know about you. There are steps in the wall to your right." Slate hooks his foot into the first rung and clambers into the loft. Though incredibly low to the ceiling, it's snug, not claustrophobic, with a large soft mattress covered with silken cushions and embroidered blankets. The fittings make him feel they were made for him, and the thought quickens his heart in panic.

"Who lives here?" There's a slight quaver to his voice until he brings his emotions under control.

"Once it belonged to your father." The caravan rocks

under Barnabas's heavy tread as he steps towards the back. "Malice uses it when she's home. Her room is down here, but this is your home now. She can always find some other place to stay." The suggestion sounds more like a threat against Malice, and Slate is reminded of their cold conversation in the car park.

"I don't mind sharing. I'm not used to being by myself." Surrounded by the trappings of a backward society, it's clear to him that his father left because, like Slate, he realised how crazy his relatives were, hiding away from the real world to reclaim a life from a forgotten time. "Where do you sleep?"

"Amongst the trees."

Slate doubts he means metaphorically.

Taking on a more serious tone, Barnabas says, "Now, I'm glad you're here, but there are a few rules." He waits for Slate to sling his legs over the edge of the loft and land heavily on the floor beside him. "First, don't leave the caravan at night alone. It's for your safety. It wouldn't do for you to get lost, and for the past week, a pack of feral dogs has been sighted. They are being tracked, so they shouldn't be a problem for much longer." Strangely, his eyes crinkle with pride. "Second, you may wander around in the day, but it might be a good idea to have a guide 'til you get used to us." Stroking his beard, he mutters: "If I'd known…never mind, soon enough to sort out tomorrow."

Turning his attention back to Slate, he grabs him into another uncomfortable hug. Unsure how to return the overwhelming familiarity, Slate leaves his arms dangling by his side "Unpack. Make yourself at home. I'll be back in the morning to show you around."

With his grandfather's departure, Slate is bereft of warmth but his other senses take up the fight for domination. The caravan trembles underfoot, and his mouth fills with acrid saliva when he picks up the scent of blood. Despite his grandfather's warning, he opens the door and peers into the black. There's movement behind the caravan, something large but with a light tread passing close by, dragging with it the smell of a fresh kill. He licks his lips nervously and listens for the voices that would indicate the hunter was of the two-legged kind.

"Don't be an idiot; it's not like anyone is going to fire up a barbeque this time of night," he chides himself out loud, closing the door and preparing to give his new home a thorough search for food.

Ignoring Barnabas's instructions to unpack, Slate searches systematically from one end to the other, opening each cupboard and drawer to sift through the long-forgotten items within. Many of the drawers and cupboards refuse to open, though no locks are evident, and they taunt his curiosity. He sniffs each one in turn to reassure himself that they hide nothing worth eating. The unlived-in feeling to the caravan reaffirms his first impression that it has sat unused for years, perhaps all the time while Malice searched, first for his parents, and then for him. Perhaps even longer.

He leaves only Malice's room unexplored, doubting there'd be any food inside, rather than through any sense of chivalry. Driven to the point where his own fingers are beginning to look good enough to eat, he discovers an abandoned stash of tuna and soup cans, stacked at the top of a high bookcase. The can opener is an easier find, and soon he is feasting the way only a hungry person could understand.

After licking the last can clean, Slate smashes them flat and dumps them in an empty cardboard box, apparently designated as a rubbish bin. The unconventional meal leaves him full but unsatisfied. Alone in the dark, it's too much. Covering his eyes with his hands, Slate lets the tears flow. He's tried to act mature, not raging, attacking or fleeing. But now, alone with his emotions, he struggles against the urge to howl and wreak havoc. He can't deny that Barnabas is related, but the glimpses of his father in his looks and actions are not enough to convince Slate that this is where he belongs. He can't allow himself to be content here, in this place his father fled; he's betrayed him too much already. But until he can find a way to leave, Slate resigns himself to stay. He crawls into his bed, missing his parents more than he has for a long while, and he dreams of escape.

CHAPTER FIVE

A creature of light, Warnner wakes with the sky melting from night to day and his hunger threatening to consume him from the inside out. Like a persistent younger sibling he's been blackmailed into appeasing, his accelerating appetite means daily pilfering from the kitchens: a challenge needing careful planning and execution. But his constant feeding comes with the awkwardness of a rapidly changing form: arms and legs telescoping away from his body, too-large hands and feet like lions' paws. He can literally measure his increasing dimensions from one meal to the next.

A sharp rap shakes Warnner from his food-obsession.

"Let's get a move on." Noel tests for access to Warnner's room with a quick twist of the handle, rattling the door in defeat.

"Give me a mo'." Warnner pulls on a hoodie and jeans, checking for normality, before stuffing his feet into his shoes and his wallet into his back pocket. "Do I have time for breakfast?" he asks, swinging the door open to Noel's grinning face.

Sitting in the car, Warnner gazes out the passenger window at the young plants checker-boarding the fields along the windy back road and calculates how much grass he'd have to eat to feel full. The toast and cereal didn't begin to feed the hole in his stomach. Constant hunger occupies Warrner's thoughts while Noel grunts and groans in time to the intermittent stop-and-go of the festival traffic. An 'aha' punctuates his vocal repertoire when he joins the line of cars pausing to pay for parking in a muddy field. Noel circles twice, before seizing a space on the side of a low embankment under a pohutukawa tree.

"How much do I owe you?" Warnner questions as they merge with the thickening crowd of revellers heading towards a wooden gate that marks the entrance to the farmer's field and the fair.

"No, my treat, Warnner. You save your money. These places are expensive and you might want to buy a souvenir." Noel buys two tickets from a concessioner dressed from head to foot in purple, and passes one to Warnner.

"Thanks, I'll catch you 'bout one o'clock at the veggie stand?" Warnner gestures in the direction of a food trailer bearing the sign *Hare Krishna Food*.

"Um, don't you want to stick together for a bit?"

Warnner screws up his face.

Noel takes the hint and heads in the opposite direction. "At lunch, then. Go on; enjoy yourself."

The vast grounds are crowded with people in dull-coloured jackets, scarves and hats. They're a sharp contrast to the lively stalls arranged in concentric semi-circles from the front gate. Milling from one ring to the next, Warnner glances at couples walking arm in arm, sharing mugs of mulled wine as they admire the variety of goods on display or take part in the games on offer. Kids race from stall to stall in their hurry not to miss a thing. He observes them like an anthropologist, trying to make sense of their speech and actions, yet understanding neither.

At one end of the fair, away from the food and art, live

entertainment beckons, encouraging participants to dance to the medieval music or stand amazed by performers' feats of skill and strength. Among the rides and carnival games, entertainers hawk their shows at the top of their voices. Both the usual and less usual are available at a price. Caught up in the atmosphere, Warnner stops at a stall to buy a drink and a donut—a gap-stop until lunch.

"Non-alcoholic," he adds, indicating a couple of early morning drunken carousers. In return for a staggering amount of money, he's handed an unusual fruit concoction and a jam donut. All at once a commotion breaks out. The two drunks tumble to the ground in an angry embrace. Unwilling to become a casualty of the unexpected brawling, Warnner ducks behind the stall and finds himself amongst the backdrop of the festival.

Without the colour and noise to enhance their appeal, the assembled cars and caravans are disappointingly ordinary…except for one. Sitting hard against the paddock fence is an isolated miniature circus tent. A young couple appear through another gap in the stalls. They draw closer, lured and unaware, from the crowds. When they near, the entrance of the tent opens like the cape of a matador inviting the bull to best him, and out steps a tall, thin man. With a flourish, he waves, enticing his targets inside.

Intrigued, Warnner moves closer. The stranger inclines his head in subtle welcome, which Warnner accepts with a shrug. Passing into the tent, he can just make out a faded declaration embroidered in gold thread above the entrance: *Feats of Fear—Contortionists and Conjurers.*

Inside, the space is smaller than he expects, with heavy drapes encircling the interior in an intimate embrace. The gothic atmosphere is enhanced by two large, wrought-iron candelabras on either side of the stage, the light of the candles dancing seductively with the shadows against the dark fabric of the walls. The tent is full of paying guests, seated on rows of long, wooden benches facing an empty, raised platform. Warnner fumbles in his jacket for his wallet, but the stranger shakes his head and leads him to a spare seat in the front row. Around him, the audience shifts and stirs, exchanging hushed whispers and offers of popcorn.

When a panpipe begins to play, Warnner focuses on the centre of the stage, where a single performer waits to be noticed. Immediately, he realises the performer isn't wearing a costume: the tattooed pattern adorning her mottled, pale green skin shows the outlines of thousands of small scales. He turns. Have others in the audience seen the truth? They show no reaction.

The act itself is less amazing to Warnner than the performer. She's graceful, but Warnner has seen contortionists before, and though she can squeeze through tiny hoops and fold herself into even tinier boxes, the elongation and contraction of her body is no more difficult for her than it is for the average person to climb into and out of a car.

The spellbound audience is no less impressed with the following act. Three performers tumble, leap and throw themselves around the stage. Unlike the smooth, scaled performer, these three are thickly covered in dark fur, wolfish in appearance, except that each performer sports a pair of horns. Warnner can't tell their gender, but it's obvious they're aware of his ability to *see* them as they twist and turn around the stage, baring their teeth in greeting. The smallest of the trio even chances a cheeky salute.

However, it's the final act that silences the audience. The music changes to the rumbling of drums as the thin man takes the stage. Warnner isn't sure what he's seeing. He's terrified and exhilarated at the same time. Gasps of horror and screams of surprise erupt around him, the stranger disappearing and reappearing at random; or, at least, parts of him reappear. This time, the performer isn't noticeably *different* in his appearance: no scales or excessive hair.

Instead, it's his act that marks him as different. The rest of the audience are caught up in the chameleonic trickery at play, and have no idea it's coming from inside the performer and not through smoke or mirrors.

Warnner struggles to contain the epiphany. He could do that, if he was taught how. He knows without explanation that he could fade into and fuse with his surroundings to escape all notice.

Too soon, the performance is over, and the audience fans out in search of their next treat, shaking their heads as if unsure how to interpret what they have witnessed.

"Did you enjoy the show?" The voice floats across the stage, anchoring Warnner's indecision. The stranger emerges from behind the curtained wall, followed closely by the four other performers.

"That was fantastic."

The performers have lost their glamour; garbed in layered, patterned clothes they could be anyone—a university student, an alternative life-styler, or a kid testing their identity. Had Warnner not witnessed what he had, he wouldn't have given them a second glance.

"What are you guys?"

"Why do you ask?" The stranger moves closer, tilting his head as if listening for Warnner's thoughts rather than his words. "What did you see?"

"You." Warnner takes a step back. "I saw you. I think."

Amused by his uncertainty, the girl laughs, defusing the tension in the air.

"Our act is our camouflage." Flourishing her hands across her body, her unexceptional appearance transforms: her hair shortens and thickens into hollow quills that flatten against her head and down her spine. Her skin changes hue and texture, and soon an alluring serpent sways before him. The stranger throws her a disapproving look and with a sigh the serpent is gone, an ordinary girl standing before him once again.

"It takes energy to maintain, but it keeps us safe. My name's Blue." She smiles ruefully at his smirk. "I know. Sad, right? These three behind me are Rex, Max and Felix. Please don't ask me who's who. It spoils their fun."

Unlike Blue, the trio seem unable to completely transform, but with the addition of sunglasses, hats, and bulky jackets, their hairy state is less evident.

"And finally, may I present my father." Proudly, she bows low in the direction of the stranger. "Julian Apata."

"Hi. I'm Warnner…Warnner Williams." Reluctant to offer a hand and uncertain about bowing, Warnner runs a hand through his knotted hair, wishing he'd taken more care with his appearance, or at least had cared enough to take a shower. "You're like me. It's crazy that I should find you here…today."

"Crazy?" Julian asks, his face showing his mastery of self-control. "How so?"

Warnner shakes his head. "It's just that the doctor from the Centre where I live offered to bring me here—to the fair—because… It's just too much of a coincidence." Warnner returns to his seat to restrict his agitation. The performers exchange worried looks.

"Please go on. Tell me about this doctor. What did he say to you?" Julian perches on the stage and waves the others to wait by the entrance to ward off unwanted interruption.

"Well…" Warnner hesitates, wondering if where he's from might be an issue. "This guy, the doctor, he's new. Came a few months back, but I only met him recently. He's more of a manager than a therapist, you know? Had some sort of breakdown."

Julian sighs. "Our next performance needs to start soon. Perhaps you could get to the bit about the coincidence."

Ducking his head in embarrassment, Warnner continues. "Sure. Anyway, about a week ago he took over my care, and in our first session he asked me if I ever wondered why I was different… No one had asked me anything like that before. It was like he could see that I wasn't just psycho different, but different-different. You know?"

"Yes, I know. But perhaps he could see you better because you're going through the Change." Julian strokes an imaginary beard, then snaps his fingers. "Did he say he was bringing you here to meet us…this doctor…?"

"Dr Noel Ledger," Warnner supplies. "No, he wasn't even with me. It was an accident that I came back here at all. Look, at the time, I just thought he was trying to suck up. You know—soften me up with a bribe so I'd tell him all about me—for research or some shit like that."

"His name is unfamiliar." Julian's artificial smile stretches wide, like an ill-drawn caricature. "But it's of no concern. This meeting is pure chance. We were meant to be on the road a couple of days ago when we were delayed."

"So, do I tell him?" Warnner wishes he didn't sound so desperate.

"Tell him what?" Julian slips an arm around Warnner's shoulders and manoeuvres him towards the exit. "What do you have to say that this doctor of yours needs to hear?"

"I can't keep hiding what I am turning into." Warnner stretches out his arms and lifts his spine, exposing the extent of his recent growth spurt. "Look at me. I'm stretched all out of proportion."

Blue grabs his wrists, yanking his sleeves down to cover them the best she can. "Don't draw attention to yourself. To us. You'll endanger us all," she hisses. "Others are coming."

"Blue's right, bro'. Chill it." One of the triplets flips the canvas door open, surveying the area before gesturing them forward.

"So, what am I supposed to do now?" Warnner asks, angrily slipping from Julian's tightening embrace.

"Go back to your doctor; enjoy your day at the festival. Go home," Julian advises.

"It's not my home." Drowning in rejection, Warnner crosses his arms and stabs his nails through the fabric of his sleeves, warding off one pain with another.

"Fine, it's not your home. But you need to return there before you risk us any further with your lack of control." Julian waves the others back inside, then he walks Warnner away from the tent. "Go back to your *Centre,* stay a few days, and if you still feel the need to leave, then leave. Make sure you're not noticed. Don't mention to anyone what you've seen here today."

As if he would.

"Leave to where? Here?"

"No. Not here. But you're welcome to head for the Hill."

"What hill? Why can't I come back here?" Fearful of losing a chance that he's never been strong enough to admit he was searching for, Warnner bites back a desire to plead more.

"And endanger our existence by entangling us in your escape? No." Julian's voice compels him to comply. "If you can remember, follow the Southern Cross south. You'll either find us...or you won't." Julian pats Warnner reassuringly on the back and is gone between blinks.

Panicking to hold on to the words which are already reforming into a misremembered dream, Warnner blindly barges into a couple of security guards emerging from between two stalls and is sent sprawling.

"Excuse me. Didn't see you." Warnner looks at the outstretched hand and is overwhelmed by an unsettling flash of fear.

"No thanks, I've got it." Avoiding the man's proffered hand, Warnner scrambles to his feet and straight into Noel.

"Warnner. There you are."

Relieved by the intervention, Warnner backs away from the guards, whose stoic faces never change expression. He allows the doctor to pat him on the back.

"I thought I'd never find you."

"Yeah, the place is packed," Warnner replies. "Did you see anything interesting?" He steers the doctor back into the thick of the festival.

"Oh, there was some good music, and some nice paintings, but nothing to really grab my attention," Noel says. "What about you?"

"No. Nothing interesting here."

CHAPTER SIX

It's still dark outside when Siren returns from her hunt and crawls into bed. Despite her exhaustion, her family's gentle night noises are unable to mask the straining of leather harnesses, the clanging of metal buckles and the creaking of timbers as caravans roll past. Suppressing a groan of defeat, she stretches as far as she's able in her tiny loft, her hands and feet flat against the three walls and ceiling. Having long since given up changing into separate nightclothes, she pulls her t-shirt over her nose and sniffs. It smells of dirt and blood: not unpleasant. She lowers her top and casts a casual eye over her jeans and jacket. They're clean enough. Ignoring her hair, she scrambles over the bed of worn, patched blankets to the fire ladder, the only egress to her loft. There's barely enough room to stand up, but since it's hardly bigger than her mattress, crawling is the quickest way to move about. She steps onto the first rung before jumping to the couch below, and in two muted leaps she's in the kitchen.

"Siren? Is that you?" The words are mumbled, spoken from a dream.

"Sorry guys, go back to sleep," Siren apologises.

"We will if you will stop making all that noise." Nova rolls on to her side, letting her twin, Stella, continue the conversation without her.

"Thought I could get some sleep, but there's too much to do." Siren's sister peers between the exposed framing of her loft, her eyes shining like stars against the dark. "I'm going for a ride."

"Don't forget Dad wants you to help him today too." Stella unfurls her hand and they both watch as a piece of paper floats to the floor. A list.

"Bugger." His list will keep her occupied for longer than she cares. "Did you have to remind me?"

"Of course," comes the smiling reply. "We don't want it."

Sighing, Siren shoves the list into her pocket, grabs an apple and a bag of carrots, and heads out to do the one thing that she looks forward to every day.

The thundering hooves of horses greet her as they storm down the side of a hilly paddock in response to her whistle. The horses are well cared for by their various owners, but Siren has a passion for them that she's yet to grow out of. Climbing over the gate, she takes time to pat and scratch, talking affectionately to the animals and treating each one to a bite of carrot. After checking their water, Siren unslings a halter from the gatepost and walks up to a dapple-grey pony, Stamp. Her baby and best friend.

"Morning, monster. Did you miss me?" His soft, pale nose quivers in anticipation of a treat. Crunching on a shared carrot, Siren sets the halter over his nose and ears and leads him out of the gate. On the other side, under the watchful gaze of Stamp's paddock pals, Siren brushes his coat free of dust, wishing she had time to braid his mane and tail.

"What shall we do first?" she whispers. He flicks his ears forward and backwards, as if giving the question serious thought. "I agree, let's get out of here." Without the need for a bridle or saddle, Siren leaps onto his back and, pressuring his flanks with her heels, directs him away from the paddock.

Though numerous, the tracks are rough and used infrequently. It wouldn't be wise to make it easy for trampers or trackers to find their way to the Hill. The faint trails criss-cross the forest, leaving Siren on guard for recently fallen trees and low hanging branches. It's not until she's closer to the main road that she's able to give Stamp his head and let out his paces. Needing no encouragement, the pony responds to the increased pressure of her heels, racing through a natural clearing in the dense bush. With her dark, feathered hair streaming behind her, Siren clings low to the back of the galloping beast. She is a startling and awesome sight, as if she and the horse are a mythical centaur. Seeing a patch of wild flowers, Siren doesn't pause, twisting one hand in Stamp's mane, and with one foot anchored to his back for balance, she leans down to snatch up a handful of blooms.

Once more seated astride her horse, Siren sits upright, a signal for Stamp to slow, and though still in an energetic mood, they circle back to the training ring. Too soon, the grey and dreamy dawn gives way to the stark blue sky of a new day, calling a halt to their private practice. Siren returns Stamp to his paddock and, after a quick brush, she reluctantly makes her way to her next stop for the day—school.

The long and low lodge was built with roughly milled planks to blend seamlessly into its surroundings. As the heart of the community, it's a welcoming sight to Travellers upon their return to the Hill: a symbol of unity, a place of gathering.

Except when it's used as a school.

"Siren, you're late!" Plump and breathless, Auntie Rose rushes towards her across the nearly empty clearing. The red hue of her skin flashes with her heightened emotion; Siren hopes it's a signal of excitement and not anger.

"I've brought you flowers." Siren holds up the wilting blooms, halting Rose in her tracks.

"You're too sweet. Thanks." Rose takes the offered treat and nibbles on a broken stem.

"What do you want me to do?" Siren's eyes twinkle as her gift is greedily consumed.

"Oh, right. With all the excitement, it's impossible to keep the littl'uns settled. They're behaving like a pack of ankle biters, so I want you to take as many as you can for a run. Make it long and make it difficult, so it takes them a while to make their way back. In fact, why don't you go and round up a few of the arrivals to join you?" Rose indicates the procession of caravans and house trucks weaving through the clearing with a flutter of hands. They watch as, one by one, the odd assortment of vehicles peel off the main track to roll to a stop out of sight.

"No worries." Siren calculates that the return this year is the largest of her lifetime. "I'll get them loosened up, or lose them in the process."

Finished with her snack, Rose licks the sweat from her forehead and moistens her protruding eyeballs with her bright-blue tongue. "I've got to run through the Welcoming edict with the babies before I decorate them. They hate looking so plain and unchanged." She smooths her top over her abundant stomach, pats her hair back into place and squares her shoulders, readying herself for battle. "I still remember when you dyed yourself so black that when you closed your eyes and mouth you disappeared completely from sight." Rose sniffs, her nostrils widening and her eyes narrowing. "Well, enough chatting, let's get on with it." Pivoting on one heel, she hurries back to the lodge.

Siren takes in the barrage of instructions, but remembering the list folded in her pocket, a grin creeps across her face; perhaps the day won't be so bad. She puts two fingers in her mouth and gives a long, piercing whistle. The order without words is rewarded with the sight of her sisters, along with the other mini-beasts, streaming gleefully out of the lodge.

"Everyone choose a rolling home and let's see if we can drag some Travellers along with us. The sooner we get going, the sooner we'll be gone."

Within seconds, familiar figures come tumbling towards her from all corners of the clearing. Siren takes the time to touch and hug as many as possible, before they settle on the ground around her.

"Right. Today is going to be fun. Auntie Rose asked me to lose you. The Welcoming is in a few days, so that should give you an incentive to return." Laughter cascades across the group, and they begin to jostle and prod each other in their excitement.

"What do we get if we get back before you?" her sisters ask from their comfortable pile of close companions.

"Don't worry. It'll never happen! But you can try." Siren leads the way to her favourite track. Behind her she can hear the tussle as the others shove their way to a better position. Ducking her head under a low-hanging silver fern, she begins a steady jog through the undergrowth. The group quietens, attempting to put aside the pleasure of seeing each other again to focus on the challenge. Siren knows they all hope to beat her, but, in truth, only her sisters have the skills to match her over familiar ground. She waits until they're distracted again, this time by the forest itself.

Running their fingertips along the rough bark, they relish the subtle differences, while they dig their bare feet deep into the moist leaf litter. Every sense calls them to remember home. As soon as Siren feels the last follower ensnared by a multitude of sensations, she drops her jacket, removes her top, and runs out of her jeans. The cool air clings to her as she manipulates the texture of her skin to become coarser and darker. She contracts her muscles, condensing her size, and then leaps away, a wild thing on the run.

With her sisters close behind and a few more able Travellers not far away, the real chase begins. Many of the younger ones soon realise that they're too far behind; they howl and chirp in defeat before turning around, hoping to beat Siren by going back the way they've come. Meanwhile, Siren teases the rest, dropping unnoticed into a dip between two trees. She holds back a triumphant howl, as the others speed past her. Waiting until the last of her pursuers disappears, she shakes away her camouflage and manages to be waiting, fully re-dressed, on the steps of the lodge a good while before her sisters, the first of the chasers, appear.

"Thanks for volunteering to do my chores," she says, taking the last bite of her apple, chewing on the core and spitting out the seeds.

"You know how we'd love to spend the afternoon helping you with Dad's list, but…" Stella continues where her sister Nova leaves off, "…we've our own work to finish. Besides, Mum told us to let you know that she's leaving you in charge of unloading the tithe."

Siren bares her teeth at the change of plans and growls contentedly.

"See you at the evening meal," the girls chorus. They wrap their tails around each other's waists and scamper away in the direction of the Station—the family workshop.

No doubt devising devious plans for world domination.

Siren's musing is interrupted by the next arrivals, out of breath and weary. She hadn't seen them join the race, but she's glad to see them now.

"Hey, we almost got you this year." Grinning, the unmatched pair—one more bone than flesh, the other more light than shadow—rush over to clasp Siren in their arms.

"You're squashing me, you great buffoons. And you're dreaming. I've been here for hours." Unable to resist their joyful greeting, Siren pushes their cheeks together for a better look. "It's good to see you guys. You haven't changed."

"I'm hurt. We're completely Changed. Haven't you noticed anything?" Dangling a pair of double-jointed arms over Rip's shoulders, Fade roughly pries his lips apart to reveal multiple rows of razor-sharp teeth. "Look. Rip really can now."

"Show off." Smacking their heads together, Siren pulls them into another hug. "You're just in time to help me collect the tithe."

"Ugh. Do we have to? We're exhausted." Rip collapses to the ground, pulling the girls with him. "All that counting and writing makes my head hurt."

"Come on. It'll be fun." Siren rolls away and back onto her feet, tugging uselessly on Rip's gravity-struck arm. "We can pretend we're spies."

"You know, if you ever left the Hill you'd see what it's like, instead of hearing about it second-hand," Fade suggests, making no move to get up.

"I can't leave. There's too much to do here, keeping it safe so you guys have somewhere to come home to." Siren drops Rip's arm and begins kicking the soles of their feet. "So, are you going to help or not?"

"Yeah. Sure. But get some of those little creeps to help. They can unload their own stuff." Fade pushes Rip to his feet just as the tail-end of the puffing pathfinders return.

"Good thinking. You guys want to come back to my place for a quick sandwich first?" Siren asks.

The exhausted runners trail back to their caravans, accepting that, at least for this year, their efforts were not good enough.

"A sandwich? We're growing Changelings. We need more substantial sustenance," Rip groans. "Or at least I do. Fungus here grows her own food."

"I'm sure Auntie will have something still wriggling for you. Don't be such a stomach." Grabbing Siren's hand and pushing Rip in front, Fade manoeuvres them toward a pole house. "My mum's spring cleaning the caravan and Rip's brother got married last moon. Do you think your mum will let us stay at your place for the winter?"

"You only have to unload your own home…and your partner's." A groan rolls across the gathered group. "Come on. The quicker we're done, the sooner you'll have more room inside." Siren is pleased she doesn't need to hunt anyone down and hurt them to get them to help. Only the smallest haven't returned, too young to be much help anyway.

"Yeah, but why do we always have to do it? If the elders are suddenly so weak, maybe it's their time to meet the ancestors—there'll be a lot more space then."

A few nervous titters echo in agreement.

"Shut your jaw, Talon." Sensing the unfiltered hostility, Rip moves to stand a little closer to Siren. "No one wants to go back to the time of sorrow, and I'd be happy to show you why."

"You think you're strong enough to take me, nipper?" Talon leaps forward; his strong jaws open wide in anticipation of landing a serious bite on Rip's outstretched arms.

"Get down and stay down. Or I'll let you try." Fade sweeps Talon's feet from under him and wraps her arms around his throat. No one moves, even as Talon scratches desperately at Fade's arms for release, thickened blood oozing from each deep cut.

"Anyone else got a problem?" Siren keeps her tone steady, though she is willing to fight for their obedience.

"Come on. We want to play," someone grumbles. Siren isn't quick enough to see who it is, only her keen hearing allowing her to catch it at all.

"So does everyone," she says. "Look at it this way: after this, what else do you have to do for the next few months except eat, grow and beat the shit out of each other?" Seeing that there are no more complaints, Siren jerks her head in a silent command.

Fade releases her captive by throwing him to the ground and turning her back, a dare for him to attack; a dare he doesn't take.

Siren doubts they'll get halfway through the job today. Everything you own, everything you need to earn your way and keep you safe, takes up a lot of space, but for some the tithe to the Hill can be difficult to give up.

Most tithe boxes are works of art. Crafted in no standard size, they're carved with stories and symbols, reflecting the objects and the troop they belong to. Passed from one generation to the next, or specially crafted for a new pairing, they're as valuable as their contents. Some carry no more than a bolt of cloth or simple tool, while others are complicated, multi-layered boxes, unique in style, holding medicine, food, or toiletries. Each box is a tribute to their past, each tithe the means of surviving the present and a promise for the future.

Siren reaches the bottom of the steps to the storage area at the back of the lodge when she hears the sound of uneven hoofbeats pounding towards the clearing. A horse in distress.

She's the first to see it gallop into sight, soaked in sweat and blood, its rider slumped over and in danger of falling to the ground beneath its hooves. Siren drops the box she's holding and rushes to control the horse, waving her arms above her head to bring it to a stop. Rearing wildly, the animal struggles to keep its footing as the rider, hands tangled in the reins and feet twisted in the stirrups, drags the horse onto its side. Using her teeth, Siren bites through the leather bindings, releasing horse from rider. Then, speaking steadily, she guides the horse into tight circles, stroking its face and keeping its eyes locked in her gaze. Willing the animal to calm down with her low tones.

"The rest of you get back to your work." Roused by frantic cries, Auntie Rose rushes out of the school room, a trail of littl'uns snaking behind her. Seeing that Siren has the horse under control, she catches Fade by the arm and nods towards her tail. "Make sure they get home and find Hathor."

The second instruction is unnecessary. Siren's parents appear, pelting from the bush with the twins in their wake. Calculating the risk, her father places himself in front of the youths who have stopped unloading the caravans, stunned into inaction by the horror.

"Keep back, we don't need any more injuries," Cornelius commands. "Do you need any help, my love?"

"Carry him inside." Hathor uses her sleeve to staunch a serious head wound as she gently searches for further wounds among the injured man's burnt clothing.

"Siren?" Cornelius lifts the wounded man into his arms, cradling him to his chest as if he were a small child instead of a being so long his legs dangle close to the ground.

"I'm fine, Papa. I can handle this," Siren assures him, her attention never leaving her charge. She checks the horse's legs for breaks and strains. Satisfied that the injuries aren't life threatening, she finishes slicing away the straps that hold the mare captive. Once freed, she leads the horse over to the well on one side of the lodge, looking for shaky legs and a lowering of the animal's head: signs of shock.

"Siren, can we help?" Her sisters know better than to come too close to a crazed horse.

"Can you get Stamp's winter cover, a couple of sponges, a towel and some *Heal-All*?"

It's only moments before the twins return, having added Stamp to Siren's list of requests.

"We thought she'd like the company; he's handsome." Though not as fond of horses as their sister, they treat Stamp with sisterly affection.

"Thanks, guys. Good thinking." After cleaning all her injuries, Siren throws a blanket over the mare's back before walking both horses to the paddock.

"Do you think she'll be okay, Siren?" Stella asks, stepping aside.

"I don't know; horses die of fright," she replies, taking in the new horse's lowered head and lethargic gait. "See how she still shivers?"

"What do you think happened?"

Siren looks at her sisters, their tails lying limply against their legs.

"I don't know. What do the elders say? It's not safe for us in this world. They're afraid of us when they see us. He must have been seen. I hope he was travelling alone." She pauses, shocked. "What happened to the others if he wasn't?"

CHAPTER SEVEN

Slate expects to see some sort of hermit hideaway, but all he sees is more of the same: tree trunks and fern fronds.

God, I hope he's not a naturist; I'm not taking my clothes off for anyone.

"Sorry for waking you up so early, but I wanted to show you something before you meet the others," Barnabas explains, pushing aside some low-hanging vines that cover a cave entrance. Stooping to enter, he motions Slate to follow him. "Sit down and make yourself comfortable."

"No, thanks, I'm fine standing." The cave is dark, but has a warm yeasty smell, like freshly baked bread.

It had been early in the morning, the sun barely up, when his grandfather returned to the caravan and suggested they go for a walk. Slate had rolled out of bed, still wearing clothes from the day before, and trailed his grandfather around the back of a lodge. They'd walked in their own silence, serenaded by the dawn chorus. Slate wasn't in the mood for talking. Another night full of fear and pain shadowed each footstep. His mind had been so chaotic and confused that the only decisions he could make were the ones made for him.

Barnabas reaches into his pack to remove a tiny gas stove of the kind used by experienced trampers. Once lit, the flames flicker haphazard patterns onto the walls and over the ceiling, illuminating a mural which depicts a war from pre-colonial time. Some of the images show beast-like creatures being hunted and killed. In others, the creatures are the hunters. Slate relaxes as he moves from one side of the mural to the other, taking his time to absorb the detail, each new image adding to a story of terrible suffering. Years of training by his parents prevent him from tracing the images with his fingertips and destroying them with the oil from his skin. Captivated by the simple beauty, he's unaware of time passing until his stomach starts growling, due only in part to the morish aroma coming from a pot his grandfather is tending at the entrance of the cave.

"I don't need to tell you that you remind me of your father. He loved this place. That's why he took the path he did. He wanted to know more about our ancestors and what brought them here. He wanted to know if there were others of our kind, living parallel lives in other places in the world. He was driven to find out what the world knew of us, and of our shared history. Living in their world, it was no wonder he fell in love with one of them." The old man's face falls, sorrow etched into every wrinkle.

"My parents worked *together* on restoring cave drawings on the reservations in the US, whenever they could get permission. I spent my childhood growing up in caves like these." Slate takes the plate held out to him and sits on a low rock next to the cooker. "I'm sure I've seen something similar to these drawings. Not the same, but so close you'd think the same people drew them."

"Just the drawings? What about the people? What did they tell you about the drawings? About themselves?" Barnabas leans forward eagerly.

"Um, I don't know. I was just a kid. Anyway, we never stayed long. Once the work was done, we'd be on the road again." Slate crams another forkful into his mouth.

"Sorry. I always wondered…*hoped* he found what he was

looking for." Barnabas puts his plate on the cave floor and helps himself to a cup of boiling water. "Would you like to hear what we know about this story?"

Barnabas waits for Slate's nod, then continues. "Let's see. You probably don't know, but it was the Māori who call this country Aotearoa, and though they are now considered to be the indigenous people, they're not the first beings to make this country their own. The *beings* depicted in these pictures were here first, thousands of years before the Māori. In fact, our people have known these *beings* longer than the Māori."

Each time Barnabas says the word *beings* he seems sadder, as if the word hurts to say. "We know every country in the world tells stories about them, each with their own names, and reasons to fear them. The Māori call them *taniwha,* and they inhabit caves, rivers, lakes and dark places in the bush. Any place a taniwha lives is protected, considered tapu—sacred. The taniwha are feared but also respected. This comes from generations of having to find ways of living together. As you can see,"—he points to an image of the beasts and people fighting—"things weren't always easy between us. In the beginning, there were too many deaths on each side. Nowadays, there's a fragile truce, but both sides know that if it's broken, this country will see a war that hasn't been seen in at least 5,000 years."

Slate is listening, but not really understanding.

"Many of the young Māori no longer truly believe in the taniwha. They're just part of the myths and legends of their people. And even though many of the new cultures which have immigrated to New Zealand in the last 150 years have their own stories, their young have begun to believe they aren't true either. As for the taniwha..." Slate grins; the old man is certainly caught up is his romantic attachment to fairy tales. "Well, their young are restless too. They're tired of being in hiding; they want to roam the planet again in their true form." Barnabas stops and looks at Slate.

"You're right about the story. No matter where we travelled, it was as if the story travelled with us."

Barnabas shakes his head. The old man thinks the stories are true. Something else he has in common with his lost son.

Slate had lied to his grandfather. He'd met many of the people who lived on the reservations where his parents worked. His parents had encouraged it, said that children were less threatened, more observant. So, he'd asked, and the kids had done what kids do: dismissed the old stories and called him names. He wasn't sure but, after one altercation that resulted in a black eye and bloody nose, his mother had become less willing to travel. She'd argue each time, begging his father to make some place—any place—home. Slate had hoped she'd win one day but, being here, he was sure this place wasn't what she'd had in mind.

"Unless you want to stay here all day, we should be going. I've got lots of work to be done for the Welcoming, but I'm sure I can find someone to give you the rest of the tour." His grandfather's voice is heavy, as if burdened by realities.

Not wanting to seem rude, Slate gulps the last of his food and hands back his plate. "Malice said you're performers—a circus—so why are you out here in the woods?"

"Nothing so mysterious. Every year most of us travel the country, performing at small towns and settlements in both the North and South Island, some years even Stewart Island. But during the winter months, Travellers try to journey home. They use this time to design new acts, create new goods, and replenish their creative soul. Winter is also a time for teaching, celebrating bondings, and mourning death. It's the Welcoming for all of us who can return home. We've wintered this way for generations. Sadly, it's unsafe to stay together in one place for too long—that has a way of getting you noticed." While he speaks, Barnabas packs away the cooled stove and their dirty dishes. "Are you ready?"

Slate hesitates. Instead of making him feel at home, the murals make him miss his parents more.

"I guess you're excited about meeting your cousins."

"Cousins? Malice never said I had cousins," Slate exclaims. "How many?"

"You've three cousins, but Siren is a Changeling, like you."

The intrigue of having cousins prevents Slate from asking what a Changeling is, but as the trees begin to thin, even he senses that something isn't right. Stepping out of the bush, he smells burnt flesh and fresh blood. Death clings to the air like a spectre, the stench slamming him back into the nightmare of his own accident. Unaware of his distress, Barnabas pushes ahead.

"What's happened?" he bellows towards a group of odd-looking youths engaged in carrying a very large, and very heavy, chest up the stairs into the back of the lodge.

"An injured Traveller. The Council has convened and we've been instructed to continue with unloading the tithes." The boy's rows of razor-sharp teeth make him look like a piranha. "Uncle Cornelius left me in charge until Siren returns from caring for the Traveller's horse."

"Why wasn't I found? Never mind, Rip. Carry on."

The dismissed youth slides his eyes quickly over Slate before returning to his task. Normally, Slate would feel angry at being stared at, but he realises he's doing the same.

Must have been in a terrible fire to have such extensive burns. But those teeth! How is it possible for all of them to fit in its mouth?

"Slate… Slate!" Barnabas slaps him on the back, forcing him to inhale deeply. "That's right. Breathe…in…out… in…out. Keep taking deep breaths, in through the nose, out though the mouth. It's just a panic attack. You'll be okay."

"I'm fine. I'm fine." Slate wobbles and collapses to the ground, keeping his head between his knees. "I know what to do. Just haven't had one in a while." That'd been true until the plane ride. Not for years, not since he stopped hoping everything that had happened was a terrible mistake.

"I don't want to leave you here, but I need to get to the Council meeting."

Slate pulls away from his grandfather's attempt at comfort.

"Go. I told you, I've got this. It'll just take me a minute then I'll go back to the caravan." Slate senses his grandfather's internal debate. "Look if you stay here you'll just embarrass me more."

"You have no reason to be embarrassed, but if you think you're okay then I'll go."

Slate waves him away, keeping his head low, concentrating on matching his heartbeat to his slowing breaths. As his dizziness dissipates, the buzz in his ears changes from the chaotic sound of his rushing blood and accelerated heartbeat, to the sound of people moving about, carrying on with whatever they'd been doing before being interrupted. Without looking up, he knows his attack has been noticed and commented on. As soon as he is able, he returns to his caravan and crawls back to bed.

Slate is roused from his reading by the creaking of footsteps on the caravan stairs.

"Who's there? What do you want?" His voice cracks as if he has been screaming in his sleep.

An exasperated voice replies, "The maid! How about not biting my head off when I've come bringing food…*cousin*?"

Before he gives his permission, the door is flung wide, banging loudly against the wall. A girl about his age strides into the caravan. Peering through half open eyes, Slate is thrown back against the bed as she flings herself into a chair, dangerously rocking the caravan. Her face is drawn and tired. She tosses one of the twin paper bags onto the adjacent seat. Then, pulling her knees up below her chin, she stares at her own bag of food without enthusiasm. Slate can't believe he's related to such a stunning creature. She is dressed in a stained t-shirt and frayed jeans, but her feet are bare. There are numerous beaded leather thongs wound around her neck, emphasising the whorls painted across every exposed piece of skin—her face, neck, arms and feet.

Must be a Gypsy thing.

"Hope you like sandwiches. I didn't want to waste time cooking when Grandfather said I should visit."

Slate can't help but feel an affinity for the newcomer, a mutual sharing of deep resentment for being told to do something they don't want to do, but powerless to disobey.

"You cook?" He swings down from the loft to join her, opening the paper bag.

"Sure. Everyone does everything. We take turns with the mundane stuff. It's fair. But, we young ones should really be given some slack. The old ones don't have to go to school, unless they feel the need 'to part with wisdom'."

Slate concentrates on his sandwich.

"Do you want something to drink?" The muscle in her jaw tenses as she waits for his reply.

"Do you have any water?" he asks.

"Good thinking. Let's go to the river for a drink and a swim." Noticing his hesitation, she reassures him. "It's never too cold for a swim, don't you think? This is Aotearoa, and it's full of wonders. Besides me." She smiles wanly at her attempt at humour. "Anyway, there's a hot stream running into the river."

Intrigued, Slate explains his hesitation: "I don't think Barnabas would want me to leave the caravan."

"He won't care. The elders are convened. I should be helping to unload the tithe, but…" She pauses. Slate gets it. He's new here, even if he is a cousin. "Grandfather… *Barnabas*…said it was more important for me to stay with you. He didn't say we had to stay here."

Sensing an opportunity, Slate agrees. "Sounds good. Thanks for the offer." Stuffing the last bit of sandwich in his mouth, he clambers up the wall to his loft to look for his swimming shorts.

"No problem."

For the first time since she came through the door, he looks directly at her and gasps in surprise as the coloured lines and whorls that pulse under her skin darken and move lazily across her face. She grimaces at his reaction, baring her sharpened incisors.

"What the hell are you?" he shouts.

Leaping upwards, he hits his head on the low ceiling and falls out of the loft and onto the floor below, just missing the table and chairs. On his back, with the breath knocked out of him, he waits for the room to stop spinning. When his eyes focus again, he's greeted by the hard, angry stare of his cousin.

Swinging her legs over the edge of her chair, she pushes off, landing lightly beside him on the balls of her feet. Instead of a pounding, a small, but incredibly strong hand, reaches down, grabs the front of his shirt and pulls him upright.

"You've got to be kidding, right?" She tightens her grip and moves in closer, trying to read his thoughts from the expression on his face.

"I'm not a freak," he squeals, his panic attack threatening to return.

"So, I'm a freak, am I? Boy, Grandfather was right to be worried about you. You're in denial. Don't tell me that you think you're Common. I bet everyone you ever met has been afraid of you."

Each word is accompanied by a puff of warm air, a pleasurable sensation across his skin. Then, releasing her grip, she steps back and sits on the edge of her chair, leaving as much distance between them as possible in the tiny caravan.

"Look, I don't know why your parents never told you

who you are, but you're among family now. You'll never be alone again, and you should be grateful. You can never live among the Common by yourself after the Change—I mean, just look at you. It's amazing you've survived as long as you have, looking like an armadillo at a zebra crossing."

With his mind in a whirl, Slate fights his fear. He can't accept what he's seeing, what he's hearing. It's impossible… Is going mad hereditary?

Go along until you find a way out of here.

"Uh, sorry about that. It's a bit of a shock. Is everyone here like you? I mean *us?*" His voice is weak and unconvincing.

"Yes, everyone on the Hill is a relic of the people. Most are born True. Some are Blends, like you. We even find Naturals, but they're rare, and some are… oh, well, they're not important." She leaves off, seeing she's said too much for Slate to take in. He's not ready to know everything.

"Are you taniwha?"

"Taniwha. Is that what Grandfather has been filling your head with? Do I look like a mythical beast? Forget that. Of course he has. We've been called that, but we have many names—too many to remember. Look, Grandfather says I can be honest with you, so listen closely. I don't want to be here, babysitting you, when our people are being hunted to extinction. But someone has to protect you, and I guess that's who I really am: your protector." She heads for the door.

"I'm sorry. I just don't understand what the hell is going on." If he's hallucinating, it's beyond anything he's imagined before. "I mean this is crazy; there's something crawling under your skin, and your hair is alive."

Laughing out loud, Siren reaches up to let a tendril wrap around her index finger before she answers. "Don't you like it? I don't understand it completely. I often fall asleep during class, but if I remember correctly the hairs on *some* of us"—she looks pointedly at Slate's closely shaved head—"act as heat detectors and diffusers. It allows us to search out prey, and helps hide us from predators. Don't ask me the details about how the process works, though: I'm not an academic. Look, let's start again. I didn't even introduce myself." She holds out her hand. "Hi. I'm your cousin Siren. Your *elder* cousin, so don't get any funny ideas about trying to boss me around. Hierarchy of age means something here."

Slate accepts her right hand and is surprised as she grasps his left shoulder and leans her forehead and nose against his, breathing in deeply as if smelling his soul. It's an unfamiliar form of greeting.

I'd get myself committed if I ever told anyone about this, but at least the natives seem friendly.

"Now come on. I'm dying for a swim."

"Wait. Let me get my swim suit." Now that the decision's been made, Slate climbs back into his loft and rifles through his pack. "Won't be a sec." He tips his pack upside down on the bed, picking up the last two items to fall out—his suit and a towel.

"Swim suit—you mean *togs?*" she teases. "Let's go before I change my mind."

With no time to change, he follows her out the door and around the lodge to the same path he'd taken with his grandfather that morning. Siren picks up the pace, as if intending to outdistance her shadow, and Slate takes chase.

Suddenly she stops. Slate slams into her, overwhelmed at the river snaking before them. He lets out a loud sigh of satisfaction at the vista of rushing water pocked by misshapen, grey boulders and deep, dark pools. On each side of the river, trees reach across to each other, their embrace torn apart by the river. Beneath Siren and Slate, the thick undergrowth of lush green-and-white ferns fans against the breeze, giving the feeling that, here, time has no purchase.

"Luckily our winters are dry, so the water isn't too high

and the rocks aren't too slippery. At this time of the year, we could cross to the other side without getting our feet wet, but it's not permitted." Siren grabs Slate's hand and edges upstream along the side of the river, her destination a large flat boulder near the exit of a narrow stream that carries with it a layer of thick steam. Dipping a toe, Slate sighs with satisfaction as it contacts the water.

"All this land once belonged to the local Māori. Grandfather says that since the truce, they've given us sanctuary, providing we stay on this side of the river." She points back the way they'd come. "We have to leave if anyone unknown comes to this part of the river. I'm not sure how much they remember about us, but contact is discouraged."

She looks wistfully towards the other side, then she pulls off her shirt and steps out of her pants.

Trying not to stare at her barely-there togs, Slate can't help but appreciate her athletic build.

Boy—she looks lethal.

He mentally compares her to any kid he'd seen back in the States. She could hold her own against any of the jocks—or the gang members. She's scary, and it isn't because of her sharpened canines, wild hair, or the lines that roam her body. Then, contrary to the menacing image in his mind, she pushes him playfully to one side and leaps into the water, splashing and rolling around like a frolicking Labrador. Not needing further encouragement, Slate changes into his suit, and plunges in beside her, causing a tidal wave over the ledge of the pool, soaking their clothing.

"This is fantastic!" Slate sinks to the bottom of the pool and counts. He bursts to the surface, and is greeted by his grinning cousin.

"Got gills?" she teases.

"Nah." He blushes. "Just great lungs."

"I can tell. How long was that? Five minutes?" she guesses.

"Um, no… I mean…" He panics. Had he stayed under

too long? What would she think of him?

"Calm down, it's fine. You're safe here. You're a *freak* among freaks." Shoving a wave of water in his direction, she flips over the edge of the pool and slides into the river. "Come on. Race you."

"How far does the river run?

"Well, there are several sources upstream; I've tracked a couple myself." She smiles smugly. "Downstream leads to the ocean, but you need to wait 'til heavy rain if you want to use a kayak, and even then, it'll take you days."

Days? I'm going to need supplies if I head out this way.

Too soon, the day turns colder, forcing them to put their still-damp clothes back on. Wrapped in their towels, they crouch on the boulder, neither wanting to leave.

"So…where did you get the name 'Siren'?" His emotions are conflicted. Here he is, trapped in a country he doesn't know, with monsters that claim him as family. It's too difficult to believe, even though he's always been different. Trusting them, accepting them, is too big a risk to take, no matter how comforting it'd be to stay.

"I could ask the same of you, but…" Siren begins. "The story my parents tell anyone who asks, is that when I was born they thought my cry was so awful people would dash their heads with rocks to stop the sound. But now that I've met you, maybe it means you and I will always fight." Slate lets a disbelieving laugh escape his lips. "Makes a cool story but the truth is I was named after an ancestor. After the First Great War with the Common, our kind took refuge on an island. There were so few us left and many were afraid there was no place safe enough to hide. *Siren* was a child with the gift of persuasion. They say she used the wind to carry her voice to approaching sailors, convincing any who sailed too close to the island to either turn around or to drown. Without her, our kind may never have survived." Siren suddenly tensed and looked towards the opposite side of the river.

"Kia ora, Siren. Is your dad about?" hails a distinguished elderly man stepping out of the trees into the late afternoon light. Slate is surprised to see that his face is covered with real tattoos, no less disconcerting than Siren's, even though his don't move.

"Kia ora, Matua. Kei te pei he koe?" The old man works his way across the river, stepping lightly from boulder to boulder, using his carved staff for support. "May I introduce you to my cousin, Slate? He's come to stay with us. Slate, this is Matua Panui."

"Haere ra, Slate. Welcome. It's good of you to keep Siren company." He makes his way onto their rock, but discreetly ignores Slate's hand held out to help him. "I'm on my way to see your dad, but I'm glad I caught you. Some hunters have found a pack of wild dogs. They won't be a problem anymore, but perhaps what killed them will be." He looks over her shoulder as if expecting to see the worst he imagines.

"I'm certain it's nothing. But I'll let Grandmother know, so she doesn't worry." She steps back to ease his passage to the bank. "Have you heard what's happened? The Traveller being attacked?"

"Here? No. That's not why I came, but it can only make my real news harder to deliver."

Slate looks quizzically from man to girl, but Siren shrugs her shoulders and mouths the word "later". Picking up their soaked togs, the cousins wrap themselves tighter in their towels and fall in behind the old man, who is already heading back up the stony path towards the community.

When they reach the back of the lodge, the kaumatua stops. "Thank you for accompanying me, but I'll go on from here alone." Addressing Slate, he adds. "I hope you enjoy being with your whanau. I know you have a lot to accept, like I had to in the beginning. Maybe I will see you again before my final journey." Before Slate can reply, the old man turns, grasps the railing, and struggles up the steps into the lodge.

"He's not one of you—I mean us—is he?" Slate asks.

"No, but he knows us and he believes in us. I wonder what his news is," she says. "I don't suppose you want to go and listen? No, wait. I need to go to Grandmother's house first."

"You could listen first, and then go visit your grandmother, *Red*." Slate can't dismiss the fact that he likes his cousin, despite her delusion. It's not her fault she's been raised in a cult.

"Red, huh? More like wolf." She gives him a wicked grin. "But you're right, I can visit her later. Perhaps I'll have more to tell her."

Behind the lodge, they sneak under a window and climb onto a pile of abandoned timber to peer into the meeting room. Straining their ears, they listen in on the discussion.

"I'm sorry it's come to this. I wanted to wait until all the Travellers had returned for winter before coming to talk to you, but not too long, in case it was too late." Sorrow clings to the kaumatua's words like a lonely child.

"It's good of you to come."

Slate has never seen such a strange pairing before. The kaumatua, with his facial tattoos, had seemed formidable, but he's nothing compared to the other man.

"Is that your father?"

Siren scrunches her face and nods. "Cornelius."

He'd thought Siren was scary, but he needs a better description for his uncle. Twisted horns emerge from his tangled mane of hair and his face is no less lion-like, with an enlarged jaw displaying enough sharpened teeth to tear through the flesh of any sacrificial feast. The only other parts of his body visible from beneath his clothing are his hands—or monstrous paws, to be precise. Slate sees nothing of his own father in his uncle. Did the two brothers have anything in common? His father had never spoken about a brother.

But, then, he had never spoken about anyone.

The kaumatua speaks slowly, warming to the conversation. "I saw Siren and Slate by the river. It appears a missing piece has been returned. It's good he's here now."

"Yes, it's good that he's here. I haven't met the boy yet. Barnabas didn't want us to overwhelm him too soon." Cornelius strokes a horn for emphasis. "I have heard that he behaves like food on two feet."

"No. He's just learnt to be cautious." Slate ignores Siren's pointed jab punctuating the exchange, and continues to listen.

"I've come to tell you it's time for me to go north, back to my people's heartland. I've valued my time learning from your kind, and I'm sorry I couldn't provide you with more protection. Our young have never understood why your whanau stay on our land and yet are separate from us. We old ones have never felt that we can explain who you are, and now that I'll be leaving, we fear that you'll be asked to leave, too." He taps his walking stick as if to erase the distasteful sound of his words.

"Where will we go? How soon? Will we be able to stay until the end of winter?" Cornelius clenches and unclenches his fists as if to prevent himself from killing the messenger.

"Yes. Maybe longer. But when the Travellers leave this year, so will I, and so may your protection here."

Other elders join the discussion, arguing back and forth about what should be done. Their gestures become more and more animated, and Slate fears it will end in a physical altercation.

Beside him Siren bites a knuckle and turns away from the window. Sliding into a catatonic state, she says nothing. He takes her bloodied hand away from her unfaltering chewing and leads her back to the caravan. After changing into some dry clothes, he offers her a blanket and sits on the floor in front of her.

"My dad will work something out so we don't have to leave. But if we do, it'll be okay. Most of our people spend their entire lives travelling. It's not easy being homeless, but it has its rewards. There's the Welcoming to look forward to, and you still have to meet my sisters and parents. You'll be happy here, Slate, among your own kind." Her words rush at him like a river after a storm.

Slate's smile is sympathetic. "I'm sorry, Siren, but I'm not going to stay here and I'm certainly not spending the rest of my life travelling around. I did that enough with my own parents. I want—what I've always wanted is—a normal life, a permanent home." He sees he's hurt her, but he won't lie. He's beginning to like her too much.

"Didn't you hear what's going to happen to the Hill? I knew I'd be leaving soon, I'm too normal to justify hiding, but I assumed I'd return every year or so. Now where will I go? There are too many of us to stay together. We'll have to split up and see even less of each other." She turns her head away. "I understand you're afraid of us, but you don't need to be. We're family. We take care of each other, protect each other."

He lets his instinct take her hand, and just like he'd experienced with Malice, he feels comforted.

"You're part of this family. We're the only ones who'll accept you when you go through the Change. You need us and…and we need you. There are so few of us left that every one of us is a gift of survival."

Shaking off his hand, she storms out of the caravan, slamming the wooden door behind her so hard it makes the caravan shake.

CHAPTER EIGHT

In the main courtyard, Warnner sits with his back against a brick wall and his legs splayed in front of him. Linking his hands behind his head, he closes his eyes, and tilts his head as if to consume the sun's rays. A breeze ruffles his dirty blond hair, bringing with it the delicious, earthy smell of recently turned soil from the dormant flowerbeds. Warnner loves the peaceful slumber of winter: a chance to recharge. But he treasures it more because he knows it's fleeting.

A shadow falls across his face. Davey Chore, one of the day orderlies, leans over and shouts triumphantly. "Hey, Warnner, a couple of Destinators are waiting for you at reception. Sound like Yanks. Ya wanna be converted?"

Warnner isn't concerned by the message, or the disruption. The Destination Church is new in the area, but just about every week a couple of believers from one religion or another turn up to have a go at saving Hearth-Thorn souls; they aren't fussy. It's strange, but not suspicious that they should ask for him by name.

"Well, are you going or what?" Flecks of Davey's spit spray in Warnner's direction.

"Nope. Can't. Got a meeting with Dr Ledger. On my way now." Warnner unkinks his body, rolls his head around his shoulders, and stretches his arms across his chest, his joints cracking like firecrackers. Ignoring Davey's sullen look, he strides towards the patio doors.

In the lobby, Warnner risks a glance through the archway at the two people waiting for him. They look familiar; but they don't feel friendly. The one thing you normally can depend on is a happy face from a converter. In fact, their presence makes him want to disappear into his surroundings. Deciding he was right to avoid their attention, Warnner hastens up the stairs, early to his appointment with Dr Ledger.

When he arrives, the door to the doctor's office is open. Inside, Noel is talking loudly into his phone. He waves Warnner towards a seat in front of his desk and turns his back to continue his conversation.

"Ahem… No, that's out of the question. Please tell them I'm happy to talk to them but we have our own chapel if our residents choose to worship… Yes, just note it in the visitors' book… Thanks." Noel struggles to return the phone to its cradle, swearing when it slips from his grip and knocks the framed photograph off the desk. He finally gets the phone under control, only to bang his head on the corner of the desk as he retrieves the photograph from the floor.

"Warnner, why do two Destination disciples want a chat with you? Did you call their help line?"

"Nope. I've never been inclined to ask for spiritual guidance. I try not to take sides." It's the truth. He has never felt the need to be saved.

"Well, even if you did, I'd advise you to find your spiritual enlightenment from somewhere else." Noel repositions the photograph of the girl to face away from him and takes a seat. "They are a cult—a dangerous cult who tear families apart and destroy lives."

His vehemence leaves Warnner wondering what secrets he has to hide.

Sunday is a day of rest at Hearth-Thorn and the permanent residents are encouraged to spend the day visiting friends and family, or go on organised trips. Warnner hates Sundays. He has never had feelings for his father and brothers and no need to foster close ties with anyone else, so Sunday is the worst day of his week. It seems to him that even the most troublesome teenagers, the most mind-damaged, the cruellest, have one family member or friend to take them out on Sunday, while Warnner is left alone with the few staff unlucky enough to be rostered on.

At an early age, he'd accepted the fact that his mother left him and his father forgot him; and at times he enjoyed the power it gave him. Nothing gets you what you want quicker than guilt. What he didn't like was not understanding why. As he grew older, he discovered that his situation was unique, and no matter how many times they'd been forced back together to play happy families, he remained an unknown, as if any memory of him was wiped rather than stored. Then, when he was released into the care of the Centre permanently, his choices were severely limited.

Despite his best efforts, the more people who are responsible for him, the less forgettable he becomes. It's as if the constant reminders, through his file and their frequent communications, keep his presence in their memories. But he has discovered he can persuade individuals, the weaker-willed the better, to forget or change their minds over short periods of time. It's a useful skill, which he uses to avoid most of the treatments prescribed him, and any other activities he wishes to shirk. He likes to think he maintains a certain ethical code when conducting his forays into the minds of others, but his power only adds to his isolation.

Alone in his twin room, a luxury enabled by the inability of staff to remember there is room for two, Warnner lies on his bed, staring at the ceiling, trying to remember something he shouldn't have forgotten. But the thought stays just out of reach, taunting his efforts. He's unable to explain his growing anger, a feeling he had worked hard to overcome as a child. He's about to dismiss the emotion as being triggered by the lonely Sunday when he notices a scrape on the palm of his hand.

The memory rushes him, filling in the gaps left vacant by Julian's persuasion. The fair, the others, even the fall.

"Shit… I can leave." Hearing the decision out loud doesn't bring relief from his deepening anger. He's twisted by indecision; there was no warmth in Julian's invitation and he'd done his best to avoid giving it. And there's Dr Ledger. At first, he dismissed Noel's interest in him as coming from someone with a strong scientific mind. Like Dr Charity, Noel's no weakling to play with. Warnner has even let himself be lulled into fantasies of the two doctors taking a parental interest in his welfare. But the mistrust remains. Noel's curiosity could be a problem, because it's one thing to recognise a nightmare, but another to be one.

If I'm gone, he'll have nothing to be curious about.

The doubt lingers. Warnner rolls off his bed and onto his feet. Too much thinking is making him hungry and giving him a headache. It's still too early for breakfast, but he has a few hidden supplies to munch on. Savouring the crisp crunch of a fresh green apple, Warnner scans and itemises each object in his room, deciding what to take with him. Unlike the other inmates at Hearth-Thorn, he has few belongings. There's no one to send him gifts for his birthday or Christmas and for Warnner shopping is a necessity, not a hobby. The majority of the money he receives from the state is safely tucked away in his wallet. He's never been interested in clothing or books, and the few things he's collected over his stay are mainly for show—because staying unnoticed means not standing out, and no one chooses to have no possessions. Warnner likes the idea of travelling light, leaving his past behind. His backpack has room enough to hold a couple of changes of clothing, his music notebooks, and his pipe.

Tapping the slim metal pipe on the palm of one hand before tucking it in his shirt pocket, Warnner remembers Dr Ledger's interest in his talent. Music, like everything else he can't explain, is a part of him. But instead of it being an acceptable inclination, it too had become a point of difference. When he was about four years old, watching the music channel, his father had commented about "soothing the savage beast". The beast reference has never fazed him, but he'd rejected the idea that music could control him: he knew better. Since that moment, he'd kept his interest, and then his talent, hidden. He doesn't know why he played in front of the doctor, but toying with him to see how far his control goes is part of the game.

Perhaps music will give him a way in with the others, as a performer. He's good enough with any instrument to earn his keep. But first, he has to find them again. With that thought in mind, Warnner finishes his packing.

About an hour after the last bed check, Warnner leaves Hearth-Thorn. It's disappointingly easy. After stealing some more food from the kitchen, he simply walks out the side doors and into the courtyard.

Slack supervision.

He briefly fantasises that a raging Dr Ledger will fire every one of the night staff when he's discovered missing. But why would the doctor care? He was the one to point out that Warnner is almost old enough for it to make no difference. Warnner doubts anyone will prioritise resources to look for him with no family or friends to care.

The night is clear and welcoming, every star cutting shapes into the black sky. Warnner is closing the door behind him when a lone car pulls up and parks just outside the main gates. After the headlights dim he waits; it's too late for visitors. But the doors of the car stay closed, leaving him to take the quickest trail away from the Centre unseen.

After a couple of hours, Warnner has to admit that travelling at night is a good idea. Following Julian's ambiguous, paranoid instructions, he uses the Southern Cross to navigate southward. Not one to spend time out of doors after the sun goes down, he's surprised how still the night is. The air is cool and a light breeze ruffles his hair, wisps of cloud drifting along the distant mountain range. He's comforted by insignificance. Despite what he told Noel, he'd never needed a reason to leave, just a direction to travel.

To avoid ditches, streams and roaming paddock dwellers, Warnner keeps the main road to his left and he hikes from one field to the next. He bypasses the nearby township, the darkened buildings standing like giant tombstones in an abandoned graveyard. As the stars fade with the dawn, he spots an area of bush fenced off from the rest of the well-grazed farmland. After tunnelling through thick bracken, he uses his bag for a pillow and his jacket for a blanket, while munching on a stolen muffin. Then, wiping crumbs off his jacket, he squirms into a comfortable position. The last thought that crosses his mind before sleep overtakes him is what might await him, wherever he's heading, whenever he gets there.

What if they don't want me?

It's difficult to sleep the entire day. The sounds of a tractor dolling out winter feed, along with dogs barking at a herd of cows, keep him on edge. He hasn't forgotten Julian's warning to stay hidden, but where's the harm in being spotted by a farmer? Now that he's on his way, he's tempted to keep going during daylight hours. He props himself up on his elbows to peer through the bracken. Just as he decides that there's no one around, a car drives slowly by, the way someone does when they're looking for the number on a mailbox. This shouldn't have drawn his attention, except this is the country; side roads and houses are few and far between, and mailboxes are clumped together at irregular intervals.

No one drives slow on a country road.

Warnner's uneasy. He hates to jump to conclusions, but what if Julian was right about endangering them? What if he'd been seen at the fair? What if he's wrong about being missed and a search party has been sent to bring him back? Whatever the reason for the car's unusual behaviour, Warnner can't risk being caught. He forces himself to lie down and wait for darkness.

The day seems endless. Every sound, every movement, keeps his anxiety high. The need to stay silent and still is driving him mad. As soon as dusk approaches, he grabs his bag and shoves another muffin in his mouth. While he walks, he adds to the list of things he doesn't want to think about. What if he doesn't find the others, or they decide that he isn't one of them? Does he return to the Centre? Then what? The events of the festival aren't clear; he's unsure exactly what he saw or heard. Maybe he's disturbed and he only saw what he wanted to see, heard what he wanted to hear, like Dr Ledger suggested.

His eyes, glowing green in the dark flick from the road to the sky to check his direction, then to the front to avoid any obstacles. Using the rhythm of his movements to compose himself, Warnner focuses on placing one foot in front of the other, planning his next meal and finding his next place to sleep.

The second night lasts even longer than the first. The terrain is getting steeper and more difficult, the well-maintained paddocks giving way to rocky, gorse-covered slopes and other low-lying scrub that catches and tears at his jeans. Warnner's legs are heavy. His sturdy, butt-kicking boots cause his feet to drag over the small stones. Stressed and tired, he looks for a good place to rest.

"Would you like a ride?"

Startled, Warnner curses loudly. He stumbles and falls hard on his arse.

"Take it easy. If I wanted to hurt you I'd have done it with more skill. Boy, are you a heavy breather." From the shadows behind him, comes a young, oddly reptilian woman. "I'm Malice." She slides towards him, sunrise reflecting in her yellow eyes. She reminds him of Blue. "So how about that ride?"

"Malice? Really?" He feels foolish for being frightened of such a tiny woman, but her name makes him think that his first impression may not be wrong. "A ride to where?"

"The Hill. When I was retrieving my horse, I caught up with some friends of yours who said you might be heading this way. So, here am I, and here you are. Shall we go?"

Without thinking, he takes her outstretched hands and lets her pull him sharply to his feet.

"Um, yeah, I'm sure. Did you say *horse?*" Dropping her hands, he reaches to pick up his fallen pack.

Malice laughs and purses her lips, piercing the air with an ear-splitting whistle. A horse lopes from behind a copse of trees, whinnying in reply. Warnner is saved from taking another tumble by Malice's strong grip.

"Here's our transport. This is Snuff. Isn't he beautiful?" With a graceful leap, Malice mounts the house. The saddle is a stack of blankets tied around its girth with a thick leather strap.

Warnner's not used to animals larger than a dog. He has no idea what to do.

Malice extends an arm. "Come on."

Warnner grabs her forearm, once again amazed by her strength as she pulls him up behind her.

"I'm beginning to feel like a postal worker. You're the

second delivery I've made this week. Barnabas must be right; more things are changing than Changelings." She kicks Snuff into a jog.

The horse leaps forward with a sudden jolt, forcing Warnner to cling to her jacket. He's never been on a horse before, or so close to a girl. He doesn't know where to put his hands. Malice solves the problem, reaching around to grab both his arms, which she pulls around her waist. She doesn't recoil from his touch; instead, she pats him on the leg and clicks her tongue at Snuff.

"Hold tight. I'd never live it down if we fell off." She laughs again.

"How long before we're there?" He's thrilled, and not just because he's riding behind Malice. She'd been sent to look for him. They wanted him, he belonged with them, and he can't wait to meet them!

"Not long. You've covered most of the distance already. We should be there by midday, in time for a nap," she answers, covering a yawn with the back of her hand.

"Don't we have to hide in the daytime?"

"Sure, if you're travelling solo, it's best to be cautious. But you're with me now, buddy boy, and there's nothing odd about a couple of kids riding tandem on horseback around the Hill. Most folks don't see us anymore; we've become part of the scenery. I don't suppose you can play your pipe one handed?"

"How do you know I have a pipe?" He shifts uncomfortably, creating a space between them.

"I'm not psychic," she says. "I dropped by the Centre to see if you'd left yet and I overheard a bit of a mountain man speaking to a police officer, saying you probably wouldn't be back as your pipe was missing."

"That must have been Dr Ledger. What did you say to him?"

"Nothing. I was just there for a sneak peek." She turns

her head to reassure him. "Julian was worried you wouldn't remember in time to leave."

"He wanted me to leave? He didn't act it." Warnner loosens his grip. Should he slide off and go back?

"Maybe my sister made him change his mind." She places his hands on her waist again. "Besides, you left in good time. There was someone from the local church there too, suggesting you had probably run away to Auckland. That will have helped to confuse the police."

"From the church?" Warnner's glad she can't see his face as he tries to piece together a memory of faces. "Yeah, they're always around, trying to save us."

By the time they've moved off the well-worn trails and onto rougher terrain, Warnner has had enough of bouncing bareback with the ferns and cutty grass raking along their legs as snuff forges ahead. Warnner has run out of questions, Malice is unlike any person he's known before. Through the course of the day, her skin has lost its shimmer and her form has become more rigid beneath his touch, less girl and more something else entirely.

"Home sweet home," she says with little warmth, bringing the horse to a slow walk. The trees thin to reveal a large clearing. "I've been away for a while, so do you mind if I drop you off at Barnabas's place?"

"Um… *Barnabas?* What about Julian?" Now that they're here, Warnner can't decide if he's excited or scared out of his mind, but he feels better than he has felt in all of his life. Of course, riding behind a compelling creature helps.

"Oh, my dad should be here by now, but Barnabas is the man in charge. You'll need to talk to him if you're going to stay."

Throwing the reins over her horse's head, Malice swings her leg over Snuff's neck and slides to the ground. She's completed the transformation to a serpent physique, with large almond-shaped eyes, golden scaly skin, and an elongated neck and limbs. He's stunned. His captive attention means he doesn't see the girl running at full speed towards them until Malice sweeps the girl into her arms. "What's wrong? What's happened? Is it Slate?"

Warnner dismounts awkwardly.

"No, he's fine. It's worse. A Traveller was attacked. He made it here, but he died. The Council still haven't told us who he was, say they're waiting for his family to return. It was horrible."

Malice lets go of the girl and slants her eyes towards Warnner by way of introduction. The girl covers her mouth with one hand, realising she's spoken too freely in front of a stranger.

"Siren, can you take care of Snuff…and Warnner…" She hesitates.

"Um, Williams," Warnner supplies.

"Thanks. Warnner Williams. Julian found him. I need to find out what's going on. Maybe I can help."

"Yes. Of course. Go. I'm so glad you're back." Siren gives Malice another quick hug before turning to face Warnner. "My apologies for the welcome." Slapping her head, a look of horror flashes across her face. "I forgot about the Welcoming. I wonder if it'll still go ahead. Things are… well…"

Her face loses all colour and she begins to sway.

Warnner steps forward to grab her shoulder, stunned when she steps even closer, burying her head in his chest. He wraps his arms around her and awkwardly strokes her hair. The connection sends sparks across his skin, causing him to breathe shakily. A few moments pass and Siren's breathing slows.

"Thank you, I just needed a moment to hide." She pushes away from his embrace and wipes her face dry with her fingertips. "It's been a tough couple of days."

"So what happens now?" Robbed of her warmth, Warnner

longs to pull her back into his arms.

"I'll take you to Auntie Rose; she's in charge of Foundlings."

Siren picks up Snuff's reins and leads Warnner towards one of the carved caravans edging the clearing. At the caravan's door, she flicks a battered bell. The sharp ring doesn't have time to dissipate before a plump and dishevelled woman wrenches the door open.

"Auntie Rose, may I present Warnner Williams. One of Julian's finds. Malice brought him. He just arrived." The words tumble out in a mix of haste and embarrassment.

"Welcome to the Hill." Grabbing him up in a hug, the large woman drags him inside. "Oh you poor thing, you look terrible. I remember what it was like going through the Change: always hungry and always tired. You must be starved. Sit down and I'll get you something to eat. Do you want to stay, Siren? You're looking a bit pale yourself."

Clearly amused by Warnner's rapid adoption, Siren backs away from the door shaking her head. "Thanks for the offer, Auntie, but I have to go take care of the horses. I'll be round later to take him for a walk." She laughs at Warnner's look of offence at being treated like a new pet. "Warnner, not Snuff!"

"Right, something to eat and then I'll show you where you'll be sleeping," Auntie Rose says. Siren removes her sleeve from Snuff's masticating jaw, giving a shallow wave goodbye as she turns to leave.

Warnner stares vacantly at Siren's retreating back, as a chair is shoved against his legs and a plate piled high is placed on his lap.

Oh shit. That's unexpected.

CHAPTER NINE

"So, he's gone too?" Lively's question is unnecessary as Trapp slams the door behind him and throws the car keys across the room. She snatches them out of the air before they hit the wall and slide unreachable behind the unmade bed.

"Missed him by a day and no one knows anything. At least no one remembers anything." Becoming aware of his fidgeting, Trapp takes a deep breath and moves to stand in front of the window overlooking the motel car park. Using it as a mirror, he straightens first his tie, then his jacket, and finally smooths his short, wiry grey hair back into perfect place. "I told you we should have taken him as soon as we knew he was at the Centre."

"You think it's that easy? How were we going to convince him to come with us when he wouldn't even talk to us?" It's dangerous to anger Trapp, but Lively's way past tired of this chase without reward. "It was only chance we found him at all, he's not on the list. Must be a Natural."

Trapp takes a step toward her, accidently kicking a takeaway container half-filled with last night's chicken chow mein.

"This place is a tip. You could straighten it up while I was gone." He slaps at several personal files stacked on the table, sending the paperwork sliding across the smooth surface. Lively snatches up a photo of Dr Noel Ledger as it slips over the edge and towards the floor. Holding it up, she casts a critical eye over the doctor's open and honest face smiling for the camera.

"Yes, cleaning would be such a better use of my time." Lively leans back from the lime-green dinette table, flinging a pile of newspapers into an already overflowing bin. "Our employer won't be pleased if she finds out we were hunting without permission, but at least the room will be tidy."

"Don't act like you didn't agree on making a little profit on the side. You're the one who said the boy was an easy gain." He kicks the table and starts his pacing again. "All of this risk for nothing. First, we miss the boy in the States, and now the one here. It's as if they know we're coming."

Lively wishes Trapp would put an end to his to-ing and fro-ing, it's making her nauseous. "What about this doctor? Noel Ledger? Should we question him?"

"No, a third visit would be too suspicious if we had to silence him. Besides, he'll have been persuaded like the rest. We should have questioned that old relic at the festival." They both know the danger of not fulfilling their contract. Neither of them want to become the hunted instead of the hunters.

"Question him? It was too dangerous, too many people. We were lucky to get the incendiary device in his truck without being seen," Lively says, measuring her words carefully.

"It should have worked. He should've been stuck alone in a paddock when we got back." Trapp picks up the car keys, jangling them in front of Lively's face. "We'll just have to track him."

"Who? The old one? Are you crazy? You're letting our focus get divided. We need to leave this as a lost hunt and complete what we've been contracted to do." She pushes her chair back, letting it scrape against the floor, then picks up the files and shuffles them into a carrying case.

"No. I agree the old one is out of reach, but we still have time to get the boy. He can't have made it far on foot. Besides, it's obvious he doesn't know what he is, and so he won't know how to protect himself. His capture will add a little padding to our profit." Trapp crosses in front of her towards the door of their hotel room. "Well? Are you coming?"

"Do I have a choice?" Maybe they can catch up with him; the prize would be worth the risk.

"Look. Here. What do you think?" Trapp steps aside to allow Lively to see where the dirt has been disturbed in the corner of the Centre's main garden.

"How the hell should I know? It could be a footprint, but even if it is, it could be anyone's." She turns towards the main building, imagining the hundred or so inmates with free access to the grounds. "It's not like kids are going to stick to the paths."

"Oi! You two. This is private property. Get lost." The man from their previous morning visit appears around the corner of the building, a lit cigarette pinched secretively in the palm of his hand.

"Our apologies Mr…ah…" Lively says.

"Chore. Davey Chore." Dropping the cigarette, he grinds it with his heel before shaking the proffered hands.

"That's right. Mr Chore. We were here the other day, if you remember. We're from the Destination Church. We heard that a boy has gone missing." She steps away from the garden bed, covering the footprint with one of her own. "We'd like to help."

"Out here?" Davey turns around. They're completely alone and the light is beginning to fade. "It's a bit late."

"Yes. I know it seems a bit strange. We were hoping to

get the feel of the place. It's so beautiful here that it's hard to imagine anyone wanting to run away." Lively puts a hand on his shoulder, twisting him gently towards the mountains as Trapp returns to their car. "Sadly, we deal with a lot of run-aways in our work and it is always good to start in the place they were last seen. Can we ask you a few questions?"

"I'm not sure. Jobs are hard to find and this one has a lot of confidentiality" Davey looks at her, rubbing his thumb across his fingers.

"Oh, I know. And your job is so important—looking after the boys. I bet you do more than you're paid for." Lively gives a thumbs-up behind her back to Trapp.

"Well, now that you mention it, I might be able to help you out. But I just got here, about to start my shift."

Lively watches his eyes lift, up and to the left.

Liar.

"You know," Davey goes on, "every day he'd stand in the courtyard and look in that direction. When I say look, I mean *stare*. Like he was waiting for something."

Truth.

"What direction would you say that was, over there perhaps?" Lively points towards the mountains.

"Yeah, south, towards those ranges. Don't know why he'd want to go there; he didn't look like much of a hiker. If you ask me, I'd have said he was more of a city boy."

"That's what we thought too, but I feel terrible knowing he's out there alone." Trapp joins their conversation, making Davey jump. "The world's a dangerous place. But with your help I am sure we will find him soon." Trapp reaches out to shake Davey's hand, passing a folded $20 note with the other.

Ha! That will serve the little shit right, being dragged back. Davey doesn't feel the knife kiss the side of his neck, penetrating the jugular, his blood clogging his throat and thwarting any attempt to scream for help.

"Told you so. He's gone on foot to the Hill." Trapp taps the dirt free from his emergency shovel. The garden bed will not reveal its secret any time soon.

"*Told you so?* When did you do that?" Lively takes the shovel and tosses it into the boot. "Well, you're the tracker so get tracking. I'll follow the main road and see if he's been careless, like the man said he is a city boy." It's not ideal, but there's always the chance the boy has found it difficult to keep up the pace at night.

Warnner's trail isn't easy to follow, often disrupted by heavy herd tracks and tractor trails. As darkness descends, Trapp is unable to continue; he is forced to wave Lively down and return to their temporary accommodation for another night.

The next day is no better. After finding Warnner's makeshift bed among the ferns, not far from where they called the search off the day before, his trail leads them across stone-studded slopes. Where his tracks end, horse prints begin.

"He's been found, but now we know where he is. I bet the other boy's there too by now. Time to report back." Grimly, they both know that it would be unwise to delay, and not returning isn't an option.

CHAPTER TEN

Groggy from troubled dreams, Slate scratches his scalp and fights free from the tangled blankets wrapped around his legs. Shattered on too many levels to count and half-blinded by the morning light, he slips down the ladder and into the kitchenette. He roots around for food when he notices that Malice's bedroom door has been left wide open. The bed's been slept in, for at least a short time, but both the bed and the room are now empty.

"Ah, you're awake."

Slate spins, cringing at the sound of his elbow cracking into Malice's nose.

"Good reflexes. I'll have to remember that." She pinches the bridge of her nose with one hand and cups the other underneath to stop the blood from dripping onto the carpet.

"Oh, shit. I'm sorry. You scared me." He glances around for a cloth, but there's nothing. "Can I get you something—for the blood?" He pulls his t-shirt over his head.

"No, it's okay. I've got it. Keep your shirt on." One hand under her nose, Malice yanks open a drawer and pulls out a cloth. "Actually, can you get me some water?"

"Right. Yes. Of course. I have a bottle around here somewhere." Slate rummages through his belongings until he locates a half-filled bottle in the heel of a boot. "Here you go."

"Um… Maybe I'll do this outside." Malice tucks the bottle under one arm and Slate rushes to open the door for her. "Wait here," she says. "It won't take a moment, and we need to talk."

While Malice is outside, Slate attempts to tidy the caravan. In the short time since his arrival, his belongings seemed to have multiplied. His efforts are restricted to throwing anything he recognises as his up into the loft and stacking everything else in the space left behind.

Malice catches him with a book in one hand and a sock in the other. "Leave it. This is your home now. I'm just your guest, as long as you'll have me." She places the empty bottle of water and the now pinkish cloth on the bench, still pinching the bridge of her nose. "I really want to talk to you." Her voice sounds like she is ignoring a bad head cold, thick and distant.

"Sure. What about?" Slate drops heavily into one of the armchairs, letting the book and sock slip from his fingers to the floor. After wiggling around to get comfortable, he removes a tiny pillow from under his butt and grasps it against his stomach, like a security blanket.

"Everything. Nothing." Dragging her braid over her shoulder, Malice moves the other armchair to a claustrophobic closeness. "My father died yesterday."

"The guy on the horse?"

Malice nods her head.

"I'm sorry."

"Thanks." Malice gives a weak smile, sniffs and then winces, holding the cloth back over her nose. "Forgot." She checks the cloth for blood. "He was travelling with my sister and some others, but they haven't returned." She pauses in the silence.

"I don't know what to say." Slate drops the tiny pillow and kicks it from foot to foot. "I hope they're okay."

"I heard you went to the river with Siren." Malice flicks out a foot, sending the hopping pillow out of the reach of

Slate's feet. "What did you think?"

"The river's great. She's great. She's worried, too. We overheard…" Slate casts his eyes towards the pillow, trying to will it back into his possession.

"Overheard…?" Malice raises a questioning eyebrow.

"Oh, nothing." Slate remembers how upset Siren was at the news and wonders at Malice's control of her own emotions.

"Nothing. Okay." Malice reaches out to take his hands, but he snatches them away and threads his fingers together under his chin.

"To be honest. Yes. I mean, it's crazy here. I don't want to live like this. With these people, or whatever these—*whatevers* are. I want to live in the real world." He rocks out of his seat and moves to stand behind his chair. "Siren seems to think I just need time, but I don't know you. Now your dad's dead, and your sister's missing. I mean, well, it's a bit much. Doesn't make a person feel safe, does it?"

"I want to tell you that this is unusual. I want you to feel you can be safe here." Malice slides her chair back and walks towards the door. "I can't. But please don't be in such a rush to reject us." She begins to cry.

What has he done?

After Malice leaves, Slate continues to tidy, this time with more precision, packing every misplaced possession back in his bags.

"Adjust to living here? Monsters masquerading as circus performers." He thrusts a pair of dirty socks into a corner pocket and zips it up. "People dying. Secret meetings. What next? Ritual killings?"

"Not likely. Unless you're offering."

"What the hell! Doesn't anyone knock?" Slate shoves his bags towards the back of the loft, hiding their ready-to-go appearance. "Make some noise, why don't yah?"

"I can go out and knock if you like." Siren has lost the angry countenance from the previous day; still not glowing with joy, she's only a lighter shade of grey.

"No, it's okay. You're here now, but be warned I've already caused a bloody nose today." He flips down from the loft, nervous energy making the walls close in. "Feel like taking me for a walk?"

"Sure. Do you want to come meet my parents?"

He's too slow to control the panic thinning his lips and widening his eyes.

Siren shakes her head. "No, I guess you're not ready for that."

"Sorry. It's just all too much." He struggles into his jumper, flipping the hoodie over his face. He's going to need new clothes soon; he just can't seem to stop growing. "I'm barely coping with accepting my own identity."

"Yeah. A walk in the woods it is." Siren swings open the door and leads the way behind the caravan and into the trees. Her stiffened back telegraphs to Slate that, as with Malice, he's hurt her with his honesty.

"I don't know why I'm so worried; it's not as if my life has been anything other than shit for years." He waits for Siren to reply but is greeted by silence. "But this doesn't feel like a life." They walk for several minutes, his words hanging in the air between them. "I'm scared about what's happening to me, Siren. I don't want to look like this—and I don't want to spend the rest of my life hiding, always on the move, like my parents did. This is no way to live."

Siren stops her stomping and turns around. She raises her hands to his face, then leans forward until their foreheads are touching. "Living here is the best way to live." She pulls a little away, still gripping his face between her hands. "I'm scared, too. And I'm not talking about the Change. We're losing—our home, and worse."

"Worse?" Slate licks his drying lips. "What could be worse?"

"Being hunted, tortured and killed." She bangs her head against him and pushes off like a swimmer making a turn at the deep end of the pool. "You're just going to have to accept that if Malice hadn't found you when she did, you'd have wound up under some psycho scientist's scalpel by the end of the year: sliced and diced. I don't know what you'd call worse than being here with us, but that must come close." She strokes a thumb against his cheek and gives him a weak smile. "Sorry. I should be teasing you to make you feel better."

"I guess we all have stuff we have to deal with." He takes her hand and gives it a squeeze. He'll miss this easiness when he's gone. "How about that walk?"

"How about a run?"

She dashes away.

Slate shakes his head. Caught between the desire to curl up and wait for the panic to leave, and the stronger need to stay as close to Siren as possible, he takes off after her.

"Enough, enough. I can't breathe." Slate leans against a tree and pulls off his hoodie. "Ugh. And I stink."

"Not as bad I do. I smell like wet dog." Siren lifts her shirt over her nose and inhales. "No time for a swim. I've got work to do. But I'll pick you up tomorrow night."

"Tomorrow? What for?" He collapses in the shade of a large puriri tree and closes his eyes. The exercise has done more than tire him out; it's chased his fears into a corner where he can forget them for a while.

"For the Welcoming? Remember? Everyone will be there." She stands over him, kicking his thigh until he opens his eyes.

"Oh yeah. I remember. Can't wait."

If he stays.

He puts his hands behind his head and closes his eyes again.

Ignoring his sarcasm, Siren replies, "Neither can I."

Shouts wake him. Metal clanging against metal. A large group of shadows are erecting a giant sideshow tent. The marquee is so dark it erases the world like a black hole. Over the entrance, massive wrought iron braziers are connected by an arch of thick metal strands that twist into the word "Welcome". Around the perimeter, people are decorating their caravans with festive flags, and setting up seating next to open fire pits. The whole clearing is full of noise: the laughter and music of a renaissance fair.

Leaving the tree and returning to his caravan, Slate watches the work continue through a stained-glass window. Its textured, bubbled glass enables him to imagine that their disfigured bodies are a distorted reality. Eventually, wrenching his gaze from the activity outside, Slate picks up one book after another, looking for a way to spend the day. The books are an eclectic selection, as if Malice had bought them to fill shelves rather than to read. The car manuals and cookbooks seem to serve no purpose, while the books on flora and fauna focus on habitats that exist either in other countries or other times. In the end, he grabs his pad and pencils and heads outside.

Settling himself on the front steps, Slate begins to draw, letting his artistry move his pencil across the page. Intrigued by the medley of configurations—both their beauty and beastliness—he doesn't notice the growing audience until his light is cut off.

"Wow, that looks great. I never noticed that Grind was so wrinkly. You can just see his belly pincers peeking out. Better not let him catch you drawing him or he'll want it for himself. Bit of a vain one is our Grind. Can I have a look at some of the others?"

Embarrassed at the praise, Slate barely looks up as he hands over his finished sketches.

"My name's Ripple. What do you say to me grabbing you some lunch, and you drawing a picture of Little Bell here?" Even with her large manga eyes, Ripple could pass for a Common, until she turns to reveal webbed bones protruding from her spine like the undulating fins of an angel fish. So unlike her child, whose baby face marks her as nothing more unusual than a three-year-old. Little Bell peeks cheekily up at him, sucking on the thumb of one hand while clinging to her mother's skirt with the other.

"Um, sure. That would be great. I'm starving." Grinning at Bell, Slate shuffles over a bit and pats the space next to him. "Why don't you sit up here, and I'll draw your picture for your mummy? You can stay still for a minute, can't you?"

The little girl nods and climbs up the stairs, her thumb still stuck in her mouth.

"Good girl. I'll be back soon." After straightening her little girl's dress and patting her hair into place, Ripple disappears into the crowd to fulfil her part of the bargain.

Slate is finishing the sketch when she returns with his lunch and a group of others, it is obviously from their open curiosity that they have been discussing him.

"Hope you don't mind, but I told my friends how great you are, and they wondered if you were willing to barter for a few drawings." She takes the completed picture from Slate's hands and passes it around for the group to admire, before swinging Bell up onto her hip.

"Ah, I don't mind doing the drawings, but I don't know how to barter," Slate mumbles. With his hoodie pulled low, like a child pretending that being under the blanket will make him invisible to the monsters under the bed.

"That's no problem. How about we owe you a debt? Within reason, of course," suggests someone in the gathering group.

"Um, sure. A future debt. Thanks." Slate has no intention of collecting on the offer but he can't refuse the request, a compulsion to draw creatures beyond his imagination is too strong. He is soon engaged by a never-ending range of subjects that the darkening of the day takes him completely by surprise.

"Thanks, Slate. We wedded a moon ago, and it will be great having something as a keepsake. Photos are forbidden. See you at the Welcoming." Holding his shy bride's hand with one hand and clutching the drawing in the other, the final customer of the day heads away.

Scanning the nearly empty clearing, Slate stands and stretches to loosen his cramping muscles in his hand. Now that he's no longer concentrating on his drawing, he's aware of the drums vibrating through the evening air. The walls of the caravan pulse with their heavy, rhythmic beat. As if repelled by the dangerous, primitive music, he moves back inside and up into his loft. He packs away his pencils and drawing pad, then rummages through his belongings for something cleaner to wear, settling on a well-worn pair of jeans and a shirt he has no memory of owning. No one here follows fashion, and he doesn't want to stand out—he's never wanted to stand out. The day of drawing has proven that once you ignore their physical differences, the Travellers look like a mixture of farmers—with their boots, blue jeans and checked shirts—and gypsies—with their long cloaks and robes. Elaborate hairstyles are decorated with ribbons and jewels. The less complicated their outward appearance, the more eccentric their attire. He guesses it's their way of fitting in.

The tempo of the drums increases. Slate ties on a pair boots and rubs his hand over the stubble steadily growing over his head. He can barely fathom what possessed him to shave his hair off in the first place. He thinks back to the stares of the kids at school, not unlike the frightened reaction he had to Siren when he first saw her. Constantly aware that his mottled hair matched his skin, he'd taken to wearing long-sleeved shirts and pants to hide his disfigurement. But his success was limited. After one particularly embarrassing confrontation in the phys ed locker room, he'd shaved his hair off, hoping it would make the stripes less noticeable. But now he wouldn't have recognised himself in a mirror. The creature within, which the Hosts had unknowingly feared, is beginning to show. His features are beginning to smooth and stiffen, and his eyes have taken on a luminous tinge. Finished with his dressing, Slates decides to wait for Siren outside.

Reaching for the handle, he pulls back his hand as the door swings outwards, and Barnabas, flanked by Siren and another figure, beckons him down the stairs.

"We have come to be your guides and protectors." Opening his arms in welcome, palms up, Barnabas continues, "May I present your Aunt Hathor? She's been looking forward to meeting you."

The figure floats forward, as if propelled through water and not air. Even the flimsy garments she wears ebb and flow around her. Her icy, grey-blue eyes bore into Slate's own.

"You're Changing. Good." Her voice reminds Slate of the river, murmuring and bubbling over rocks and around bends.

Unlike the darker Barnabas and Siren, Hathor is as pale and insubstantial as the light of the moon, and completely devoid of hair, including eyebrows and lashes. Rather than appearing ugly, she is otherworldly.

"Um, thanks." Slate's relieved to see Siren's silent approval at his response.

Not screaming, he mouths silently.

Well done, she responds in kind.

"Come on, then. You don't want to miss your own party, do you?" His pleasure at seeing them together evident,

Barnabas ushers them towards the tent.

They walk across the open space, shadows moving ahead of them. Slate strains to make out their shapes, to see if any of them are among those he'd met and drawn during the day. But the vagueness of their bodies gives him a headache. Pausing before the entrance to the tent, Barnabas puts a hand on each of their shoulders, pulling them firmly around to face him.

"Tonight, you'll be Welcomed and Marked, numbered among us. It's a time of celebration. Don't be afraid." He strides ahead into the tent, his arm protectively around his son's wife, their disappearing backs silently commanding the cousins to follow.

Upon entering the tent, Slate is overwhelmed by the drums, the beat constantly changing as fresh players take the place of tired musicians on a stage at the opposite end to the entrance. There are drums from around the world and throughout history. Great and small, wooden and skin, round and square, the percussion seeps into his skin, releasing the part of him that had been closed off for so long, first by his parents and then by his ignorance. Slate is scared by his wild inclination to move recklessly through the crowd, but reassured by Siren's presence beside him.

A roaring bonfire in the centre, its smoke funnelling though a gaping hole in the cone of the tent, casts flickering shadows against the fabric of the tent walls. Groups cluster around the edges, leaving room for dancing, but all eyes glance at the stage from time to time, waiting for the Welcoming to begin. Led through the throng of bodies, Slate is astounded by the number gathered.

There must be hundreds…*thousands.* His artist's eye twitches.

"Why does everyone look so different?"

"Where have you been living where everyone is the same?"

"Californian Hell." Slate is pleased when he gets a smile in return.

This time, he looks more closely at the others, not with an artist's eye, but with a desire to see them as people he could know better. Everyone older has a tattoo as unique as the bearer, somewhere prominent on their face, torso or limb. Pulling Siren closer to ask what they represent, he points to the symbol on his aunt's lower back: three horizontal wavy lines across a circle.

"That's her *Mark*. When we start going through the Change, we're counted among our people and branded with a Mark," she explains, shouting over the increasing sound of the drums.

"But what does it mean?" he asks.

"It means you're no longer alone." Siren slaps his arm down, still pointing at her mother's back. "Don't worry, it doesn't hurt."

Before he can ask if he has a choice, they reach the stage and the room crashes into silence. Barnabas beckons both Slate and Siren to join the others gathered in front, while he climbs the stairs to face the waiting crowd. Standing close to Siren, Slate struggles with what he is seeing. He's surrounded by normal-looking teenagers, all shuffling and twitching, each battling an inner creature under their skin. He glances at his own hands, and his breath catches in his throat. He runs a finger over the skin on his arms. Their once mottled colour is more defined. Uneven pale and dark stripes look like shadows in the grass. Then, a sharp pain spikes from his forehead, a bony ridge thickening above his eyes and splitting his face from nose to chin. He's distracted from the pain by Siren pointing to her sharpening ears.

"You should see your head!"

Slate rubs his fingertips over his head, now no longer shaven but hairless and lumpy.

Will I be forced to hide in the shadows forever?

A lone drum strikes up a slow beat, heralding the start of the Welcoming. Three elders stand facing the audience, and change.

Terrified, Slate grabs Siren's hand, unaware how tightly he is holding it until she leans over and whispers, "Breathe."

As if from an attack of the flu, he shivers uncontrollably when an indecipherable chant rises from the audience, reaching a crescendo above the drums. Hundreds of growling, roaring, howling voices end abruptly when Barnabas raises his hands to speak.

"In the beginning, there were many; then there were only two. The Common ruled the day and the Relics ruled the night. From the air that fills our lungs, to the water that quenches our thirst, and the earth that satisfies our hunger, we are here to Welcome our newest Changelings and number them among us. Prepare to step forward and be Marked as one of the Dispossessed."

With obvious pride in his voice, Cornelius calls, "Siren. Welcome."

Slate reluctantly lets go of her hand. She twists away and leaps forward like an eager puppy, baring the back of her neck to her father. Cornelius reaches into the blue flames of a burning pyre and slowly withdraws one of the long iron brands, its fiery end glowing brightly. Slate holds his breath in anticipation of Siren's cry, but she merely twitches her nose to the offensive smell of burning hair and flesh, as her skin hisses and blackens. When she returns to her place, she winks at him and lifts her head higher. The audience howls, stomping their feet and slapping their approval across their chests.

"Slate. Welcome." Instinctively Slate steps back, away from the stage and his Uncle's extended hand.

"Slate, it'll be all right." Slate jerks away from Siren's attempt to grab his elbow.

"No. I don't want to do this." His voice is low and shaky.

"I don't want anything to do with this." He turns and runs blindly towards the entrance, knocking into bodies in his haste. He reaches the caravan before he comes to his senses. Heaving, he collapses onto the steps, burying his face in his arms.

"Slate."

"Go away."

"Come back to the Welcoming." Siren's voice is closer, but no less panicked than his own.

"I don't want to be burnt. Marked as a biohazard or a mutation of evolution." He raises his head and rubs he eyes even redder. "I'm not like you. I don't belong here. I want to go home."

He hears her sigh. "Is there room up there for me?"

Slate moves slightly, allowing his cousin to join him on the step. He lets her put her arm around him, her warmth reaching under his clothes, calming his tremors. "It's okay, Slate. No one's going to hurt you."

Her hair caresses his cheek.

"Your hair is doing that thing again." He takes in a shuddering breath.

"Does it scare you? Do I scare you?"

There's pain in her voice.

"No." He leans towards her, resting his head against hers.

"Can you come back with me and just enjoy the party?" She twists an arm though the crook of his elbow and threads her fingers through his. "All the ritual stuff will be over by now and Grandfather will be telling everyone we will be leaving soon." She sniffs. "It's funny. In our own ways, we both just want to be home. I want to stay here and you want to go. But we both want to be home."

"Except, you still have your family." He squeezes her hand and shuffles closer.

"They're your family, too." She moves her hair away from

his face to have a better look at him. "If you go back to America, where will you live? Who will you live with? You don't know how painful it would be to us here—to me—not to know what happens to you. Grandfather said he had to let Malice go in search of your father because not knowing was driving her mad… She could've… I know we haven't known each other long, but I don't know how I'd cope not knowing if you were safe. If you were happy."

"I'm sorry, Siren. I can't help how I feel, and I don't want to be here." But he's not sure if he's lying to her or to himself. He wants to tell her how much she means to him, but he says nothing at all.

"Will you at least stay until we all have to go?"

There's regret in her whisper.

"Do I have a choice? I don't even have my passport, or money for a ticket. I'm trapped." His anxiety rises and his body begins to tremble again.

"You're not a prisoner here, Slate. You can go anytime you want. You just have to let us get used to the idea. No one ever considered that you wouldn't want to stay," she says, her voice rising.

"No one asked me if I wanted to come," he counters.

"I'm sorry, Slate."

They sit, holding each other, looking at the stars.

"Siren. Are you out here?" The tent flap widens and a figure moves hesitantly towards them, then back inside.

"You're being summoned." Slate releases her hand and shifts away, the cold air coming between them.

"Oh, sounds like Warnner." Her voice is a mixture of wistfulness, longing and exasperation.

"Warnner?" Slate questions, surprised by an unexpected feeling of jealousy.

"He's new here, too. Was living in an institution. It's really amazing he was found in time…before he… Oh, never mind," she answers.

"You mean he's mad?" Slate sputters.

"No, I mean he's like us, but his parents weren't. He's a Natural. He is…who he is." Siren sighs disappointedly.

A Natural. Does that mean than anyone could become a monster?

"That's awful. He must've been devastated when he found out." Slate means to sound sympathetic, not accusatory.

"No, he wasn't… He was relieved."

The tension between them has returned. "I've never been to a dance before." Slate reaches for her hand again.

"Thanks, Slate. I'd never leave you to sit here by yourself, but I really want to go back." Siren lets Slate pull her to her feet.

Ignoring a few hostile stares and a bit of purposeful pushing, they wind their way through the celebrating crowd towards the group of Changelings still gathered near the stage like awkward wall-flowers, not wanting to do the wrong thing and not wanting to be left out.

"Hey, guys. Found him," Siren greets them cheerfully. "Now everyone play nice. I want to dance and have fun. You only have one Marking party."

The others follow Siren's lead and the tension he's been holding dissipates. He's dragged further into the dancers. Slate glances towards the musicians and sees a boy near his own age look up from his drumming. Caught in mid-laugh, his face changes from friendly to fierce. Without being told Slate knows he's the boy Siren was tongue-tied about, *Warnner*.

"Slate, I want you to meet my best friends, Rip and Fade."

Slate wrenches his focus back and extends a clenched fist in greeting.

"Nice fist bump."

"You too. I think we've met. Maybe?" Slate mimes drawing.

"Ugh. Did you draw that lovey-dovey picture of Knash and Curvia? I don't know how you could stand watching them smooching long enough to draw them." Rip makes gagging noises, while Fade rolls their eyes.

"Well they both owe me a future debt now, so I guess it was worth it."

"Cool. Maybe I can do you a favour and then you can give me their debt. They've kicked me out so that they can be alone, and I'd love to get them back." His toothy grin is hard to look at; all Slate can imagine is being consumed. "Though shacking up at Siren's is not bad."

"Sure, but I can't think of anything I need right now," Slate agrees, trying to keep his thoughts from showing.

"Enough talking, you two. We want to dance." Dragging Rip towards the dancing crowd, Fade gestures for Siren and Slate to follow.

The celebration continues, Siren leading him around the tent, introducing him to everyone they meet. While Siren preens under their compliments on her new Mark, no one makes him feel judged for opting out. He knows he won't remember their names, but the constant touching, a process of familiarisation, he'll never forget. After a brief introduction to his other cousins, Stella and Nova, he's passed along from group to group. Not all the introductions are easy. Some are friendly glances, others blank stares. But it gives him an opportunity to show Siren how he'd spent his day. After the first couple of thanks from happy recipients of his drawings, a new respect for him shows in her eyes. She hadn't been ashamed of him before, but now he can tell that she is proud to have him as her cousin.

Too soon the sun fights back against the night sky. Still high on the festive air, Slate and Siren race toward his caravan, this time trailed by Siren's parents, and her little sisters. They stop outside his door to say their goodbyes, but not before wringing a promise of meeting up again in the morning. In bed, Slate feels he'll never sleep. There's too much to think about.

"Honestly Slate, get up, you lazy boy." Popping her head into the loft, Malice whips off his blankets and draws a claw down the sole of one bare foot.

Slate wipes the drool from his mouth and looks at his arms. They appear normal— well, less abnormal than last night.

"Why the puzzled face? You lose something?"

"Um, yeah." Twisting around on his bed, he holds his hands out for Malice's inspection. "Didn't I look worse last night? And why are you here? I thought you were looking for your sister."

"Don't know to the first. Wasn't there to see. But as for the second, I did find her."

Slate slides over the edge of the loft and takes the proffered plate of food. "That's great, right? She's okay? And the others?" He takes a bite.

"Yes. Blue and the triplets are well. They knew my father was injured but he'd hid how seriously when he left to return with help. Do you mind if I don't talk about it right now? I'm not ready."

"Of course. Sorry. Um, what about this?" He lowers his head for inspection. "See anything different?"

"Right. This is all new to you. Normally, parents have the Change talk when their young are little." She crosses her legs and folds to the floor. "Let's see. The Change can take a while to settle, and everyone experiences it differently. Generally, some characteristics come and go when they're needed, like a defence mechanism." Her skin flips over from pale brown to black and back again. "Others are permanent. Like your bumpy head and face, for example."

Slate reaches up to stroke his head, confirming that the hardened ridges are still budding out of his skull. "I might need a hat or a ski mask," he muses. "Um, okay…but…"

"No *buts,* boy. Eat and begone. The fair awaits you and sadly, I have a funeral to plan." The light in her eyes fades and, she drops his empty plate onto the bench. Then, giving him a brief, tight hug, she goes into her bedroom, and pulls the door closed behind her.

Slate is drinking the last drops of water from his glass, wondering if he should check up on her, when the pounding on the door begins.

Covering his head in his hands, Slate groans, "Uh, no more. Enough is enough. My head's going to explode."

"What's taking you so long? We've been waiting out here for ages. Come on. There's so much to see and do and only a couple of days to enjoy it." Leaping inside, Siren ignores his protest and pushes him out the door into her sisters' waiting arms. Surrounded by his cousins, Slate lets his eyes fill with the sights before him. Last night had been surreal and in some ways easier to accept as just a dream, but today the view is glorious. If he'd been transported back in time, to a place on the edge of his imagination, he couldn't have conceived of a more exotic display of people and entertainment. Along with the rich, tantalising aroma of mouth-watering meals, enticing enough to make him want to start eating all over again, he's mesmerised by the startling performances of music and trickery. Egged on by his cousins, he moves from one caravan to another, acknowledging the acquaintances he'd made yesterday, while taking every opportunity to try new tastes and sensations.

At each stop he's encouraged, along with his cousins and several other Changelings, including Rip and Fade, into attempting feats of strength and skill. His younger cousins seem well suited to any act that includes sharp, flying objects, while Siren displays a talent for balance and speed. Failing many times to catch, throw, leap or fall with grace, Slate enjoys himself, but not too much to not notice that they're being followed. As the day wears on, he meets every resident, except for Warnner, who is never far away but often absorbed with any group making music. The exploration of the fair continues well into the night and again the following day, by the end of which he no longer feels a need to make sense of this new world. Perhaps he could be happy if he stayed.

As Siren had said, "It is what it is, and nothing more."

CHAPTER ELEVEN

"Slate, can you help me with these?" Malice finishes tying a thin red ribbon around her neck and holds out her wrists for Slate to tie identical ribbons around them as well. "I appreciate your support, but you don't have to come with me."

"I…I don't even know where my parents are buried." He concentrates on tying the ribbons firmly, but not too tight. "I know it sounds selfish, but I never got to say goodbye to them. So, if it's okay, I'd like to come."

"Thank you." Malice strokes the ribbon at her neck and runs her hands down the front of her dress, smoothing out the few wrinkles caused by sitting too long.

"You look great," Slate reassures her. And she does. The cream-coloured dress is woven with thick strands of cloth that are braided down her back. He'd spent the day in the loft watching the women of the community come and go, each taking their turn to add their own piece of cloth to the dress until it touched the floor and no more could be added. "Should I be wearing a black armband or those red ribbons or something?"

"Oh, these. No. They're just for descendants. I should really have some around my ankles too, but no one will see they're missing under this dress. It's silly really. They represent the struggles we overcome in life. My father was a follower of the old ways. He'd have liked me to wear the ribbons for him." She looks around the room as if searching for a reason to stay a little longer. "Right. Let's do this thing."

Outside, the clearing is shrouded in darkening clouds. The tent and festive decorations are gone, but the large fire pit remains, its pyre reset but unlit. Nearing the lodge, Slate steps away from Malice's side to allow a girl to take his place. Wearing an identical woven dress and red ribbons around her throat and wrists, despite her dark green colouring, Slate assumes she's Blue, the younger sister Malice mentioned. The pair act as if they don't see each other, but they link their pinkies like a promise. When they reach the bottom step of the lodge, they're met by several people carrying a body wrapped in dark brown woven cloth, the burden etched in their faces.

Slate is taken by surprise when the keening starts. It echoes but doesn't intensify. Just a continuous, grief-stricken note in the air. As one voice fails, another takes up its pain. The sisters follow their father's body to the pyre and stand back as it is placed on top. A torch is passed from hand to hand, even through Slate's own, until it's clasped between the sisters, who raise it together and set the pyre alight. The body is rapidly engulfed by voracious all-consuming flames and the keening stops. In its wake the pining sound of a reed flute, rises above the crackling flames. It is soon joined by the drumming of a sudden downpour as the sky bursts over the clearing. But no one moves. They stay watching until the pyre turns to ash and smoke, then the mourners approach the sisters. Hugging them tightly, tears camouflaged by the rain, no one says a word. Time seems to have both sped up and slowed down. Eventually, there are only a handful left in the clearing to watch the last of the embers flicker out of existence.

"Do you want help with the ashes?" Siren, her clothes plastered to her body, holds out a large metal bucket and a shovel.

"I thought we could send him down the river together."

"Thank you. I hadn't planned that far ahead." Malice takes the shovel and hands the bucket to Blue. "This is it."

On the walk to the river Slate trails behind, not sure if he's still welcome at this part of the ceremony, or whether he really wants to be there. Watching the sisters dig up the ash, bone and wood fragments had horrified him, and the thought of throwing the remains in the river make him ill. How many other burnt bones litter the river floor where he'd so recently swum?

The rain has petered to a light mist and the sun begins to eat away at the thinning clouds by the time they are done digging. Up ahead, Blue begins to talk, and soon the sound of laughter snakes towards him.

"It's good you're here, Slate." Siren links her arm into his, and he squeezes it against his body.

"Do you really think so? I feel…unnecessary." His voice breaks.

"Being here is enough." She pulls him to a halt. "I'm so sorry no one was there for you. I don't know how anyone copes with anything, especially the hard times, when they're alone."

"You just stop thinking about it…or at least I tried," Slate replies.

At the edge of the river, the sisters tip the bucket over. A light breeze catches the ash and sends it dancing across the surface of the water. They watch until the river runs clean, then rinse the bucket and shovel and return them to Siren.

"Will you sit with us tonight?" Malice asks.

"Of course we will. Your truck is a bit small. Do you want to do it at my house?" Siren offers.

"I was thinking we could build another fire and stay out under the stars," Blue suggests. "I don't want to look at that spot and have only sad memories."

"Good idea. Father would have approved." Malice gives

her sister a hug. "First, I want to disassemble this dress. I hope not to wear one again for a very long time."

A new fire is going strong by the time Slate finds the courage to approach. Two distinct groups have formed. A much older group have joined Malice on one side, while a group of Changelings his own age have gathered around Blue.

"Over here, Slate. Come join us." Siren waves him across, scooting over to give him a place to sit. "I think you've met everyone, except Blue, of course." Unsure whether to give her a hug or say something comforting, Slate settles for an awkward wave. "Oh, and possibly Warnner." On the other side of Siren, Warnner gives him a mocking stare.

"Oh yeah, the stalker." Slate says. The murmurs stop. Above the beating of his heart, the wood crackles under the assault of the flames. "I mean, I seem to see you everywhere: at the Welcoming and at the festival." He ignores Siren's pointed stare.

"Maybe *you* were stalking *me*," Warnner counters, sliding closer to Siren.

"Enough, guys. We're here to keep the mood light for Blue. Not to start a fight." Siren pushes the boys away from her and moves closer to Blue.

"No, it's okay. I think seeing these two stretch their muscles would be fun." Blue isn't deterred by Siren's angry stare. "Oh, come on. It's what Changelings do, isn't it? Huff and puff and knock each other around." Her laugh is hard, her white teeth shining brightly against her dark green skin. "I bet you could take them both without breaking a tooth."

"Your sister might not approve," Siren reminds her. "And besides, these guys are newbies. They have no idea how strong or fast they are. They're too used to being Common. I wouldn't want to damage them."

"How do I know what my sister would approve of? This is the first time I've seen her in years." Any sign of welcome is wiped by her cold stare at Slate. "First she was gone chasing after *his* father. And when that didn't work, she stayed to find and protect him instead of being here for her own family."

"It's not Slate's fault."

Standing up, Blue brushes off Siren's attempt to comfort her.

"No, it was his stupid, weak, Common mother's fault." Blue spits the words out, her finger piercing the air like a knife. "…and *his*, too."

"My fault?" Warnner takes a step closer to Slate.

"Didn't my wonderful sister tell you?" Blue's voice echoes shrilly in the hollow of an abruptly ended conversation. "Of course not. You're both *so* important. Must save every lost relic."

"Blue, stop it!" Malice rounds the bonfire, flanked by her companions. "You're just hurting."

"Hurting? Is that what you call having your sister tell you *she won't be gone long*? Having your father tell you *it's just a scratch?*" Blue, fully transformed, leaps towards her sister, fangs and claws extended. "Liar!"

"It's okay, Blue. I'm here now. I won't leave you again. I promise." Malice makes a grab for her sister by the wrists, but Blue rakes her across her cheek, drawing blood.

"Don't touch me! You should be dead, not father." She strikes again, but this time Malice is quicker.

"You're not yourself. Come back to the truck and rest." Malice holds firm against her thrashing sister.

The others watch, unwilling to interfere, the silence broken only by Blue's weakening cries. Finally, exhausted, she collapses.

"You guys should go. We can talk tomorrow." One of the triplets lifts Blue into his hairy arms, while Malice whispers soothing words to her distraught sister.

Slate lets Siren lead him back to his caravan. "Should I move out?"

"No. The caravan is your home. Malice will stay with Blue in their family house truck. Only the engine was damaged by the sabotage."

He wants to ask more, but she shakes her head.

"Tomorrow. Okay? I just want to go to bed. I've had enough of this sad day."

As he turns to leave, Slate is surprised when Warnner materialises at Siren's side. He watches Siren reach for him, and then pull back, as if afraid of needing his comforting touch. Slate grips the door frame, sinking his nails into its pulpy flesh, until it cracks.

"Hey Siren, do you think you could stay with me tonight? I could use the company." Warnner's looks at him in disgust and pulls Siren into a hug, kissing he top of her head.

"That's a good idea. Your cousin needs you. I'll see you in the morning."

CHAPTER TWELVE

The bell above the door gives a tired jingle, as Trapp and Lively enter. Their tailored suits and name-brand sunglasses clash with second-hand furniture and appliances so old they can't be given away. After a cursory glance to check for other customers, Lively flips the sign from open to closed, and locks the door.

"Welcome to Destination's Second-Hand Depot." The voice startles them. "Can I help?" An old man, looking every bit as decrepit and neglected as the shop he's minding, lifts his head above a pile of dusty books stacked on the customer counter.

"We're expected," Lively informs him.

"Out the back." The shopkeeper dismisses them with a jerk of his head and returns his attention to his jigsaw depicting Salome delivering John the Baptist's head on a platter to her mother, Herodias.

Trapp and Lively leave the old man to his diversion, and thread their way to the back of the store. Behind a maze of tables and towering bookcases, they push through a sticky, fly-specked, plastic-strip curtain and enter a small, windowless office. The room smells like unwashed gym clothes and the ghost of a heavy smoker. The walls are plastered with yellowing calendars, while faded postcards and numbers scribbled on scraps of paper are layered like découpage across a large pinboard. There's barely room for the two of them as every flat surface, and most of the floor, is stacked with papers.

"Where the hell is she?" asks Trapp.

"He said out the back. Maybe he meant outside." Lively opens another door. This one leads into a warehouse. An enlarged version of the interior of the shop, the space is full of storage racks reaching to the ceiling, each stuffed with the refuse of daily life.

"Who the hell would want any of this crap?" Trapp mutters. He kicks a deflated football into a broken bucket.

"No one. Maybe that's the point." A chilling draft caresses their faces. "Let's keep going. She has to be here somewhere."

Stepping carefully, they head deeper into the gloom. The only sounds are their footfalls and the hiss and spit of the overhead lights, flickering erratically and leaving them half blind.

The aisle ends with a choice. The first is a battered steel door; set in a larger roller door, haloed by the light shining through the gaps in the frame. No less elegant, the second option is a roughly hewn plywood door hanging awkwardly from its hinges, an empty hole where a handle should be. The final choice is a metal staircase, rising along the inner wall of the warehouse to a mezzanine floor above their heads.

"Your pick," Trapp offers.

"Up."

The stairs sway and creak under their weight, pulling away from the wall to reveal rusted metal bolts and bracing. At the top is an opaque glass door, caked dirt obscuring the view inside as much as the tempered glass. With no space available on the landing for two, Trapp is forced to teeter one step below.

"She's not going to be pleased," he says, reaching around to bang on the door.

Too late, Lively smacks his hand away and points to a surveillance camera. "They already know we're here."

On cue, the door swings inward to reveal a modern open-plan office space with cubicles branching left and right off the grey-carpeted corridor. Everywhere they look, people are chattering into headsets, typing at their computers, or flitting in and out of offices with files under their arms and serious looks on their faces.

"Destination Church thanks you so much for your support. Every little bit helps."

"We're grateful for your concern. Ms Stone's mission has always been to reach out to the most vulnerable in our society."

The intense activity seems to take a breath, then the volume is turned back on as the sea of people part to reveal a glass cubical at the far end.

"Here we go," says Lively.

The head of the Destination Church, Ms Stone, looks fragile behind her large glass desk, her face a lattice of fine scarring. She waves them in without lifting her eyes from her work, her pen stabbing viciously at the piece of paper, circling, crossing out, and scribbling changes in the margins.

They try not to fidget as they wait.

Finally, with a sigh of surrender, she lays down the sheet in the middle of the glass desk, places the pen on top of it, and speaks into her headset: "Mary, the ad is still not right. I'll give you my notes when my guests have left, but we really need it to appeal to young people. They are, after all, more pliable."

"I hope you don't expect me to wait for your report." The see-through desk is adorned with an array of broken artefacts more suited to a museum, and is the only protection Trapp and Lively have from the danger on the other side.

Staring at a spot on the wall behind her, Trapp stands rigid and speaks like a little boy reciting a half-learnt poem.

"We did not find his trail. Or the creature assisting him. We think he must have gone straight to the Hill."

"*Think?* You don't need to think! All you need to do is bring me a confused child." Ms Stone rises from her chair, her eyes narrowing. She takes a step towards them, and they take a step backwards. "I'm beginning to wonder if you believe in what we're trying to do here. We're trying to save this boy. Too many innocent children have been stolen and corrupted, but it's not too late for this one." The damage her body has suffered is well hidden by her clothes, but as she caresses one of the little figurines on her desk the cuff of her shirt pulls back, revealing a trail of puckered skin, evidence of a terrible burn.

"Of course we believe," Lively protests. "It's as if they know we're coming—the Relics."

"I don't need to hear your excuses. I need—we need—you to do what you have been hired to, which is to rescue him, *now*." Turning to the back wall she unrolls an aerial photograph covered in crooked black lines. "Fortunately, I have planned for your incompetence. I have Search and Rescue teams prepared to traverse these known trails to see if an emergency evac is possible. What I need you to do now is to patrol the main road. If anyone leaves, let us know. But do not approach," she warns.

"Just the two of us? That's miles of road. It's impossible to cover all the exits." Trapp hates the politics of their cause; he signed on for the thrill of the hunt and the pleasure of extracting information from reluctant captives. So far, the only challenge has been keeping himself alive. The Church could forget about saving souls. He wanted a trophy.

"Don't question me." Ms Stone has the conviction of a born-again believer. "You have your assignment. Do not fail me again. There are plenty of other trackers who'd like the chance to hunt an unknown species. You don't want to be their price of admission."

"Yes, ma'am. I mean no, ma'am. No problem."

Lively kicks Trapp in the ankle, reminding him of how they got the job in the first place.

"Good. And don't worry, I won't forget our deal." Ms Stone rolls up the map and returns to her seat, picking up the pen as if her work had not been interrupted. "Once we have the boy, you can do what you want with the girl—as agreed."

CHAPTER THIRTEEN

"Hi, Auntie, can I come in?" Siren steps onto an overturned feed bucket to get a better view, but still has to stand on her toes to peer in through the caravan's kitchen window.

"Hi, sweetie. I heard what happened last night. Are you looking for somewhere to hide?" Rose reaches out to stroke Siren's cheek.

"Yeah. I wanted to talk to Blue, but she's refusing to see anyone. Malice is really worried about her." Siren bites her lip and looks over to a nearby house-truck. Waves of charred metal panelling are the only remaining evidence of the burnt-out motor that left Julian with a mortal wound.

"Grief takes time. I thought the girls were trying too hard to get happy too fast." Rose picks up a cloth and begins to chase grime out of the crevices of her intricate stained-glass window.

"So? Can I come in?" Siren points helpfully to a small spider web and a cluster of fly specks.

"Oh, sure. Where is my mind? You come right in. I might pop over and see the girls while you're here." Rose shakes out the cloth, sending a cloud of dust and bug bits in Siren's direction.

"Hey, Warnner." The inside of the caravan is crowded, but not claustrophobic. At one end, the bed has been folded up into two couches with a table pulled up between them. The storage space above is closed off by trellised doors, creating a 1950s diner atmosphere. Along one wall high shelving, full of books and personal items, hangs above a long, narrow, wooden bench. Below it, Warnner sits cross-legged on the floor, half in sun and half in shadow.

"Hey, Siren," he answers, not taking his eyes off his little charge, who is attempting to pull himself up on Warnner's knee.

"Babysitting?"

Warnner holds out two fingers for the baby to steady himself as he works towards improving his new-found stepping. "Yeah. Never seen one of these before." He rubs his thumbs over the soft, fat, baby hands gripping his fingers. "Looks delicious."

"A baby?" Having two, much younger sisters, she's seen enough babies to last her a while.

"Yeah. Social Welfare tends not to put babies in holding cells or detention centres. They still have hope for them." He gives her a twisted smile, his face shifting from gentle to fierce and back again.

"Sorry. I keep forgetting you're new. It's just that…well, you know. You're not like Slate." She sighs her cousin's name like a lost prayer.

"Glad to hear that." Warnner picks up the baby and pops him into a cage erected in a semicircle around the back doors. "Here you go, buddy; keep yourself busy while I entertain my friend." Warnner empties a basket of toys and waits long enough to see if his offering will be accepted.

"You know what I mean, and now, after last night… What am I going to do?" Fear and hate mingle in the air, the tension so thick it presses against her, making it difficult to breathe.

"Whoa. Calm down. Why do you have to *do* anything?" Warnner leads her over to the couches, sliding in across from her.

"He's family. He has no one but us." Siren plays with her bracelets, pushing them up and down her arms before trailing her fingers along the agitated swirls on the inside of her wrist.

"Believe me, sometimes it is best to make your own family. Just because they're related doesn't mean you have to like them." Warnner reaches out and takes her hands. As with the baby, he rubs his thumbs over her knuckles.

"Ahhh, no more. I didn't come here for this." His touch is like static electricity, sending all the hairs on her body to attention. She slips from his grip and smooths her palms along her thighs under the table, dissipating the tingling.

"Then why did you come?"

Siren ignores the question and stares out the window. Outside, a rough wind is tossing the trees from side to side, sending their leaves dancing across the clearing.

"Siren?"

"I actually came to see Uncle Blaise." Her voice is muffled, as if it, too, has been caught by the wind and tossed aside. "Do you know where he is?"

"Ahh. A man of few words but a great many eyes."

She smiles at his teasing.

"He left early this morning," Warnner offers.

"Oh. I should have noticed. He's the herd master. You know, in charge of the horses and other 'food on four feet' on the Hill." She draws a target on the dusty window. "I wanted to ask him about Julian's horse."

"Ugh. Animals. I don't understand your fascination with them." Warnner sticks out his tongue, pretending to rid himself of a bitter taste.

"They're my friends. They listen to me when no one else does. They keep me from being lonely."

Warnner holds up his palms to ward off her short, playful punches to his shoulder.

"Ouch. That hurts. You're stronger than you look. I know

what you mean. I've always had my music. I guess everybody needs something…or someone."

Her breath catches. "You're right. I'm going to speak to my dad. Slate just needs to feel independent: needed, not just wanted. The only way he's going to feel that way is if we teach him how to look after himself. Maybe then he'll choose to stay." Siren shuffles out of her seat and leans over to kiss Warnner on the cheek. "We can't lose him. Despite what Blue said, Julian was right. There are too few of us to lose even one."

Siren spins out of the caravan leaving Warnner wishing Rose would come back for the baby so he could follow her.

"Don't worry, little man, I'm still here," he calls as the baby begins to grizzle.

Siren finds Slate at the river, pad in hand, sketching the scenery with a few added details. Looking closely, Siren can see the barest hint of something more in the shallow water: faces of death.

"That's a little gruesome don't you think."

"Go away. I just want to sit here and draw."

"Well, I won't and you can't. Come on, Slate. It's the only way for you to be safe in the Common world." She picks up a couple of stones and skims them across the surface, disturbing Slate's muse.

"What you're really saying is it's not safe for me here either. Blue's not the only one who wants me gone. And that's fine with me." Slate flips over a page and draws an outline of her hand, stone in mid-flight above another unwary creature lurking behind a half-submerged rock. "You don't need to look after me. You've got what's-his-name to worry about."

"Warnner. His name's Warnner. What do you have against

him, anyway?" She taps the drawing, pointing out a missing feature.

"Nothing. I mean, I'm your cousin, but he's all over you like he owns you." Blowing off the lead sharpening, he uses a moistened forefinger to smudge thick lines into delicate shading.

"Aww, Slate—you called me cousin. I like the sound of that." She clasps his head and shakes it roughly.

"So?" He brushes her away, grinning at her affection.

"So what?" She scoops up another handful of stones, using her fingers as a sieve to shake the smaller ones loose.

"So, what's up with that guy?" The creature in the drawing is beginning to take on the characteristics of Warnner's face, the stone descending towards his forehead.

"Stop changing the subject. Come and work out with me and the guys." She snatches the pencil from his grip, holding it to ransom. "It'll be fun. I promise."

"Okay, but he better keep his hands to himself." He folds the cover back and threads the returned pencil through the spiral binding.

"I don't think he's that into you." She laughs, tossing the rest of her stones into the river.

"I didn't mean…aww, shut up."

"Sorry we're late, guys. Slate was fixing his hair." Tucked in an area off the main clearing, a number of Changelings are engaged in a range of athletic activities. From Slate's hesitation, Siren can tell that some of them are familiar to him, others less so.

"No worries. We were just playing around with a few ideas." Though way past the Change, Siren is relieved Rex insisted that his brothers come and help. Unsupervised and untested, Changelings often end up needing serious medical attention.

"So, nothing traditional?" She casts her eye over to Fade and Rip, who are timing some sprinters. From the looks of it, it wouldn't be long before one of them is faster than her. Well, she has other abilities she could develop. A loud cheer erupts from some of the bystanders. Siren steps in front of Slate, blocking Talon's gleeful carnage as he tosses away one opponent after another, using a combination of Thai boxing, jujitsu and capoeira fighting styles. Past experience has taught her that Talon enjoys leaving a mark with each victory.

"Criminal ideas." Rex clips his younger brother Max, sending him stumbling backwards into a back flip and back onto his feet. Slate, who hasn't seen them perform, gives an impromptu clap of appreciation.

"Survival ideas," Rex clarifies, shaking his head in disgust at his brother's antics and Slate's response.

Siren stops Max from crashing into Slate with another impromptu move. "No funny ideas. This is supposed to be *in*structive, not *de*structive."

"Look, you lot haven't been out there like we have." Rex has always been the most serious of the three brothers, but Felix is the one who feels Julian's death the most. She knows that if his brother hadn't expected him to be there helping her with Slate, he'd have been with Blue, or at least as close to Blue as he could get.

"Guys, you're not helping." To keep the mood away from such dark thoughts she clenches her fists and raises them above her head like a body builder. "Think *empowering*." She relaxes into a defence pose as Max squares up for his attack.

"Siren, I'm not saying we shouldn't try. But we do have other things to worry about. The old people are no help; all they care about is staying hidden." Rex grabs his brother from behind and pins him to the ground, ignoring his imitation of an asphyxiating fish.

"Plus, there's all the littl'uns and no one is talking about...."—Siren gives Felix a deft kick to his ankle and jerks her head in Slate's direction— "... how we're going to be able to support this many of us on the road."

"So, what exactly do you want me to do?" Slate has been watching the whole interchange like a new kid at daycare, both afraid and eager to join in.

"We want you to learn how to be one of the wild things." Rex yelps as his brother resorts to nipping his leg for freedom.

"Yeah. Roar that terrible roar and gnash those terrible teeth and...um, what's that line about the claws?" Max's roar causes everyone in the clearing to pause and look. "Oh yeah, show their terrible claws. That's kinda stupid. Why show and not use?"

"Really, Max? Not helpful." Siren watches Slate's paling face. It is both exhausting and pointless trying to protect him. "Um, maybe we should go somewhere less graphic?" she suggests, leading her cousin towards the edge of the bush as a group of Changelings rush to stem the flow of blood from the torn limb of Talon's last opponent.

Built amid the trunks of giant tōtara, the pole house rises into the canopy like a wooden castle. Slate has never been to Siren's home, but the triplets are very familiar, calling out to see if her parents or sisters are around, scampering up and down stairs, over railings and in and out of doors.

"All clear. We can practice out here with no one to bother us." Like the pole house, the surrounding area is so different from the homes Slate was fostered in. The plants are all natives, allowed to grow where and how nature intended. Even the lawn is unmowed, clumps of long and short grass creating a wild checker-board, edged with sculptures half hidden amongst low-growing ferns and vines.

"Okay, so what does every one of us need to survive?" Rex loops his arm around a statue in the shape of a woman on fire, and draws a claw through his facial hair.

"A way to hide," Siren offers. Picking up a wild daisy, she begins plucking its petals in a private game of *he loves me, he loves me not*.

"A way to fight," Felix counters, his eyes darting in Slate's direction.

"Yes, if you can't hide, you must fight." Rex pats the statue and wanders over to the group seated in a loose circle.

"So, how do you practice hiding?" Warnner ducks out of the shadow of the bush and into the light, grinning at their startled reaction. Siren glances from the boy to the tortured daisy in her hand. She quickly throws the naked stem over her shoulder while brushing the petals from her lap.

"You have to know what you're good at." Rex opens his arms to Warnner as if greeting an old friend, and performs a complicated handshake ending with a back thump and a nose press.

"Like what? You don't mean like good with animals or music?" Warnner repeats the greeting with Max, but wisely skips Felix and Slate to join Siren on the ground.

"We're not Common. Siren, have you ever shown Slate what you can do?" Rex picks up a small twig and holds it out on his palm. It isn't a plant at all, but rather an insect: a walking stick.

"No," she mutters.

"Well, go on." He places the walking stick on a branch and waits.

"Okay, um… Let me think. I need to plan." She scans the group, looking from Warnner to Slate and finally at each of the triplets. "Okay, I'm ready."

She lifts her chin and shakes her head. At first, it looks like just her hair is growing but it covers her face, her arms, her hands. Her hands aren't the small childlike hands he drew but long, thick muscular hands. In fact, she no longer looks anything like herself. She's metamorphosed into a fourth identical sibling to the triplets.

"How's this?" She rubs her arms, fluffing up the newly grown hair.

"Shit. No. No. That's wrong." Slate stumbles to his feet and backs into a tree, before tripping over and falling on his butt again. "You can't be doing this. It's not real."

"Shush. It's okay, Slate. Don't panic." Siren holds out her hands, now monstrous paws with deadly looking claws. "Look. I'm fine. See?" She shakes again and turns back into herself.

"No, it's not okay. None of this is okay. This shouldn't be possible. I could become accustomed to birth defects but that was…just wrong." He sticks his head between his knees and breathes quick and deep.

"What are you talking about, Slate? That was seriously cool. Can I do that?" Warnner reaches out to rub a hand along Siren's now smooth arms, the connection causing sparks to arc between them, and ignores the triplets shooting mocking grins.

"We don't know. Some of us are mimics, chameleons, like Siren. But in the Common world it won't do her much good to look like us," Max explains. "Others are incredibly fast or incredibly strong."

"What about persuasion?" Talking to the ground, Slate has recovered enough to remember how easily Malice removed him from the Hosts.

"Oh, you mean the voice?" Felix rolls his eyes. "Yeah, a few of us can do that, but Julian was the best—and Malice. That's why she's always sent out to do the Council's dirty work. No offence, Slate."

"It's what the Change is all about. Finding yourself. No, that's not it. It's about finding your own way to survive," Rex explains.

"I can't do that." Without raising his head, Slate points in Siren's general direction. "I don't want to do that."

"We don't know what you can do. That's what we want to help you find out, so that you can survive when you leave here." Siren flicks Rex a worried look. "Look, sometimes it helps to play a game."

"What kind of game?" Slate asks.

"That was a good try that time, Slate." Pushing her hair away from her sweating face, Siren holds out a hand to help him up from the ground.

Slate spits out a mouth of dirt. "Can I go now? I think I've eaten enough earth today." His lip swells where he wasn't quick enough to dodge the incoming ground. "If we're the hope, then there is no hope."

Taking advantage of the break, the triplets have wisely settled themselves far enough away to avoid being entangled in another argument between the cousins.

"Come on, Slate, just one more time. Stress and fear, physical activity, and strong emotion should make your body react defensively." Siren gestures to Max, Rex and Felix to re-join them.

"Well, at least we know your head is hard, but as for the rest of you…" Rex trails off.

"I can't do this. I don't need to do this." Slapping aside her helping hand, Slate flips up his hoodie and limps stiffly away.

"Yes, you do. You need more than clothes to survive in the Common world," Siren yells after him. Frustrated, she turns to her companions, "I really need to stab something."

"Good idea. We haven't actually *tried* to hurt him yet." Rex brushes off a few leaves and twigs that have become entangled in his fur in their attempts to push Slate to his physical limits.

"Why isn't this working? We've been trying all day. I mean, when did you know what you could do?" Siren flicks her gaze over to Max and Felix.

"Us?" Rex turns. His brothers are engaged in a series of jumps and twists as they tumble effortlessly about the clearing. "We've being fighting since before birth. Our poor mum said she had to send us to our own area of the womb just so she could get some sleep."

"I knew really young, too," Siren whispers. "I remember entertaining the twins, as babies, by changing from Mum to Dad and back again. I used to get worried they'd choke with laughter."

"So maybe it'll take longer for him. Don't forget his mother was a Common. His skin could get thicker." Rex sticks out a foot, tripping one of his brothers and sending the pair into a half-sprawl. "What are you really worried about?"

"What if he *turns?*" She keeps her voice low so that only Rex can hear, only Rex can see her shake.

"You can't stop that. No one can," Rex says, leaning so close their heads rest against each other. "But if he does, we will be here for you and for him."

"Don't mean to interrupt, but now that the dead weight is gone, can I get in some practice?" Not welcome to participate, Warnner has only been an audience while they tried to get Slate to show his true self. "I want to see what I can do."

"Go ahead without me. I'm not in the mood anymore." Siren gives Rex a hug and waves goodbye to his brothers.

"Can I come?" Warnner brushes away a hair trailing across her face.

"No. Besides, the boys here can teach you some tai chi. Very good for channelling aggression."

"What's did she mean by that?" Warnner asks.

"It means she's noticed you needling her cousin, lover boy, and if you don't stop she's going to rip you a new one." Rex slams a paw onto Warnner's shoulder, making him wince.

"You've got a thing to learn about how to treat your split-apart," Max adds.

"My *what?"* No longer needing to hide his growing frame, Warnner doesn't look like a teenager any more. His long limbs allow him to tower over the brothers, but they still have the greater mass.

"Don't they teach you anything in the Common world? You've read Plato, right?" Felix asks, as he cracks his neck from side to side.

Warnner shakes his head. "But I've read *The Wolfman Cometh*."

"Ah, a classic, I'm sure. *Not*." Over the afternoon, Felix has joined Warnner in his cryptic remarks about Slate's lack of aptitude for anything that would help him survive. Now it looks like Warnner is going to have to pay up or shut up.

"So what you're saying is that, if I want Siren to like me, I've got to leave her cousin alone, read the classics, and practice old people's martial arts." Warnner sweeps his arms in front of him, locking them in an offensive pose.

"It is a way to a woman's heart, my man," Max says, squatting between the combatants, ready to drop an imaginary red flag.

"Well, Slate's not here, and I don't see a mobile library, so teach me so I may master the ultimate fist." Warnner makes a mock bow, first to Max, then to Felix, before sailing through a series of movements copied from the brother's earlier efforts with Slate.

"Yes, well done, smarty pants. Don't rush, follow each action through slowly. You need to feel the power of the movement from start to finish. Speed is of secondary importance. Mostly, combat is won with your head. Now, try the sequence again but watch for my blocks."

"Yes, Sensei. Show me how to do the teeth to the throat move again. I think I'll be needing to use that one soon." Warnner had been bored watching Slate fail time and time again, but now he relishes the feel of his body contorting into positions of strength and defence.

"It is called 'white crane spreads wings', weirdo." Stopping mid-movement, Felix gives him a quizzical look. "Are you humming?"

"Yep. It's a new composition. I call it 'De-stressing with tai chi'." Warnner hums louder, matching each movement with a different score.

"I don't think de-stressing is a word—and besides, look at you—or what's left of you." Felix steps back to admire Warnner's transformation. "I think you've found your talent."

Warnner holds up a hand.

"Cool!" His skin has changed to blend in with the trees and bushes around him. "Siren's got to see this. I'm barely here."

"She'll be at the station." Felix points. Metal clangs, then a rapid series of thuds—like something penetrating deeply into a wooden target—echoes towards them.

"What's going on there?"

"That'll be the twins. They have a knack with knives." Max pantomimes throwing a knife, followed by gripping his stomach as if suffering from a mortal wound.

"Knives?" Warnner grins, as Felix pretends to remove the non-existent knife from Max's body only to begin repeatedly stabbing him with it.

"Everyone needs a hobby." Rex rolls his eyes, and Felix falls to the ground, joining Max in his death antics.

"Their parents let them?" Warnner ignores the brothers' calls for the kiss of life. Was it supposed to have been like this between him and his own brothers?

"Let them? Their dad's the master craftsman. You need something sharp and pointy, he's your guy." Rex walks across his brothers' stomachs, smiling as each one lets out an *oomph* before popping back to their feet.

"So, Siren will be there?" He checks his hand again, disappointed that he hasn't managed to maintain his manipulation.

"Probably. I'll leave it to you though, I prefer girls of a gentler persuasion." Rex jerks his head in the direction of the river and jogs away; his brothers follow him.

Warnner holds an arm against a tree trunk and hums. Once again his skin changes, fading so the deeply grooved bark can be seen clearly. Grinning, he shakes his arm, like he'd seen Siren do, and it becomes familiar once again.

He finds Siren in front of an old railway station, working her way through an eclectic collection of weapons under her sisters' watchful gaze.

"Scary," he says, careful to let her see him before she begins her next throw.

Siren raises her arm and throws a knife, end over end, into her target. "Just helping my sisters out." She walks over and prises the knife out of the centre, tossing it from hand to hand. "Guys, this one's a bit light on the back end."

The twins take the knife and lay it down on a bench littered with a series of similar weapons of increasing size and width.

"Do you guys need me anymore? My arm's beginning to tire," Siren says.

"No. Thanks. You've given us enough to go on with." Nova and Stella exchange whispered giggles when Warnner approaches.

"So, you like knives?" He picks one up and runs a finger down the blade. "Sharp."

"No. Not really. It's just that I'm so..." Siren pulls her hand back from stroking a wicked-looking weapon on the edge of the table.

"Angry?" he suggests.

"No," she says defiantly, stepping away from the table, and her sisters' close observation.

"Frustrated?" He smiles wickedly.

"No," she says, unable to hide a weak smile.

"Constipated?" her sisters offer.

"Shut up. No. *Accurate,* and if you don't want to be my next target you might want to remember that." She nudges Warnner away from the station and her sisters' eavesdropping.

"What about a swim?" he offers. Folding one arm behind his back, he sweeps a branch out of their way.

"Race you," she counters, taking off before he has a chance to answer.

The sound of splashing and laughter tells them they're not the only ones who've had enough for the day. Jogging around the bend, Warnner sees that the river has taken on the appearance of an impromptu out-of-school beach bash—minus the beach.

"Not bad." Shedding his shirt, he follows Siren, leaping into the middle of a dark, slow-moving section of the river, and sending a small tidal wave of water over the edge of the rocks and onto a pair of feet tapping impatiently at the side.

"Siren, can I speak to you—in private?" Malice emerges from the bush looking like a dark cloud on a sunny day.

"Yeah, sure. What's the matter?" Siren slides out of the river and struggles back into her pants, which cling to her still-wet legs.

"Is it anything I can help with?" Warnner asks, treading water at their feet.

"Yeah, if you don't mind. I could use some help."

Desperation clings to Malice, smothering the strength and power that had greeted Warnner the day they met. "Blue's missing."

CHAPTER FOURTEEN

The inside of the house truck looks as if it has been hit by a mini tornado: bedclothes are strewn about, cups and bowls knocked over, and knickknacks swiped off shelves.

"What happened here?" Siren bends to pick up a fallen book. She flattens the creased pages and places it back in the bookcase, then unable to stop with the job half done, she straightens the rest on the shelf.

"I don't know. When I went to wake her this morning, it was just pillows under her blankets. The place was fine." Malice scoops up the traitorous pillows and blankets and piles them back on the bed. "She must have come back after I left to look for her."

"Have you told anyone? I mean besides us." Following her lead, Warnner begins to clear the floor, putting the pieces of broken plates, a windup clock and a bag of apples on a bench lining the far wall.

"No… It's just that I've let her down too much, and if she's…" Malice gestures to the room. Though less messy than when they arrived, Siren understands the implications.

"I'm sure she's fine. Just needed some space to think. There aren't any other signs she's in trouble, are there?" Siren joins Malice on the bed, shifting the bedding against the window to make room.

"Yes, there are. This isn't the only scar she's given me."

Pointing first to her face, a reminder of the previous night, Malice raises her shirt, exposing deep scratches criss-crossing her belly. She twists so that Siren can see they reach around to her back.

Warnner sucks in his breath at the deep, bloodied lacerations.

Siren ignores him. "Oh Malice. I'm so sorry. What do you want me to do?"

"I need to look for her, but I'm supposed to be removing trails." Malice pulls her shirt down, wincing as she tucks it back into her jeans. "There have been sightings along some of the more defined trails. Probably just hikers, but the Council wants to make the way impassable until we need to leave. Can you do my trails?"

"Sure, where are they?" Siren doesn't check with Warnner, she doesn't need to, she knows he'd do anything for her just like she would for him.

"I was given the back trails, over the range. You know the ones?" Malice unfolds a roughly drawn map, with a couple of trails highlighted in red ink. "You can cover one on your way out and another on your way back."

"No problem. I'll go now." She can feel Warnner's eyes burn against her skin. "*We'll go,* as soon as we're packed."

"I hated to ask, Siren, but thanks." Malice hands her the map. "There's one more thing."

"Sure. Anything." Siren folds the map and slides it into her back pocket.

"Can you take Slate with you?"

"Slate?" She glances at Warnner, who shrugs his shoulders in reply. "I don't know. He's being a jerk at the moment."

"Can't you work something out? It's just Blue's so angry at him, I'm afraid she might hurt him." Malice unconsciously strokes the raw claw marks that decorate her cheeks.

"I'm sorry, Malice. Of course we'll take him with us." She pulls Malice's hand away from her face. "I'm sure you'll find her."

"Why are we heading out in the dark?" It'd taken more than persuasion to get Slate to come with them. When they found him he had been repacking his bags, his *go to* reaction to stress. In the end, she suggested that the trails were a way to reach the Common world, and he agreed to accompany them if she showed him the way.

"Because we don't know when anyone will have to use these trails; if they can find them at night, they can find them in the day." She's beginning to hate the sound of his voice. If she wasn't so worried about him, she'd quite happily murder him and drag his dead body behind them to sweep the path clear.

In silent, but total agreement, Warnner falls in beside Siren. Leaving Slate trailing behind. "Couldn't we have left him with the triplets?"

"Ahh, will the two of you just shut up?" Siren stops and spins around. "Listen to me carefully. The both of you. We are doing this, not just for Malice, who has enough to deal with, but for everyone on the Hill."

She stares from one to the other, her warm breath condensing in the cold night air and wafting away like smoke. But even in her distress her heart and her hair betray her, reaching to caress Warnner and Slate's cheeks. "I need the both of you to be on my side. I'm not asking for the world, just a couple of nights out under the stars." A shaft of moonlight cuts through the canopy and splits her face in two. Neither side looks friendly. "Now this is the really important bit… If you're unwilling to help me and we fail, I will never speak to either of you again." Awaiting their response Siren bends to dust away the shallow indentation of her grinding heel, it wouldn't do to destroy the good work they've already done by leaving a trace of their passing.

Slate ignores the proffered hand to make peace, instead

nods his head and ushers Siren to continue her lead through the bush.

"Fine. I'm counting on you both to get this done before everything and everyone I love is lost," she says.

Warnner shrugs off Slates dismissiveness and steps lightly behind her, leaving silent Slate to bring up the rear like a bad dog waiting for his next beating. They walk for hours, silently copying her as she removes scuffs in the leaf litter, adds fallen logs and strokes low-lying foliage closer to hide their trail.

Nearing dawn, Siren halts and points at the ground in front of them. There is no mistaking the unnatural pattern of broken leaves scattered across the path. "Someone's been here recently, but they've turned back."

"So what? That's good, right?" Slate looks nervously over his shoulder. "Means they've given up."

"I don't know. I'm too tired to think. We'll have to rest here for a bit. Warnner, you take the first watch. Slate, you take the second, and I'll take the third." Unslinging a tiny, tightly fitting pack from underneath her coat, she sits against the nearest tree and takes out her water and food. "It could be hikers or hunters…or worse." After taking a few careful sips, Siren wraps herself in her jacket, checking first to see that Warnner has positioned himself a few metres away and a couple of metres up a totara tree, before willing herself into a shallow sleep.

"Siren, your turn." Regretting her decision to take second watch, she shakes herself awake and waits to see that Slate is some distance away from Warnner, before scaling the same lookout tree. From her perch, she has a clear view of the surrounding area. but it's her keen hearing that will alert her to any unexpected visitors. However, her initial regret soon morphs to joy, as she reveals in the natural noises of the night and the starts piercing the canopy. She is almost reluctant to wake Slate for his shift, it has been a while since she has been able to be alone with her thoughts.

"That's enough sleep, guys. Time to get going." She pockets a packet of peanuts and raisins and pops the lid back on her drink before re-slinging her pack over her shoulders, taking care not to tangle the straps in her hair. Seeing that the other two have sorted themselves out, storing away their jackets and adjusting their packs, Siren takes one more glance at the scattered foliage, removing all evidence of their makeshift camp.

The second night is like the first. There are more signs of others' passing, more than Siren expected for the time of year. After a brief dawn meal, they compare notes.

"I thought maybe hunters, but there are no dog tracks and they don't usually travel alone," Siren concludes.

"It's probably hikers," Slate offers, stiffening at the harmless cry of a possum.

"Don't be stupid. What kind of hiker goes off alone and never stops to put up a tent or cook a meal?" Warnner catches Siren's look and modulates his tone. "Well, no hiker I've ever heard of."

"Doesn't matter who they are. Now that we've worked on the trail, they'll never find their way back this way." Throwing a last handful of nuts into her mouth, Siren rotates her head from side to side to release the tension in her neck. "I suggest we have a short rest now and loop across to the other trail. If they choose to re-use either one, they'll find themselves turning back on themselves without knowing where they went wrong."

The boys barely grunt in agreement, offering no suggestions of their own. Warnner slides to the ground, and leaning against a tree trunk, closes his eyes. Staring a moment longer, Slate moves in the opposite direction, choosing a partially exposed rock to create a barrier between himself and Warnner. Sighing at their continued antagonism, Siren again locates a lofty position from which to keep watch.

"Siren, wake up. Slate's gone." Warnner keeps his voice low so it doesn't carry. Siren takes a second to become fully alert. The moon is high. They've overslept, which should have been impossible. After her watch, she'd woken Slate and had seen him take his position in the tree, before going to sleep herself.

"Why?" Slate's pack is missing from his rock.

"We had a bit of a disagreement after you fell asleep. I had no idea he'd do this." Warnner moves away, perhaps fearing Siren will fulfil her threat from the day before.

"Disagreement? About what?" Siren barely manages to keep her voice to an angry whisper.

"Um, you, *us*… I don't know really. The usual. I told him to just accept how lucky he is: he has family, he has you…" he trails off.

"How could you?" She picks up her pack and swings it back on her shoulders.

"I'm sorry," he says, but she can tell he isn't. "All his whining about wanting to leave. To be Common. It makes me sick."

"You had no right." Pacing back and forth Siren chews on a tendril of hair, sucking the end into a fine point. "Okay, we should change trails before going home, but I don't trust Slate to leave this one unmarked," she says. "What a waste of effort. I'll just have to come back and finish by myself… once I find that…*cousin*. I want you to know that I'm going to be mad at the both of you for a very long time."

With only the two of them, they pick up the pace, careful to hide their passing as they close the distance between them and their prey.

"Hey, I think it's…" Siren reacts, tripping Warnner and

smothering his outburst with her hand before it can leap fully formed from his lips.

"Do you want her to attack us?" she hisses in his ear.

Shaking his head, he drags his lips across the inside of her palm, firmly held against his mouth.

"Stop that!" Loosening her grip against his caress, but leaving her hand in place, she continues. "Blue won't be expecting us; she's definitely been following Slate."

"Should we leave her to it?" Warnner asks, peeling her fingers gently away from his mouth.

"No. We should go and find Malice. But I have a better idea." Siren rolls off him, and pulls him to his feet. "Show me what you can do."

Grinning, Warnner steps away, puts his pack on the ground, and begins to blend into the light and dark of both his camouflage clothes and the forest flora.

Siren can't drag her eyes away: he's perfect. Then, embarrassed by her admiration, she sends her swirls across her face to hide her blush. "Okay, now be good bait. I've got your back."

She slips into the shadows. It isn't long before she hears Warnner's fake cry and catches a glimpse of her target taking flight at a ferocious speed. She's known Blue all her life. She's like an older sister. Julian was the reason Warnner isn't lost or crazy, and yet it could be too late for her. Siren triangulates Blue's trajectory. Establishing Blue's position in relation to Warnner, she manipulates her skin tone and texture while mimicking the other girl's muted footsteps. Not carefully enough, though. Sensing her, Blue turns to attack but hesitates when she sees her own surprised face staring back at her. In a heartbeat, it's too late for Blue to take evasive action and, as fast as she can turn to flee, Siren has her face-down on the ground, her arms twisted behind her.

"Nice trick. But what's the plan now? You're just going

to sit on me until *what?* My sister arrives?" Blue laughs, contorting her body until Siren is forced to let go.

"No, I just wanted to talk to you." Siren moves to shield Blue from Warnner's body, which is still blended into the low growing ferns.

"You mean to see if I've lost my mind?" Disappointment flashes across her face.

"I won't let you hurt him." Siren can't believe this is the same girl who used to babysit her, telling her stories of the Common, easing her fears about the world beyond the Hill. "You can't blame Slate for what happened."

"I don't. I blame all of you. Your family has brought us to the attention of the Common with your stupid need to find others." Glaring at Siren, Blue's green scales darken to black. "I've seen the trails. I know why you're here. We've been discovered and they're coming to get us all. But not if I can help it." Blue bounces onto the balls of her feet and shoulder-charges Siren, knocking her over onto Warnner's prone form.

"Shit." Siren lets Warnner pick her off the ground, removing the bracken from her hair as Blue disappears towards the Hill.

"Should we go after her?" As if he's been doing it his whole life, Warnner shakes the camouflage from his skin and resumes his normal appearance.

"Yep. At least she's heading in the right direction." Siren gives him a pained smile.

CHAPTER FIFTEEN

Nearing the Hill, Blue's trail becomes more difficult to follow. The hardened earth leaves few clues of her passing, but there's little doubt she's closer to Slate than they are to Blue, and that both of them are taking the quickest route back. Siren had let the soft pattering of their footsteps distract her from all the *what ifs*. But now, taking a break against the ribboned trunk of a great rimu, she needs to make a decision.

"Warnner?"

"Yes?" He's so close she has to fight the desire to curl up in his warmth and sleep. She gives rein to the urge without giving in: a painful delight.

"How much do you really know us? What we are?" She peers around the trunk. His eyes are closed and his chin is raised in communion with the sun.

"Malice told me some stuff…you know…the genetic divergence. Said I'm one of the newer evolutions. Then there was Julian's death, and Blue blaming me and Slate for somehow exposing everyone to some sort of monster hunter." He pauses, raking his fingers over the loose dirt and grinding desiccated leaves to dust. "The rest I just feel… you know… *different*. But a good different. Why?"

"Would you like to meet Grandmother?" Siren omits the unwritten rule that no one visits without an invitation.

"I think I met her at the Welcoming. The moon lady?" He smiles and picks up a twig to draw his Mark in the dirt.

"Harsh. 'Moon Lady' is my mother. I am talking about *Grandmother*. *The* Grandmother. The oldest of us." She emphasises *old*.

"So, we aren't going to protect Slate?" he asks cautiously, smoothing away his pattern with the flat of his hand and replacing a few leaves to remove all signs of his meddling.

"We'll never catch up to Slate before Blue, so we can't stop her from hurting him. But when we do find them, I think we'll need reinforcements. The only problem is that Grandmother likes to be left alone." Lowering her voice, she adds, "It's safer."

"Safer? She's just an old woman, right?" Warnner's fingers walk towards her hand like a hesitant spider.

"Yes, but... You must meet her yourself. I'm not good at explaining," Siren replies, keeping her hand just out of reach.

"So, a visit to Grandmother's house. Best thing you've suggested since trying to capture Blue." He stands, dusts off his jeans and reaches over to pull Siren to her feet. The simple gesture sends shocks rippling through both of them. Siren's hair flares and waves madly around her head, while Warnner staggers backwards, reaching out for the trunk of the rimu for support. "What the hell was that?"

"Nothing," she responds angrily. "I must have built up some static electricity from the fabric of my jeans rubbing together."

"Yeah, well, you seem to have static electricity every time I touch you. You might want to get that looked at."

She hears his hurt and disbelief, but she can't explain what's going on between them. It isn't the right time and it isn't the right place.

If he were born here, his parents would have told him.

"Please just drop it," she says.

"For now," he concedes, but she knows she's going to have to explain soon. "How far to Grandmother's house?"

The further they walk, the darker and more menacing the atmosphere becomes. In all his weeks on the Hill, Warnner has never lacked light—whether it was sunlight or starlight—and only now does he realise how much he craves it.

"Not far." Her encouragement is matched by a hasty, almost desperate, increase in her pace through the undergrowth.

"What's she doing out here? Practising dark magic?" He laughs, untangling himself from a trap of supple-jack vines. He has yet to master her ease with their surroundings.

Siren doesn't reply. She doesn't laugh, either.

"Really? Magic?" Warnner asks.

"Don't be stupid. There's no such thing as magic. But she is guarding a dark secret. One that means leaving the Hill is more difficult than you can imagine."

Siren has to make a decision: trust him, or turn around and accept whatever happens. Shortening her stride, she lets Warnner catch up.

"Grandmother keeps us, and the Common, safe from the worst of ourselves." She hates the way her voice shakes. "I'm afraid for Blue; her anger is getting out of control. But I'm more afraid for Slate, because he doesn't understand the risk...doesn't even *know* there's a risk. There are worse things than hating your life," She explains. "When we lose control, when we allow ourselves to be consumed by our anger, we become Lost. It's the Lost who are the source of legends of mythical creatures. The ones who drink blood and kill without thinking. It's the reason the Common are afraid of us. They see us at our worst, and would have us forever gone to save them from their nightmares."

"Why didn't anyone tell me?" Warnner's hair falls over his face, his nose flaring and eyes narrowing. "Why didn't *you* tell me?"

"We don't talk about it." She bends a branch, then releases it skyward, sending dry leaves flying like a kaleidoscope of butterflies. "There are so few of us. It's unbearable to lose anyone, let alone when they're dead… and I've never been afraid of losing you."

"I'm glad of that." Forcing her to look at him, Warnner tugs her hand away from the branch, sending a hail of leaves into their hair. "So, why are we really going to see this Grandmother?"

"Sometimes, only sometimes, she can stop someone from becoming Lost. That's why she needs to come with us." She twists the leather bands around her wrists, anxiously watching for his response. "To help Blue. To save Slate. Will you come?"

"You don't need to ask. I thought I've made myself clear. Where you lead, I will follow."

A pair of kereru swoop by, the downbeat of their wings sending whirlwinds against the ground. The birds come to rest, exchanging a series of whistles. They cock their heads when Warnner joins in their conversation, mimicking them flawlessly.

"You sound like you know what they are saying," she says, admiring the iridescent green and white feathers.

"Music I understand." The birds launch off their branch and continue their flight below the tree tops.

"We should get going. We're already so late." But the urgency is leaving them, replaced with a sense of uncertainty. "Her cave should be over there."

A group of large boulders rises defiantly from the hillside on the other side of a narrow stream. The two of them descend a gentle slope onto a wide, flat area, totally devoid of any plant life as if the ground has been swept clean for some unknown purpose. In a semi-circle, away from the cave, a row of widely spaced trees rise high above them, their branchless trunks standing guard against unwelcome visitors.

"Where you lead, I will follow," Warnner repeats, swallowing. They walk towards the cave and into its generous entrance.

Scanning from side to side, Siren sniffs deeply and shakes her head.

"Maybe she's asleep," she muses as their eyes adjust. "This doesn't feel right. We shouldn't be here without permission."

"Oh no, you don't. We're here now, so let's keep going. Besides, it would be rude to come all this way and not say hello." Warnner waves her forward, blocking the exit from a possible retreat.

Rolling her eyes, Siren squares her shoulders and leads on into the gloom. The arching sides of the tunnel curve to the ceiling far above their heads, where glow worms form unnamed constellations. The further they delve into the deep, the more the tunnel opens up, eventually dividing into smaller and smaller passageways.

Siren flicks out her tongue, tasting the air. "She's down this way." The irregular beat of water dripping from the walls into puddles at their base, gives way to the sound of metal on metal.

"Do you think someone is training down here?" Warnner asks.

"I wouldn't have thought Grandmother needed to train. She must be two hundred years old and she's spent most of that time alone."

The passageway ends abruptly, opening into a cathedral-sized cavern. A shaft of light from a skylight illuminates a solitary figure lying on a plush, chocolate-coloured couch, right in the middle of the cavern. Her eyes are closed, with one arm resting on her stomach, the other dangling off the couch towards a book that has fallen open on the floor. Her *Sleeping Beauty* posture is accentuated by the elaborate gold and red medieval gown she wears, but her long grey hair shows she's no youthful princess to be woken by a kiss.

As they approach, inhabitants of the cages embedded into the circular wall begin to shriek and bellow. The beasts reach through the bars, grasping at their targets, who remain tantalisingly out of reach. Ignoring their rowdiness, Siren and Warnner approach the woman on the couch. She does not move, and she isn't asleep.

"She's dead," Siren confirms after touching the forehead of the elderly woman.

"Maybe she's just meditating."

The woman's greying face seems so calm; she'd look almost human, if it weren't for the gill-like slices across her cheeks and throat.

"People don't stop breathing when they meditate. We will have to tell the Council we came, so her body can be claimed." She trails her fingers through the dead woman's hair, combing it neatly into place. "How will we survive without her. There is no one who can take her place."

"Why do we have to tell anyone? Surely someone will come and check up on her soon."

Grandmother's is the second death in less than a week and Siren wants to weep without end. But she knows the grief will have to wait, there is too much to do.

The clanging starts up again as the Lost rattle their cage doors. "I wonder when they last ate."

"Don't look at me. I'm not feeding them. They might think I'm dinner." Warnner steps a little closer to Grandmother, hoping that even in death she can control her wards.

"Yes, they probably do." Siren sniffs back her tears and then laughs out loud. "No matter who they once were, they're just animals now. Why don't you sing to them, to calm them while I go and look for their food? It must be down one of the other tunnels."

"Sing to them? Sure. Why not? I can do that." His gaze flicks from one to another, finally resting on the tunnel entrance.

"You'll be fine. I have faith in you." Smothering another

laugh, Siren takes off back down the tunnel.

A few moments later, a flute plays.

She locates dinner for the inmates in an adjoining tunnel, and knowing Warnner's aversion to live food, she quickly dispatches two goats, hacking them into meal-sized pieces. She hopes there's enough to go around. She doesn't relish staying too long.

The trouble she's going to be facing when they get back!

When she re-enters the cave carrying two baskets of meat, she finds Warnner has seated himself next to Grandmother as if she were his audience. The Lost, in their cages, have responded to his talent, calming their cries to an occasional yelp and a weak rattle of their bars.

"Don't stop, and you might want to keep your eyes closed. This won't be pretty. Once I've finished here we'll leave. I promise."

Nodding his head in agreement, Warnner continues to play as Siren throws slabs of meat into each cage. She keeps the final piece for herself, tearing a chunk of bloody meat from the bone before tossing the remainder to the last permanent guest. Still licking her fingers clean and sucking the strands of meat caught between her teeth, Siren is the first to hear hurried footsteps approaching.

"Sounds like we're going to have to explain ourselves sooner than I planned." She wipes her mouth and squats, rubbing her hands clean of blood in the dirt.

Warnner stops playing and returns his pipe to his pocket. The Lost are too busy enjoying their meal to pay any attention to the new arrival; chewing on the bones, they growl contently.

It isn't who they expect.

"What are you doing here?" is the only thing Siren can think to say.

"I was coming back to meet you. To apologise and to explain. But then you came here, so I decided to follow."

Slate notices the other occupants in the cave. "What's going on here? Is that a dead body? What are those things in the cages?" His voice becomes shriller.

"Calm down, we just got them settled." Warnner's tone is disdainful.

"I won't calm down until you answer me. Siren?" Slate's breathing is shallow and ragged. He's hyperventilating.

"It's okay. You don't have to worry about them. Grandmother looks after them. *Looked* after them. We came to talk to her about you, but she must have died during the night."

A look of horror spreads across Slate's face. "About me? You came to ask her about me? Is this why you've been so kind to me? Is this what I'm to become?" He backs up, knocking away Siren's outstretched hands.

"Stop," Siren shouts. "You've got it wrong, Slate. You'll be fine. Everything will be fine. Come on, let's go back to the clearing and I'll explain." She moves towards him again.

Terrified, Slate turns to make his escape, but in his haste, he stumbles and falls forward towards one of the cages.

"Careful," Siren and Warnner call out in unison, but it's too late.

As Slate tries to correct his fall, a confined beast grabs him, tearing at his clothes. Screaming, Slate struggles as the Lost snarl in response, their hunger re-awakening. There's a loud rip, and Slate is free, abandoning his shredded jacket. His eyes are pools of black when Slate picks himself up off the ground and flees.

CHAPTER SIXTEEN

"Well, that didn't go as expected." Warnner re-joins Grandmother on the couch, now leaning into the corner with her eyes closed and her hands resting lightly on the book returned to her lap. She could have just dozed off mid-conversation. "You don't look a day over 199," he whispers in her ear.

Over the tearing flesh and crunching bones of the Lost, who have returned to their easier-to-catch lunch, Siren hears him and giggles. If she doesn't stop, she'll get full-blown hysterics. Inhaling deeply, she slowly calms down and wiggles a place for herself between Grandmother and Warnner.

"Why can't Slate be like you? What's so wrong with being like us?"

Knowing no answer is required, Warnner lets himself relax against her side, revelling in her warmth. He stares towards the spot where Slate had stumbled.

A symbolic struggle.

The beasts are less agitated, settling to an afternoon nap. Warnner doesn't know if it's because they have live company, because of the food, or even because of the music, but they're less frightening now. *Well, a little less.* The strangeness of their appearance ranges from odd colouring to monstrous, extra limbs, massive claws, spikes, spines, and huge jaws accommodating too-numerous teeth. While he is giving a quiet prayer of thanks to whatever good fortune had given him a chance to blend into the Common world, a glint in the dirt catches his eye. Reluctantly leaving Siren to her anguish, he wanders to where Slate had fallen and picks up a bronze disc attached to a broken leather thong.

"Hey Siren, look at this," he calls over to her, holding up the necklace. "I think this belongs to Slate."

Siren lets go of Grandmother's hand, which she'd been absentmindedly stroking, and walks over for a closer inspection.

"I think you're right. He was wearing it when we went swimming." Taking it from Warnner's open palm, she traces its unusual designs with her forefinger. "Look at this side. It has our Marks on it."

"Are you sure? Let me see. That's spooky. There's yours, and mine. Slate never got one, right? So maybe this third one would have been his. I thought our Marks were unique," Warnner says as he hands it back. "Where did he get this?"

"I have no idea." Flipping it over, she tries to make sense of it. "This side is a jumble of symbols I don't recognise. I wonder if his parents gave it to him."

"We can ask him when we give it back," Warnner suggests.

"How? I think he's left." She stuffs the necklace into a pocket and picks up Slate's torn jacket. Folding it over her arm, she pats it as she would a child in need of comfort. "I mean left the Hill, with no plans to return."

"We'll have to go and find him. Who knows what trouble he'll get himself into without us. It's not as if he's learnt anything of how to survive."

"You'd do that? Go after him?"

Warnner nods.

"Thanks, Warnner. I…" She blinks rapidly to chase away a tear. "Let's get out of here. We need to inform the Council of Grandmother's death..."—noticing Warnner's raised eyebrow, she adds "—in writing, and then track down my pain-in-the-arse cousin, to work on him until he admits he wants to be with us. With big love, of course."

"Yes ma'am." Warnner makes a mock salute. "Where you lead, I will follow."

Siren surveys the cave. Layers of multi-coloured sediment roll across the walls, a reminder of the waves of ancient seas. She imagines the years Grandmother spent here, often alone, caring for the Lost. The Common owed her for her service as much as her people. They didn't deserve to keep Slate, as well.

"Let's check his caravan. If he's not there we'll leave a note and check the trails," Siren decides.

"What are you going to say?" Warnner asks, his long legs working hard to keep up.

"That Grandmother has gone and we're still working on the trails," she suggests. She makes room for him at her side.

"Sounds weak..." Warnner stops mid-sentence. "Shit, look at this mess." Clothes, books and torn drawings are spread in a wide arc from the caravan's open door. "Someone's had a tantrum."

"I don't think this was Slate." Siren picks up the scraps of paper, hopping from one piece to the next before the breeze has a chance to disperse them. "I think this means that Blue didn't find him either. But the question is, did he get here first, or did she?" She anchors the stack of papers to the front step with a large stone, carved in the shape of a squatting toad. It looks annoyed; perhaps the change of job from garden ornament to paperweight demeans him.

Following Siren's example, Warnner attempts to complete the tidy-up by tossing the larger items in through the caravan's swinging door. "Do you think Malice has seen this?"

"Who knows?" She grimaces when she steps on a pencil that's been snapped in half, pointy end up. Using the back of a broken book, she slips a less crumpled piece of paper from her pile and begins to write. When she's satisfied with her missive, she folds the note in half, intending to attach it to a window in clear sight of any future visitors.

"Warnner…"

"What?" His mouth is full of broken biscuits.

"It's worse than I thought."

Warnner chokes, crumbs blowing out in all directions. "What's worse?" He wipes his lips and tosses away the empty packet.

"This is worse." Siren passes the note to him. "What if Slate's seen it?"

"How can he have seen it? You've just written it." Siren's writing flows across the page like ancient Sanskrit. She's written words he cannot read. He's got so much more to learn.

"Look at the other side." She snatches the message from his hand and turns it over.

"Shit. His mum's mad?" Warnner squints to make out the faded print: a copy of a copy, hastily scanned. "Wait. Didn't she, like, die years ago? This report isn't that old."

"But what if she didn't die? What if Blue is right and my family has screwed us all?"

"This isn't your fault, and it isn't mine—or Slate's." Warnner folds the report and hands it back to her.

She slips it into her back pocket. "We need to find Slate, and then I think Malice has some explaining to do."

Snickering, Stamp paces in front of the paddock gate.

"I don't see why we have to ride. What's wrong with walking?" Warnner groans. His last, and first, trip on horseback wasn't terrifying, but nor was it comfortable. He can still feel the impression it made on him, days later.

"If we want to catch up, we need to go on horseback. Now get on." Leaping effortlessly onto the horse's back, she reaches down to help Warnner up behind her. Bracing himself for the shock of touching her, he's not disappointed when a surge floods his senses. He clasps onto her forearm and groans. Siren drops the burning connection between them as soon as he's seated safely behind her.

"Um, Siren?"

"Still not a good time, Warnner," she interrupts, and kicks the horse into a fast trot. After all she has tried to teach him, it's hard not to be disappointed when she discovers that Slate has made no effort to hide his trail. He's taken the same route he used when he arrived, and so has Blue. It's not an easy trail to manoeuvre on horseback, the trees and ferns causing them to bob and duck under branches and away from trunks while they eat up the distance between them and their targets.

"I can hear traffic ahead." Warnner leans dangerously to one side. The horse stops. "And voices."

"I've never come this way before… It's kinda off limits. In fact, I never ride close to the Common world. I've never even seen a real road before." She sneaks a conspiratorial look over her shoulder.

"Well, get ready; you're going to see more than a road." He pats her shoulder encouragingly. "I do believe we're not alone."

"Shush." Swinging a leg over the horse's neck, Siren passes the reins behind her back into Warnner's reluctant hands. "Wait here while I check it out."

Siren disappears into the undergrowth.

"Nice horsey," Warnner whispers, patting Stamp's shoulder. The animal's restless. He's at its mercy if it decides to bolt.

The arguing voices change to frightened shouts, then doors slam and gravel sprays as a car speeds off. Then there's the heavy crashing of someone heading towards him. Before he can think of what to do, Siren emerges, her haunted dark eyes even darker against her pale skin.

"They've been taken."

"Taken? Who?"

"Blue and Slate. They were arguing, fighting, and this car just pulled up and... It was weird... I don't understand."

"Can you describe them?" Warnner hands back the reins.

"Who?" Siren pats the horse's nose, her trembling causing his ears to flick back and forth.

"The people in the car," Warnner says.

"Um, a man a little taller than you, dark hair. And a woman. She was driving. About my size with lighter hair. They both looked fit. Strong." She twists to look to the road as if to dispel her disbelief. He wants to hold her, calm her, but she's not ready to be calmed by him.

"The people at the fair!" He slaps his forehead. "The Destinators."

"The who? The what?"

"Look, Blue was right. I did get Julian killed," Warnner says. "But I didn't realise it."

"Explain yourself." She grabs his elbow, gripping tightly.

"When I met Julian at the fair, I bumped into this couple. A man with dark hair, about my height, and a woman with blond hair, about your height. They felt wrong to me at the time, but then later two people from the Destination Church, a man with dark hair, about my height..."

Siren releases her grip, but phantom fingertips remain on his skin.

"Yeah, I get it. They found you," Siren interrupts.

"They must have followed me to the Centre. They probably followed me to the Hill. Figured that this is where I was." He keeps his feet wedged between Siren and the horse, but only just.

"Even if it's the same people, that doesn't mean they killed Julian or were following you. And it doesn't explain why they decided to take Blue and Slate." She looks as unsteady as he feels, but there's no accusation in her tone.

"That doesn't matter. What matters is that I know where they could be." He brushes a stray hair floating across her face and tucks it behind one ear.

"Okay." Her warm breath moves against his cheek.

"Okay, what?"

"Okay, let's go get them."

"Wait, are you crazy? We can't go chasing after them on horseback," he exclaims. "We need to get backup."

"What backup? We don't know where Malice is, and besides us, who's going to be able to hide what we are in daylight? There's a reason we work the fairs, in the back, in the dark." She pauses. "Anyway, I think they wanted Slate, not you."

"What?" Why is she shifting the blame?

"I mean, I think they're looking for Slate. Before they took them, they were asking something, and Blue pointed to Slate."

Stamp snickers and butts his head against her hand.

"That doesn't mean anything." Not satisfied with Siren's offhand affection, the horse transfers its weight from one foot to the other, leaning heavily against Warnner's back.

"But what if it does?" She stops stroking her horse's nose and leans into its neck. "I told Slate I was his protector. I told him I'd keep him safe."

"It'll be okay." Warnner lets a tendril of Siren's hair wrap around his finger. "Right. How do we get to town from here?"

He's rewarded with a hint of a smile.

"We follow the road."

Trailing Siren, who's leading her horse, Warnner does his best to pull the battered foliage back into place behind them, but his efforts are rushed and wanting. They emerge from the shelter of the bush into full sunlight. In the centre of a car park, a shallow trench outlines where the car sped off, dislodging clumps of grass growing on the ungroomed surface. The area's low on the Department of Conservation's list of priorities; the single picnic table has long since been burnt down to its moss-covered concrete slab.

"I like what you've done with the place." He motions towards a sign declaring the natural wonders of the area, defaced to read only that 'ogs' were 'hibited'.

"Yeah, works better than a map saying 'here be no monsters'." She looks at him. "So, where to?"

"If they are who I think they are—and I'm sure I'm right—we need to get to the nearest town." From Hearth-Thorn Centre you could drive in one direction to a lonely pub along the state highway, and in the other direction there was a gas station which sold basics just before a major turn-off to a popular coastal holiday destination. None of which were on this side of the mountain range. "My therapist at the Centre had a real thing against these guys; even warned me against them. Hard to avoid when they seemed to be everywhere."

"Okay. Let's go left, I think." She bites her lip.

"You think left?" He stares pointedly at where the road divides. "I mean, you can barely call either direction a track, let alone a road."

"Yes, left, unless you know better." She nods, agreeing with some internal cartographer. "Besides, the best way to make someone feel lost is to not let them know where they are." Siren hops back onto her horse and clicks her tongue. "My grandfather has someone check entry points like this regularly, and remove signs of life. But the Common have not been so careful." She points to a second set of parallel trails in freshly turned gravel.

"Good eyes. Which way do the tyres lead?" He kicks at a pile of stones, sending them scattering against the back of her legs.

She shoots him a grin. "Left."

"We're going to have to take a break. Poor Stamp's not used to carrying one, let alone two, for so long." Siren runs a hand down his sweaty neck, and the horse flicks his mane from side to side like a feathered fan.

"I'm happy to walk, give him a break, but I think we should keep going." Warnner's thighs and butt are less painful than the sharp pounding in his head. "The town can't be much further; the gravel's gone."

The road wound its way down the hill and cut deep into a valley, slowly enlarging as the land flattened to a plain at the base of the mountain range. The verge widened, giving their unshod horse a relief from gravel, then merged into asphalt adorned with white stripes.

"Good guess." Siren points to a sign, battered and bullet-riddled, stating only five kilometres to go.

"Not much traffic," Warnner comments, as the second car of the day, a beaten-up flatbed containing one barking dog and a dead deer, speeds by.

"Not many people. Land's too hard to farm. Too swampy." She waves a hand towards the lines of deep ditches, full of stagnant water, separating fields with too few cows. "They've been trying to drain this area for decades."

"Speaking of water…"

"Fine. We'll go on foot from here. Stamp should be safe in a paddock. Besides, if he's captured by the landowner, you can charm him back for us." She leans forward, and lets

Warnner dismount first, careful not to laugh when his legs give way and he collapses.

"There's got to be a better way to travel," he groans. "I am not made to bend this way."

Slipping the rope halter from the horse's head, Siren pushes him through the paddock gate. "Hey, we're not alone." At the far end of the field, another horse is grazing peacefully in the shade of a stand of puriri trees. "It's Snuff. What is going on?" She inspects the horse, laying a hand against its side. "He's cool. Been here a while. But where's Malice?"

"Let's just find her and ask," Warnner suggests. "Change that. Let's find Malice, and let *her* rescue Blue and Slate."

"If only." Siren gives her horse a final pat as Warnner struggles to his feet like an old man.

"How do I look? Common?" she asks.

"Not quite. Kids our age don't generally have facial tattoos or look as beautiful as you."

"Right." Ignoring his compliment, she rubs her hands across her face and arms, her whorls thickening and blending with her darkening skin. "How's this?"

"Perfect, you'll blend right in. Just remember, no teenager wants to look an adult in the eye. That would be too respectful," he adds. "And try not to smile."

Siren uses her fingers to brush her hair over her face and glares through the thick strands that hide her eyes. "Better?"

Warnner can't say. She makes his heart beat quicker. "Um, maybe you need to practise scowling so people don't attempt to talk to you. What about me?" he asks, hoping for a compliment.

"You look Common enough," she says dismissively.

Now was not the time to flirt.

They hop the fence and walk along the verge for a few hundred metres, where the grass morphs into a cracked sidewalk overgrown with weeds. The nearly empty paddocks give way to old villas in various states of disrepair, merging into two rows of shops flanking each side of the main highway. Several of the shops look as if they've been empty for years. They pass an old-fashioned café, takeaway bar and bakery. The last two shops are crammed with unwanted second-hand goods, but only one of them displays a freshly painted sign declaring it a *Destination*.

They walk past the large front window, casting brief glances, but their view is hampered by dirt and the remains of faded and torn signs advertising everything from retail opportunities to visiting bands—decades out of date. Crossing the road, they return to their starting place to sit on an abused-looking bench at a sorely neglected bus stop.

"If nothing else, setting up a church here shows that these guys aren't thinking clearly. Who are they planning to convert?" He looks around the nearly abandoned town. An elderly couple chat next to a postbox, while a harassed mother pushes a hand-me-down pram into the small convenience store. A trail of children follow her in descending order of height, holding hands like cut-out paper dolls. "This isn't a town. It's barely a village."

"But where are they?" Siren's voice trembles.

"You didn't really think she'd just be sitting around waiting for us, did you?" His attempt to lighten the mood misses the mark. "We just need to look around a bit more. Or more precisely we need to have a look inside that Destination shop."

"We should have never come here by ourselves. If they die, it'll be our fault." She ducks her head as a group of teenagers walk past.

"Die? Do you really think they'd go to all that trouble to just kill them?" He moves closer, pressing his thigh against hers.

"What about Julian?" she whispers.

"Yeah, what about Julian? Just because his engine catches fire doesn't mean it wasn't an accident." He'd been thinking about it, obsessing over it, since he put Blue's accusation together with the recognition of her kidnappers. Julian's death made no sense.

"So?"

"We can do this. We *are* the help. Just like you said." His urgent tone covers his fear.

"Okay. I need a moment to think."

"I suggest we think and move at the same time. The indigenous population is getting curious." Converging into a spontaneous neighbourhood watch group, the teenagers join the elderly couple and the busy mum at the postbox, taking it in turns to throw worried glances in their direction.

As they stand to move, Siren gives a sharp tug on Warnner's pant leg. "Wait. Front door or back? No, not front. We'd be trapped. Maybe there's another entrance, or emergency exit, somewhere else."

"Do you think that's likely?" Warnner asks.

"I didn't read *The Art of War* for nothing. Even on the Hill we have more than one way in and one way out. Why would these people be any different?" she counters.

Steeling herself against unbidden shocks, Siren threads her fingers through Warnner's and leads him around the back of the bus shelter and into a forgotten playground. A solitary swing dangles, one-sided, from a fraying rope. Next to it, only the centre of the see-saw remains embedded in a wedge of concrete, a tombstone to a history of childhood memories. A metal carousel twists back and forth under the caress of a gentle breeze.

The park falls away to a duplicate street of even less prosperous buildings, taunting each other across the divide in a race to be the first to decay. This time the collection includes a car lot, with rusty and broken mechanisms, sitting cheek-to-cheek with a lumber yard selling firewood, and a nursery edged with dying plants for sale. Walking slowly, scuffing their boots, they kick the dust from the dirty gravel road until the lower parts of their legs have turned a pale shade of brown.

"Don't stop. This is it. Keep moving." Standing between a dilapidated *Housing New Zealand* home and an old church is a warehouse. A banged up, but intact, lattice fence encircles the yard and buildings, complete with rolled barbwire at the top and two hungry Rottweilers roaming purposefully behind a padlocked gate. Besides the dogs, the yard contains a few cars, including a dark blue sedan.

"That's the car I saw."

They continue to the end of the road and loop back to the main street, relieved to see that the mob has dispersed for the day.

"We can't just keep walking in circles."

"I know. Let's get back to the horses and wait until it's dark." No longer holding hands, Siren rubs her fingers together until the last of the tingling leaves.

Back with the horses, they lie in the deep grass, hiding from passing traffic. They avoid discussing what they'll do if they can't find Malice.

"Is it dark enough yet?" Warnner chews on the sweet end of a piece of grass, flicking the seed end from forehead to chin between nibbles.

"It will have to do. I don't want to wait any longer."

"So, what's the plan?"

"We wing it."

"That's a plan?"

"Warnner, I'm sixteen years old and I've never been more than a couple of kilometres from home." She wraps her arms around her legs, hugging them tight. "I've never seen a road, a shop or even a playground until today. Everything I know about the Common world comes from books and stories brought back by Travellers."

"Sorry, I forgot." He tosses the grass aside and rolls onto his knees.

"We need to get past the dogs, and whatever else might be between us and the inside. Then, in a building we've never been in before, we have to find our way, without being discovered, to wherever they're holding Blue, Slate and maybe even Malice." She mumbles into her forearm. "This is so stupid. We don't even know if they are inside. They could've been taken anywhere."

"Siren, we've got this. You're right. We can't prepare for what we don't know, so we'll improvise." He stands and savours the buzz as he pulls her up beside him. "We don't know what we don't know, so let's find out."

The main street is poorly lit by flickering lights, casting dim orange polka dots down the centre of the road. A few of the storefront displays are illuminated by blinking fairy lights tacked around the inside of the windows, while others are plunged into darkness. At the far end of the street, country and western music beckons them from inside the sole pub. A few cars are parked outside.

Rounding the corner, they're caught in the high beams of a truck turning out of a driveway. The driver peers into the night, the passenger studying a large map by headlamp.

"They're driving very slow."

"Does it matter?"

"Don't know. Trampers don't usually head out at night. Maybe they're hunters."

This time, Siren and Warnner stop in front of the old church, using its incomplete picket fence as cover. The dogs are still patrolling the inner edge of the fence, joined by a lone sentry, who lights a cigarette next to the open gates. Clothed in similar apparel to Siren and Warnner—jeans, shirt, jacket and butt-kicking boots—there's no mistaking the glint of the rifle slung over his shoulder.

"I've got an idea. Follow my lead." Siren links her arm through Warnner's and leans into him as if returning home from a night of hard drinking. The obvious connection between them puts the guard at ease as he moves to close the gates.

"New plan. Call the dogs." Letting go of his arm, Siren staggers into the gate, knocking the guard back.

The dogs' growls abruptly change to howls, then whimpers, as Warnner's high-pitched whistle breaks through their conditioning. "Good doggies," he praises, as they crawl on their bellies towards his feet. Leaning down to scratch between their ears, Warnner misses Siren's sweet words as she persuades the guard from his gun with a violent elbow to the temple.

Warnner helps Siren drag the guard between two parked cars. "We're just going to leave him here?" he asks.

"Yep. Unless you think we should feed him to the dogs," she suggests. Quickly checking her handiwork, she pats the guard's face. His eyelids flutter and he moans. "You are very sleepy," she tells him, and is rewarded by a deep sigh as he returns to unconsciousness.

Warnner completes the guard's job of closing the gate, briefly wondering who he'd opened them for, and sends the dogs back to patrolling.

"I think the entrance is over here." Indicating with her elbow, Siren pulls her hair into a severe knot at the base of her neck, then covers it with a woollen hat, borrowed from the guard. "How do I look?"

Warnner shakes his head at her quick change into a heavy set, muscular man with a gun slung over his shoulder. "Terrible." He eases the gun from her shoulder and kicks it under a car. "I think we'll just leave this here. I'm all for the art of passive resistance."

"Fine. Now you." She waits while Warnner takes on a less defined appearance. Anyone trying to take a good look at him would find his features less than solid and difficult to describe; they may even wonder if they had seen him at all. "Perfect."

The door to the warehouse stands open.

They step inside.

"What's wrong with this picture?" Through the low lighting, they make out rows and rows of widely spaced storage shelves filled to busting. Cat-scratched couches are stacked under chipped porcelain sinks and toilets, which in turn are shelved below warped door frames and battered kitchen cabinetry. The racks tower towards the ceiling, where boxes and old suitcases overflow with second-hand clothing. "What is all this stuff?"

"It's camouflage," Warnner exclaims. "Like your broken signs and destroyed trails. These guys are using donated goods to hide."

"But what are they up to? And where are they?"

"Let's go find out. Left or right?" Warnner offers.

"Left."

Leading the way, Siren heads up a steel staircase set against the outer wall of the warehouse. At the top, the office door hangs open. It's been kicked from the inside. "Okay, this is getting weird," she says.

Inside, the camouflage of an overfilled storage facility gives way to the shell of what must have been a very busy office space. Even without the presence of any living creature, there's no mistaking the purpose of the empty cubicles.

"Looks like they left in a hurry." Warnner tugs at one of the cables that snake across the empty desks. Blank spaces in the dust are evidence of missing laptops, printers and landlines. Along the floor, thin strips of paper trail from one end of the room to the other. "They must have shredded everything they couldn't take with them."

"But why?" Siren pushes away a chair left in the hallway and walks towards the far end, peering under desks and running her hand down empty pinboards, as if hoping to read their missing messages by braille.

"Visitors." Warnner ducks into a room behind the desk, pulling Siren with him. Two men dressed in camo, small packs slung over their shoulders, inspect the damaged door. They rummage through the scraps of fallen paper.

"We're trapped. They're going to find us."

"Fight or flight?"

One of the men laughs and unfurls a map in the other's face. The other man gives him a friendly punch to the shoulder and the two of them bolt from the room as if late for a bus. "Flight it is."

"Wait. Not yet." Siren pulls Warnner closer. "Let's give them time to get good and gone."

"Anything you say." Warnner covers her hand. The pulse of an electric fence beats in rhythm with his heart. "A curious sensation. It only hurts when I let go."

"Does it?" Siren scrapes her teeth against her top lip, turning it pale.

"I'd never expect you to do anything you didn't want to do." He pulls off her guard's hat and unties her hair, dragging it slowly through his fingers.

"We're only sixteen, Warnner." She leans back, leaving his hands empty.

"I'm seventeen, and we won't be young forever."

She doesn't pull back when he cups her face, drawing his thumb slowly across her cheek. He leans forward. Their noses and foreheads touch. She closes her eyes but the kiss never comes.

"Let's go," says Warnner.

"Door number two, then." Retracing their steps down the staircase, Siren opens the plywood door to reveal a large hall. At one end a raised stage is partially hidden behind half-closed curtains, gently swaying as if ghosts of long dead performers dance in their shadows. In front of the stage, steel-legged plastic seats form a series of incomplete circles. At least half a dozen doors are inset into the remaining three walls at random intervals, barring the way to the unknown.

"What is this place?" Siren asks.

"The back of the church," Warnner replies. "It's where they hold functions for funerals or wedding receptions. You know, for Sunday school and youth clubs. Fun stuff like that. Not that I've ever participated."

Siren sweeps her arm like a presenter on a game show. "Okay, your turn. Which door now?"

His eyes flick towards a white-and-green exit sign screwed above a door near the stage. Siren wiggles her eyebrows in response.

"If they're here, what we need is a reason for them to leave." Warnner grins, his hand poised over a fire alarm. "You might want to put your hands over your ears. You're about to have another new experience."

CHAPTER SEVENTEEN

"Come back to me." Slate wakes to dripping water and a voice whispering so close to his ear the hairs on his cheek quiver.

"What?" He tries to sit up, but the cool hand against his forehead is not the only thing holding him down. "Let me go." He struggles against the straps across his chest and hips, then tries to wrench free of the bindings pulled tightly around his wrists and ankles.

"Don't hurt yourself. You're safe," the voice coos.

"Let me go." He bangs his heels against the table and claws at its pulpy surface. He's in a kitchen, strapped to a dining table. His mind races.

"Shush. I will. As soon as you're better." The woman strokes his skull, pulling back sharply at the row of budding horns as if the points aren't blunt. "I'm so sorry, Slate. I wish I could save you from this pain."

It's not until the saw blade takes its first bite that he begins to scream.

"What are you doing to my friend?"

"Friend, is he?"

Dragged through a maze of rooms before being tossed into an office and tied to a chair, Blue hasn't had enough time to get her bearings. There's been even less time to see where they have taken Slate, but he is close. She can hear his screams.

"You don't see many friends beating the shit out of each other, or selling each other out to strangers."

Blue winces. She'd been so angry, she could only think about finding him, so it had taken her by surprise when their captors swept into the car park and asked for Slate by name. She'd answered without thinking. Slate had been quicker to react, trying to headbutt the driver. But the woman had been faster still, using her gun to force him into the back of the car, and her animal taser to keep him there.

Blue had done nothing.

"See, me, I like a friend who has my back, not one who uses it for target practice." Trapp tightens the rope between her ankles and wrists, forcing her to arch her back to release the pressure. "Or at least one who shares the same interests."

"Like torturing children?" she asks.

His eyes dilate as she changes from green scales to pink skin. She's out of practice and the pain in her shoulders makes it hard to maintain, but she's not going to die without trying.

"Children? Is that what you think you are?" He caresses her cheek, tilting her head back, studying her. "Monsters to frighten children is what you really are."

"And yet I'm the one being frightened." Her shuddering breath is not a lie.

"Frightened? You have no idea what being frightened feels like. But you will." He tips up the chair, sending her flying backwards, her head cracking onto the wooden floor. "No sleeping. I mean to get my payment's worth."

"Don't cry, baby. I'm all done now."

Slate whimpers while the woman bandages the raw ends where his horns had been.

"They'll pay for what they've done to you. My sweet boy."

My sweet boy?

"Mum?" He mouths the word and raises his bloody and blackened head towards the woman. "But you're dead," he whispers.

"Oh, Slate. What lies they've told you." She presses one hand to her own heart and hovers the other over his. "They stole you from me. I always knew they'd try. Your father wouldn't listen, and they murdered him."

"What are you talking about, Mum? Dad wasn't murdered, we were in a car accident." Slate struggles uselessly against the restraints. "Where have you been?"

"They lied to me, baby boy. Said I needed treatment. Said they'd keep you safe." She laughs, raking her nails sharply against the inside of her arm, reddening the lines of pale scars. "It took me so long. I had to be clever. Had to make friends. But I'm here now."

"You hurt me." His head is throbbing.

"I know, and I'm sorry I was too late to stop them turning you into a monster." She glances towards the door.

"I'm not a monster. They didn't do anything to me." A sob catches in his throat. "They didn't do *anything*."

"Oh yes they did, baby. You're not thinking clearly." She stops scratching and yanks down her sleeve; pinprick lines of blood soak through the pale material like footprints in snow.

"I was leaving."

I should have stayed.

The throbbing in his head morphs into heat that spreads like an acid burn. It flashes across his flesh and then dissipates, leaving him panting.

"I know. I'm so proud of you. But you left too late. They'd already released a demon inside you." She unfurls her fingers, revealing his bloody horns. Like the buds on baby goats, they look so harmless in her hand.

"A demon?" The heat washes over him again, this time hotter, longer.

"Don't be afraid. We are going to drown that demon out of you." She tips her hand, the horns falling and scattering across the floor.

"We?" The dripping water is louder. His mother grabs hold of his head and someone jams a hosepipe into his mouth.

"You're making this too easy. Now where's the fun in that?" Trapp makes a hop and kick to Blue's face. Her last-minute contraction moves his target, and his foot delivers only a glancing blow to the side of her head.

"Untie me and I'll do my best to kill you." The pain is making it difficult to maintain her little girl camouflage.

"No, you're doing this all wrong. You should plead for your life..."—he leans down and drags a knife down her cheek, poising it below her eye— "...beg for my mercy."

"Sorry, I don't speak French." She pushes her face against the knife, feels the point slide into her skin and waits for the beating to continue.

"Please. Mum. Stop." Slate wrenches his head from his mother's grip and coughs the water from his lungs. It steams from his skin like raindrops on a hot pan.

"Almost." She twists his head and ties it back into place, the rope cutting into his forehead. "Again."

At her command Lively shoves the hose back down his throat.

"Not dead yet. Good."

"It's weakened. The demon's weakened. You can wake up now, son… Slate… Baby … You can wake up now. Momma's here."

"Stop playing around."

"What?" Trapp pauses, his foot resting firmly on Blue's sternum.

Lively steps into the room. "She's just about killed the kid and now she wants to test him against the other one."

"What do you want me for then?" Trapp increases the pressure on Blue's chest, grinning into her defiant face.

"I can't handle it alone."

Trapp turns his gaze towards Lively, framed in the doorway, his grin widening. "Oh, that's right. How's the face?"

Instinctively, Blue darts her eyes from Trapp to Lively. The woman's face is divided by four parallel lines that run from hairline to chin.

"Shut up and give me a hand. You can toy with that one later."

Blue catches Lively trying to hide the fresh scars with her hand and is rewarded by the woman's frustrated parting punch into the wall on her way out.

"Yes, lots more fun to be had. Let's see if you can think of something to challenge me by the time I get back."

Trapp laughs. Using Blue as a step, he crushes her to the floor on his way out. Blue holds her breath and listens to the lock sliding into place.

"Challenging is not the word I would use for what I have in store for you," she whispers to the empty room.

"Here you go. Package delivered. Apologies for not handling with care." Trapp throws the woman to the floor.

Slate recognises the new voice and stiffens. He twists his head painfully towards the rope scraping his forehead, and it takes a while for his vision to clear through his sweat and tears.

"Malice?" A gasp escapes Slate's lips. She's unconscious. One leg is bent under her at an unnatural angle. Her untied hair sweeps over her body like a shroud.

"This is the demon that stole you from me. Whispered in my ear that she'd keep you safe when they locked me away. They drugged me until I couldn't remember your sweet face." Spit sprays from his mother's lips.

"Mum?"

"Didn't she tell you?" Trapp and Lively take position on either side of the door, folding their arms and leaning against the wall like bored bouncers. "In the beginning, she visited often. Asking me questions. Telling me lies. Oh, she thought she was so clever."

"But not clever enough, eh Mum? You found me." He chokes, bile clogging his throat.

"Yes, yes. There was a nurse, a Destinator. She helped me. It took me months, but I got out and found real friends, people I could trust. *Real* people." Her smile doesn't reach her eyes and her eyes don't meet his. "People who know demons."

"Every day I waited for you to come, and you didn't. But I didn't blame you, Mother. I never blamed you." This time the heat moves slowly, deeper, he can feel it burning against his restraints, weakening their hold. "I'm feeling much better. Can we go now?"

"Soon, baby boy. Soon." She unbuckles the straps across

his chest and hips and unties the ropes from his head, wrists and ankles. "You feel a bit hot. Are you feeling sick? Can you sit up?"

Slate swings his legs over the edge of the table. His head has stopped throbbing under her warm caress, leaving his mind clear. The heat expands, stretching through his body. It feels good. He feels good. "No, I feel much better. Thank you mummy."

"Good. I only need you to do one more thing and then we can leave." Smiling at his childish response, his mother points at Malice's prone body. "Bring her here."

Trapp flicks a disdainful glance in Lively's direction, but she doesn't move from her place on the wall.

"Now," Slates' mother repeats impatiently.

Trapp picks up Malice's listless body and half carries, half drags her towards the table. She hangs heavily across his arm.

"If she's dead, we'll have to use the other one."

"Hey, that's not the deal. The green one is payment for services rendered," Trapp protests. "Services I've worked hard to provide."

Blue. No, not her, too.

The emotion surprises Slate. He'd being dying since the day of the accident, but after hearing his mother's voice, her words, feeling her pain, he is finished with dying. He wants to live.

"No worries, she's alive. Just needs a little encouragement." Wrestling her body upright, Trapp grabs Malice by her hair and pulls her head back. "Now open your eyes, sweetheart, or your little friend here is going to be in a lot more pain."

Slate can almost hear her skin rip as she forces open her bloody eyes.

"Good beasty," says Trapp.

"What do you want me to do, Mother?" Slate lets his smile shine through his eyes. He's ready.

"You have to kill the demon. She made you, so only her

death will bring you back to me." She hands him a knife.

"I don't know how to do this." His skin tastes the knife's cold surface. The metal cuts an outline into the palm of his hand. Slate absorbs its hostile intention, slowly curling each finger around the handle, until it is no longer an object but a purpose.

"Trapp?" His mother ask, looking for suggestions.

"Does it matter? Stab as many times as you like. You're bound to hit something important eventually," he replies, his mind wandering to unspeakable plans.

"Is it getting hot in here?" He releases his grip on Malice's hair and wipes a trickle of sweat running from his forehead before it reaches his eyes. Before anyone can answer an alarm sounds.

Malice is the first to move. Head-butting her captor, she snatches the knife from Slate's open hand and throws it at Lively, pinning the woman to the wall by her throat.

"Nooo," Trapp yells, holding his broken and bleeding nose. Slate's mum's screams join his outrage. Lively tries to free herself, choking on the blood welling into her mouth.

In slow motion, Trapp flicks out an expandable baton, drawing his arm back to complete a deadly swing to Malice's head. Slate grabs the man's wrist in mid-flight. Heat leaps from his skin, dances from his fingertips, and dives hungrily into the man's body.

Trapp stops. Stunned, he drops his baton and stares at the blisters bubbling across the back of his hand. Slate releases his hold on the man's wrist. Together they watch wide-eyed as Trapp's skin slides away from his bones.

The smell of cooking flesh permeates the room, complementing the horror of Lively's lifeless body dangling from the wall, mimicking Malice's most recent performance of unconsciousness to perfection.

"Slate. We've got to go." Malice grabs his shoulder, using his body as a crutch.

"My mum?" he asks weakly, relieved that Malice remains unaffected by his touch.

"She's gone." Hopping forward, Malice peers into the hallway. "I'm sorry Slate, but we have to get out of here now. That alarm could bring the police. We can't be found here."

Propelled like leaves before a gathering storm, the two of them limp towards the end of the hall.

"Stop." Slate twists around. The hall is full of closed doors.

"What? No." She winces, tugging him back into motion.

"Yes. We have to find Blue," he says.

"Blue? What do you mean, Blue? She's here? No. She can't be." The words are spoken as if they are more painful than her injuries.

"Try the doors. She has to be here somewhere."

Lurching from door to door, they find one empty room after another.

"She's not here." Malice slumps heavily against him.

"She has to be. Where else could he have taken her?" Simultaneously, they reach for the final door handle just as it twists and opens.

"What took you guys so long?"

Slate struggles to speak as Siren half strangles him in a hug.

"Quick, we've got company." Warnner steps from behind Siren, with Blue cradled against his side. "Outside. Now!"

CHAPTER EIGHTEEN

"Did you have to bring the dogs?" Siren helps Warnner reposition Blue on the horse in front of him, the dogs whining at her heels.

Blue moans. Too bruised to grip any tighter, she leans stiffly back into Warnner's arms. They can only imagine what she'd had to do to free herself. Blue had been the first to answer the call of the fire alarm. They'd caught her blindly running for the exits and pelted angry questions against her silence before they noticed her injuries. Whatever happened, she isn't saying. Siren has done her best to bandage her friend's wrists. They are a bloody raw mess, the teeth marks where she had to chew herself free clearly visible.

"That's what you're worried about?" It is an instinct Warnner can't explain, whistling for the dogs to follow as they escape away from the town.

"No—sorry." Siren grabs the reins of both horses, galloping as fast as she dares, not wanting to cause more pain to their riders but needing to get them all safely home.

Malice, too, has refused to answer any questions, urging them away from the church just as the oscillating lights of the local fire engines send them spinning into the dark. With only two horses she'd argued she could walk, but Siren had put an end to that, forcing her to sit behind Slate, who is shaking with delayed shock.

Siren shivers and tries not to wonder about what's hidden under the blood-soaked bandage on his head.

With the sun creeping over the edge of the mountains, Siren leads them from the open fields into the protective canopy of the forest. Blue leans forward to untangle a vine of clingy bush lawyer from Stamp's mane, allowing Warnner to wriggle for a more comfortable position. On the other horse Slate, no longer shaking, breathes deeply, consuming the flavours of earth and the leaves crushed by their passing. The forest compels her to slow, but Siren digs deep to keep going.

When at last they break into the clearing on the Hill, nothing has changed. People are waking up, breakfast is cooking, children are being chased from their beds; morning bustle envelops them. It's a sharp contrast to the tired and battered bodies of the returning group. Like a game of statues, one by one the clearing dwellers stop in mid-action. Worry flitters across faces, but none interfere in the group's procession to the front of the lodge.

The dogs collapse against the steps, their tongues hanging out and their chests heaving in unison. Though still on their feet, the two horses hang their heads, harrumphing for breath. Only Siren appears unaffected by their ordeal, as if she had only just hit her pace when the race had come to its end.

"I'll go first." Malice leans on Slate and he helps her slide to the ground. "I have a lot to explain."

"No."

"Blue?"

"You don't get to explain what you've done." Before anyone can stop her, Blue leaps at her sister, biting, scratching until she is pulled, screaming, from Malice's fallen form. A wild creature denied her prey, she spits and struggles against their hold.

"Let me go."

"What the hell is going on here?" The sisters' fight has raised more interest from the others in the clearing and they draw nearer.

"Blue… I'm sorry. Forgive me. Slate…" From the ground Malice looks up, pleading, fresh scratches bleeding down her face. "I needed him so much and he just left me…for a Common woman." She wipes the blood from her lips, wincing at the touch of the cuts and bruises. "He wouldn't listen…said he didn't feel what I felt."

"It's true, then. My parents were running from you." Slate tightens his grip on Blue's arm, half to prevent her surging forward again and half to keep himself in place. "You caused the accident?"

"No. No. I would never hurt him. I loved him." Malice struggles to her feet. Her damaged ankle gives way, sending her sprawling on the ground again. No one steps forward to help her. "It was raining. He was driving too fast."

"I know. I was there." Blue untangles herself from his grip and threads her fingers through his, sharing his betrayal. "My parents were afraid… Afraid of you."

"Malice, tell them you were just following." Letting go of Blue's other arm, Siren steps in front of them as if to hold back the storm. "Please."

"She can't. My mother…" Slate winces as he reflexively smooths a palm over the raw-ridge of absent horns. "She told me you had her locked in an asylum. You kept us apart."

"You should have been mine. *My* son. Not hers," Malice whispers. She drops her head, her hair curtaining her face. "She didn't deserve you. She was afraid of you."

"You crazy bitch. You ruined my life." Slate pushes past the crowd and heads for his caravan.

"Can we talk?" Blue asks.

Like him, Blue has taken the time to have her

wounds patched but her long-sleeved shirt is unable to hide the thick bandages wrapped around her wrists. The rest of the damage to her body is covered by clean clothes; even the bruises on her face are camouflaged by the natural tones of her green skin.

"Sorry," Slate says. "Just tidying up." There's organisation in his chaos: a pile of unrepairable items by the foot of the stairs, a stack of easily fixed books on the table, and his packed bags, waiting at the door. "Give me a sec." He slides some clutter into a drawer, closing it with his hip, and wipes his hands clean on his jeans.

Outside, Blue sits cross-legged by a small cooking fire and sifts through the pile of torn paper, laying the pieces out. "I was just so angry. I miss my dad." She gives up searching to complete the puzzle and tosses the scraps into the flames.

"I know. Me too." Tidying the caravan has given him the space he needed to calm down. The chairs and books, even the loft, are no longer strangers easily left; now they are old friends who've welcomed him, made him feel he was home. It is all he can do to stop himself from staying.

"I'm sorry about your mum." Blue avoids looking at him. She pokes at the fire, sending a distress signal of embers burning towards the sky.

"Thanks. I'm sorry about your sister." He joins her, adding more of his ruined sketches to the flames, the rough drawings disassembling into ash in a flash of heat. It seems like another life when he drew them, years since he discovered them shredded and strewn across the ground. Distraught from the conflict at the caves, he'd expected the demise of his drawings to destroy him, but he'd been beyond anger, even beyond fear. All he could think about was leaving. So, he'd left, Siren's plea for him to stay haunting each step he took. Now he doesn't think he can be that strong again.

"Do you want to talk about it?" Blue points her stick at

his head, the bandages firmly covered by his hoodie. "About what happened? About your mum?"

"No. Do you?" Finished with his drawings, he throws a couple of broken books onto the fire, letting the ash choke his voice and the smoke burn his eyes.

"No." She hesitates. "I can't. I'm so ashamed. I'm so sorry, Slate. I just wanted you gone, wanted my sister and my dad back."

"Me too. I wanted so hard to see my parents again, to be normal, to get away from here." With nothing left to burn, they watch the fire die down to smoking embers. "You know, when my mum first spoke to me in the church, I didn't recognise her voice. That was my one wish after the accident, to hear her voice again. Hear her tell me that she loved me and that everything was going to be okay."

"I'm sorry." Tapping the ground with her stick, Blue flicks dirt and shortened winter grass in a semicircle around her bare feet. "I seem to be saying that a lot today. Guess I'm going to be saying it for a while." She stabs the ground, snapping the twig in half; it dangles from her hand like a broken baton. "Your mum, she gave me to that guy—as his reward for finding you." She breaks her stick into smaller pieces, throwing each piece as far as she can in a furious rhythm. "He told me I was going to live longer than everyone else here, but he'd make me wish I hadn't."

"Well, we're all still here." He offers her another stick.

"I'm barely here." She tugs it from his grip and continues digging.

"I've spent years like that: not living. I don't want to be like that anymore." He watches a couple of fantails flitting from one branch to the next. "She's out there still, and I know she'll come looking for me again. I have to find her first. I have to talk to her…to finish whatever this is."

"Don't do it. She's not your mum anymore. She's like the Lost."

He looks at her sharply.

"Yeah, Siren and I've been talking too, but I'm right," says Blue. "She'll hurt you again, only next time there might not be anyone there to save you."

"Save you from what?"

They both jump as Siren drops her hands on their shoulders and plonks herself between them, knocking Blue's rising wall of dirt back into the hole.

"Slate wants to find his mum." Blue plants her stick in the ground. "He wants to find her, even after what she did to him… To *us*."

"I think he's right." Siren returns Blue's startled look. "None of us are safe as long as she thinks she needs to save Slate."

"We are if we stay clear of her." Blue pushes aside Siren's restraining touch, and shakes the dirt from her feet. "I'm tired of asking people not to leave…but I wish *you* wouldn't."

"What's changed?" Slate asks Siren.

Blue and Warnner meet in passing, one leaving and one arriving. Warnner places a hand on Blue's arm, but she just shakes her head and keeps moving, like old friends who have nothing in common anymore.

"Malice. She didn't stop talking just because you left." Siren hands Slate his token and the hospital report. "These are yours."

Slate glances at the hospital report before tossing it into the fire; it browns and curls before dissolving into ash. "I don't want to think of her that way." He eases back his hood and loops the cord of his necklace around his neck, stroking the coin flat against his throat. "This, I'll keep."

"So that's it. We go through all that effort at being heroes and then we're supposed to just let him leave again?" Warnner holds out a hand to pull Siren to her feet.

"Yes, but this time I'm going with him." Siren uses her other hand to help Slate up beside them.

"Then I guess I'm going, too," Warnner says, eyeing Slate until he drops Siren's hand.

"Fine. Anyone else you want to bring along?" Slate takes in their easy connection, their fingers intertwined, the way their shoulders lean into each other. Instead of feeling excluded, their closeness radiates, and he knows that, more than family, he longs for friends.

"Now that you ask, yes." Siren disentangles herself and grabs Slate's bags, tossing each one back inside the caravan. "But these are staying here."

"You know that some of us prefer to sleep in the day, right?" Rolling his shoulders, Rip yawns and peers over lowered sunglasses. His lazy stare is met with an impatient sigh as he cracks his neck and leans back against a fallen punga log. "Just saying."

"And some of us look better in the dark." Fade leans over and flicks the sunglasses back up the bridge of his nose. "You didn't have to come."

"Hey, at least I was invited. What about them?" He points towards Stella and Nova who are criss-crossing silently between the trees in a confused game of predator versus prey. "Do they have to be so energetic?"

"They threatened to tell." Siren looks over her shoulder, scowling at her sisters until they stop. "It was either let them come or have my parents lock me in a cage next to Malice."

"Poor Blue." Even with her arms folded across her chest, Fade looks like a walking stick pretending to be a leafless twig. "Her dad dead. Her sister mad. At least she has the triplets."

"She has us, too." Siren crawls forward on her elbows, joining Slate and Warnner at the edge of a steep drop.

"Can we all focus on this for a while?" Slate slides back to give Siren an unobscured view of a man and a boy engaged in a game of catch below. Though the boy is dressed suitably for a companion of the devil, his father is more sensibly attired for days of rough terrain and variable weather.

"Those two?" Warnner tries to rise above the overhanging foliage, then yelps as Siren yanks him back to earth. "Why are you stressing about a father taking his son for a little walk in the woods? We can easily slip past them."

"That's not the point. What are they doing here?" Siren has anticipated Slate's desire to find his mum, and the best way to go, but Slate knew that she hadn't anticipated the unwelcome company below. "I mean, do you usually get a lot of trampers here, this time of year?"

"No. Not any time of the year. There are no trails, no huts, nothing to see and nothing to do. Sometimes we get people trying to find the caves, but they never do." Siren motions for them all to wriggle back from the edge. "We keep this area a black hole of nothing."

"What about hunters?" Warnner retrieves a leaf trapped in Siren's hair and sends it floating to the ground on his breath.

"Oh yeah, sometimes, but they never catch anything so they don't come back." Still focused on the pair below, Siren shakes her head from his teasing touch.

"Never catch anything?" He redoubles his efforts and strokes an unruly strand around his fingers.

"Nope. No deer, no pigs, no possums." Siren rakes her hair out of his grasp and weaves it into a rough braid. "We keep the critters down in these parts."

"Wild dogs?" Watching the interaction between the two, Slate's not the only one smiling.

"Yeah, we take care of those, too." Siren kicks Warnner away, moving closer to her cousin for protection.

"So, what's it going to be?" Eyes closed behind his sunglasses, Rip looks like a tired jazz player, skin leathered by too many years in smoke-filled rooms, now being forced to participate in daylight activities. "Are these guys nobody or somebody?"

"There were those other guys." Warnner throws a piece of bark at Siren's back to capture her attention again. "In the truck and in the warehouse. Could be the same ones."

"I didn't see a boy in the truck." Siren leaves the bark where it lies and crawls back to the edge for another look. "And there definitely wasn't one in the warehouse."

"So, go up and introduce yourself and get it over with." Warnner taps Slate's foot with his own, but doesn't miss Siren's look of disbelief. "What? He wants to talk to his mum. If they work for her, mission accomplished."

"I know what I said, but this doesn't feel right." Slate leaves them to their staring contest and has another look at the couple. "Why would she send hikers to grab me before we escaped? This is something else."

"Something else as in 'Oh shit, we're all going to die'?" Rip stretches and pushes his sunglasses on top of his forehead. Slate remembers the panic he felt when he first saw Rip: the puckered skin, wide mouth and numerous teeth. He remembers first his empathy and then his fear, and smiles at his ignorance.

"Not helpful, as always." Fade chucks a stick of jerky at Rip's head, which he grabs from the air without opening his eyes. "Why don't you eat something while the grown-ups talk."

"Rip may be right. The guy who had Blue…" Warnner grimaces at the tearing of meat, followed by concentrated chewing—"He told her that she would live longer than the rest of us. Maybe these guys are here for us."

"If she was planning to kill us—no offence, Slate—she'd need a lot more than a couple of trampers like these two." Fade nods knowingly towards Rip. "I mean, how could they ever be sure to find us all, and what kind of sicko would send a little kid?"

"What about the other trails? The ones Malice was supposed to work on." Slate glances guiltily towards Siren. "The ones we didn't finish covering—because of me. There could be people coming from all over the place."

"So, we go and look. See if there are more of these guys," says Warnner. "Cover up the trails at the same time."

"What do we do if we find them?" Rip pops the last piece of meat into his mouth and holds his hand out for more.

"No eating them." Fade teases him with another strip of jerky by tossing it towards him and snatching it back before it reaches his mouth.

"Not even if I'm really hungry?" Rip makes a grab for her wrist, but not quick enough. "You're seriously going to make me beg, I'm starving."

"When are you not starving?" Fade shoves the food in his mouth and pats him on the head. "Good boy."

"Willow wisps." Not even slightly out of breath, Nova drops to the ground, completing their informal circle.

"Yeah. Willow wisps. Good idea." Siren motions for Stella to join them. "We cover trails and make new ones to lead them away. Tramping in unknown bush can be dangerous if you get lost."

"Sounds like a great plan and all, but they can't be stupid enough to rely on trails. Surely they'll have GPS, maps..." Warnner snaps his fingers and whistles low. "The first pair had a map, and the second came to find theirs, so there are at least two more out there."

"Yeah, but unless they've been to the Hill, they won't know exactly where it is. Even with a map, they'll have to search." Siren smooths a space in the leaf litter and draws a rough sketch. "So all we have to do is change the trails a bit, curve around the Hill and lead them out the other side. That way they'll think they're getting close, but..."

"But never close enough." Fade tugs Rip to pay attention. "Good plan. I'm game. Come on boy, let's play."

"There's so much ground to cover. I wish there were more of us." Siren rocks back on her heels and pokes at her drawing.

"We have to work with what we've got." Fade glances over at Rip, an arched brow implying they lack more than numbers.

"Okay. Warnner, Slate and I will do the trails on this side. Stella, Nova, you two take the road, and that leaves Rip and Fade to take the back trails—the ones we missed."

"What about along the river?" The long, wavy line in the dirt reminds Slate of his first plan to leave, using the river as his guide.

"We have to hope that our neighbours are still awake and looking out for their own borders." Swiping the image away, Siren brushes back an uneven distribution of leaf litter. "After all, they've kept us safe from strangers for generations."

"You worry too much. We've got this." Stella copies her sister's lead and checks to remove any sign of her presence. "First one home wins."

"Last one home gets caught." Taking up the chase, Nova follows her sister, the pair mimicking the lightness of startled deer.

"Show offs. Come on, our turn." Rip pops to his feet, dispelling any impression of lethargy.

"No rest for the wicked." Fade pushes Rip back to the ground and takes off in a sprint. Rip bounds back to his feet as if gravity is a myth, leaving Slate in no doubt that neither of them will leave an impression of their passing.

"Yeah, I know what you're thinking." Warnner has stepped up behind him. "We really need to work on our game."

"Well, now's your chance." Siren moves back to the edge, taking another look at their targets. "We'll take care of these guys, then we'll go find your mum."

"No."

"No? You don't want to take care of these guys or you don't want to find your mum?" Siren turns slowly.

"I mean, yes, let's get these guys to leave." Slate rocks back on his heels, unwilling to return Siren's stare. "But no, I've changed my mind. I don't want to find my mum. She died in that accident. Despite what Malice may or may not have done, I always knew that my mum was beginning to be afraid of me. Hell, even afraid of my dad, long before the accident. I just didn't want someone to show me it was true."

"Yeah, it sucks." Warnner crouches beside him and pulls him into an awkward hug. "Been there, done that, bought the t-shirt." He looks over at Siren. "But trust me when I say, we've got something better here."

"Yeah, we do," Siren says. "Time to blaze some trails."

As if their trip on the trails had never been interrupted, they back track, removing any sign of their passing, an increasingly strong wind adding touches of its own.

"Just checking that the plan is to leave them here and hope they take the wrong path?" Creating a trail is more difficult as time is short and they're getting tired. Even Warnner is reluctant to get too close to the pair despite his ability to blend.

"No. You heard my sisters. We are willow wisps in this." A gust of wind beats at their bodies, sending their clothes flaring and forcing them to duck behind a tree for shelter.

"Willow what?" While Siren appears recharged by the squally weather, Slate ramps up his core temperature to *nicely toasted*.

"Wisps of something to chase." She jogs on the spot and wiggles her head mischievously.

"Sounds dangerous." Warnner reaches out as if to pull her to safety, but Siren dances out of reach.

"I promise not to hurt them." Without warning she runs

towards the hunters, bashing through the forest so even the deaf could follow. "Just get them lost enough to want to leave."

CHAPTER NINETEEN

"Help."

The trampers look up, as Siren runs towards them. Clothes in disorder and covered in dirt, she casts fearful glances behind her.

"Please. Help me." She trips on a blind root and slams into the boy, knocking the rifle out of his hands as he braces their fall.

"Are you all right?" Her saviour rolls on his side to take the impact, and they land heavily in a pile of deep mulch, soaking dark patches into his thick black hoodie. Up close Siren realises he's a lot younger than she first assumed: a frightened child.

"There's someone after me." Her body shaking, Siren scrunches her eyes, forcing tears to streak down her face.

"Who's after you?" The older man has reacted quicker to Siren's intrusion, sidestepping her fall and taking up a defensive position, his back to a tree and his eyes on her path.

"I don't know. I was hitchhiking and my ride dropped me off at the crossroad." Siren lets the boy help her up, noting the slight reluctance to touch her. "I'm sorry. I'm just so scared."

"That's okay. You're safe with us." Turning his body away from her, the boy retrieves his rifle from between two moss-covered rocks wedged deeply in the soil and checks it for damage. His hands shake. He's unfamiliar with the weapon—perhaps even repulsed by it.

"Are you hunting?" Siren whispers breathlessly, the trembling of her words not entirely fake.

"No." The boy steps a little further away. "My… Uncle Jake is taking me—"

"Shut up, Ash. She's doesn't need to hear your life story." The older man splits his attention from the trail to them. He rubs his knuckles against his stubble covered jaw. "You're a long way from the road."

"I was waiting for another ride, but I had to pee. I guess I got turned around. I couldn't find the way back to my stuff." Siren shifts her weight from foot to foot, like the urge to pee has returned.

"Didn't anyone ever tell you that running and screaming has a way of getting you killed?" The man caresses his gun, sliding a finger over the trigger guard.

"I'm not an idiot, but I got scared when I heard…" Siren pauses as if deciding whether to trust them. "Look, I know it sounds crazy, but there was this noise, heavy crashing — like a bear."

"In New Zealand?" The boy's easy grin transforms him into a fey creature, at home among the wilds. "Not likely."

"I told you to shut up." Jake's eyes sweep over Siren, from her bare feet to her wild hair, and over her shoulder to Ash. She can almost see him calculating the odds that she's not what she seems. The same calculations run through her head about them.

"Do you know what it is?" Siren ducks her head, fighting against the creeping itch along her skin. It wouldn't help if she lost control now.

"We can take you back to the road, but then you're on your own." Jake motions Ash to take the lead and for Siren to follow. "I'm not paid enough to babysit two."

"Oh, thank you." Siren steps forward eagerly, just as a

crash sends startled birds rising towards the sky. "Oh my god, it's here." She steps behind Ash, grabbing onto his shirt and pulling him in closer. "It's going to get us."

The crash comes again: louder, closer. "I'll take a look." Jake rifles through his pack and stuffs a few extra cartridges in his pocket. "You stay here with her."

Siren feels a strange affinity watching Jake move like a hunter, checking his blind spots and keeping his rifle in a loose grip, the weapon an extension of his own body. In moments he's gone, the forest closing behind him in a sinister embrace.

Inviting Siren to stay close with a subtle head nod, Ash takes up Jake's position. Poorly mimicking his uncle's movements, he sweeps the edges of their clearing, as if to catch an attack on all sides. Siren moves restlessly beside him, playing with her hair.

"He's not coming back. Whatever's out there has got him." It takes all of Siren's acting to get her body trembling like a leaf caught in a spider's web.

"Don't worry. He can handle himself. My uncle's been on African safaris, and even navigated the Amazon River." Ash stands straighter, shoulders back with the rifle crossing his body as if pledging his life to a cause. "He's a freaking firefighting hero."

"Please, I'm so frightened. We should leave. Can you take me to the road?" Siren grabs Ash by the sleeve.

"No. My uncle said we should stay here." Ash shakes off her grip and holds tighter to his rifle. "He won't help me if I disobey orders."

"If you won't take me, just tell me how to get back to the road." Siren takes a hesitant step forward as if deciding which direction leads to safety. "You do know the way out of here, don't you?" She breaks off a branch of a silver fern. Shredding the leaves between her fingers, she taps the stem against her leg.

"Yeah, 'course I do. But I really think it'd be safer if you stayed here with me." Ash stops his sentry duty, distracted by the mesmerising tapping of her stem.

"Please, I just want to get home. My parents don't even know where I am." Siren is getting tired of being hysterical. It's not working.

"When my uncle gets back we'll take you to the road—"

Gunfire rips through the campsite.

"It's coming. We have to get out of here." Siren takes flight from the steady boom and pause.

"No. Stop," he calls after her, taking chase. Siren picks up the pace, keeping the boy on her heels but staying just out of reach. She's played this game before.

"I didn't take you for being a screamer." Warnner offers Siren a bottle of water and a wry grin.

"Ugh, thanks. I think I'm losing my voice. Growls are more my thing." She takes a sip and pours the rest over her face. "You're sure you covered our trails?"

"No worries." Warnner looks at the empty bottle and sighs. "It'll be hours before they find each other, let alone find their way back here."

"So what have we got?" Siren dries her face with the edge of her t-shirt and hunkers down to join Slate on the ground. In their haste, the trampers have left their backpacks, the contents of which are now laid out before the group.

"Not much. A map, some snacks and fire starters." Slate picks up each item as he repacks. "The map could be something. There's an 'x' circled where we found them and some numbers. I think it's the time."

"They must have been eager to get here." Warnner makes a grab for the map, but Siren is quicker, snatching it away to take a closer look. "They're way ahead of schedule."

"Maybe that's not when they're supposed to *be* here."

Seeing nothing else of interest Siren hands the map back to Slate, who folds it neatly and returns it with the rest of the belongings. "Maybe that's when they're supposed to *do* something."

"The only thing they'll be doing now is waiting for *Search and Rescue*." Warnner throws the empty water bottle at Slate, who catches it and adds it to the pack. "So what's next?"

"I'm shattered." She feels clammy, her cooled sweat itching along her skin. "Let's go home. The others should be finished by now, too."

Despite carrying the extra packs, Slate has led a quick pace back to the Hill, allowing Siren and Warren a bit of hand-holding privacy. They reach the edge of the clearing as the first stars make their appearance.

"What's going on?" He is the first to speak.

Infants and children are being thrust into the arms of youths barely older than their charges. Everywhere they look, parents are giving no more than a quick stroke of a hand and a brief kiss on a cheek, before the youths split away and vanish into the trees.

"What the hell?" Siren winces. Warnner grips her hand tighter, as if afraid she too will flee.

"Oh, shit. Look." Slate, not so firmly anchored, points above the tree-line behind them.

Against the remains of a sunset shot with pinks and golds, dark plumes of angry smoke draw a line across the sky.

"Fire." Siren's whispered words are whisked away in the beginnings of a storm. "I've got to find my parents, my sisters—the horses…"

"You go. We'll stay here and help." Warnner releases her hand and gently pushes her away. "We'll go ask Aunt Rose what she needs us to do."

Torn between old and new loves, Siren first kisses Warnner, then Slate, before taking off in the direction of the pole house.

"Oh, you're safe. I was beginning to worry. I've had Blue out looking for you." On one hip, Aunt Rose is clutching her baby; a couple of hastily packed bags lean against her leg.

"What's everyone doing?" Warnner takes the baby from her arms. The baby coos and clutches at Warnner's hair, then yanks hard with glee.

"Taking what we can, leaving what we can't." Aunt Rose picks up the bags and offers them to Warnner. One is full of the baby's belongings, the other is his own.

"Where are the kids going?" Swapping the baby from one arm to the other, he jerks his head towards the remaining group of youths heading into the bush.

"To the main caves. They'll be safe there, even in a total burnover. They go pretty deep." Aunt Rose staggers, grabbing hold of the door frame in time to stop herself from tumbling. She brushes away Slate's help and mops her face with her thick tongue. "I'm okay."

"What about everyone else?" Warnner cuts off the baby's impending grizzle with a jiggle and the offer of a toy to suck on.

"We can't risk leaving yet." Aunt Rose squeezes her eyes tight, her pink face deepening into a devil red. "If we're discovered, it won't matter that we survived."

"You're going to burn your homes." Slate is quicker to catch on, noticing the bales of hay, previously used as outdoor seating, stacked against the front steps of her caravan. He scans the clearing. Similar piles are stacked near every dwelling.

"If we must." Her body tenses and her gaze hardens. "Now hurry, head for the caves with the others. Siren knows the way." Warnner holds the baby out for Aunt Rose to reclaim, then tightens his grip as she shakes her head and closes the door behind her.

"We screwed up," Slate mutters. The line of smoke is longer but no higher, burning its way to encircle the Hill, but still a distance away. "They weren't here to find me. They were here to hunt us. We might have chased them a bit further away, but they still started the fires."

"My parents are staying." Having raced back to join them, Siren fights for every breath, fear and exhaustion squeezing her lungs. "They've sent my sisters to the caves, but they said I have to leave the horses." She juts out her chin and swallows hard. "I can't. I just can't let them burn."

"If you free them, won't they run to safety?" Slate leads the way to his caravans. Swinging the door open he's relieved to see that his bags are packed and ready to go, just where Siren had thrown them, not so many hours before.

"Where's safe?" Siren asks. The wind whips across the clearing, bringing ash and smoke with it, and the low roar of fire getting closer. "They'll get confused in the smoke without someone to guide them."

"The river! Siren, you can take them across the river. It doesn't look like the fire has reached there yet," Slate suggests, kicking at the bale of hay leaning against his steps and wondering who'll set fire to his caravan once they leave.

"I can't… We can't… It's not allowed." She sniffs. Her eyes are red but she refuses to cry. "Besides, I have to get you guys to the caves."

"Stuff the rules." Blue slips from around the back of the caravan, weighed down with a heavy pack of her own. "I can take the guys to the caves. You go get your horses."

"I'm going with you." Warnner hands the baby to Blue and tosses the bags to Slate.

Slate catches them in a rugby hold, dropping his own in the process.

"Yeah, off you go while I play Sherpa again." Slate waves them away while Blue, still clutching the baby, helps him layer the bags across his back.

"I owe you, cousin." Siren throws her arms around Slate, knocking the bags back to the ground. "What would I do without you?"

The forest is thick with resinous smoke, hiding the path and causing the horses to baulk.

"It's no use. The horses are too frightened." Siren's hair streams behind her, like dark flames licking the night air. She's kicked off her boots and discarded her jacket to cope with the increasing heat, but still her body is coated in sweat and ash.

"Copy *them*." Warnner points to the two dogs, who are nipping at the horses' heels, worrying them to keep moving forward.

"What about you?"

"I'll keep up."

Siren gives him a thankful glance and begins to shake. First her jaw lengthens, then her muscles shorten, with thickened hair pushing through her skin. Transformed into something neither fully beast nor fully human, she is forced onto all fours. She lifts her muzzle, smelling the river not far ahead, but with the fire close to cutting off their access to the other side. Trusting Warnner to keep up, she growls at the hysterical horses, harassing them through the smoke and down a steep embankment, plunging after them into the icy water. The sudden chill sinks into her furred flesh.

Beside her, Warnner coughs and splutters as he struggles to keep his head above the fast-flowing water. "Keep going, you've got them on the run," he calls when she slows down for him.

A dense haze blankets the river, concealing the other

side. Siren raises her head and howls. The two dogs join her. Breaking left and right, they corral the horses, preventing them from losing their way. The dogs' claws scrabble across half submerged rocks, keeping the horses just out of range as they prance and kick against the water.

The last to reach the farthest shore, Warnner drags himself onto the crumbling bank. Still gasping for breath, he waves her onward. After giving his face a grateful lick, she leaps after the horses. Using the last of her own reserves, she propels herself upwards to the crest of the bank, where both the trees and the smoke are thinning, revealing a loose fenceline. The relief of having made it almost overwhelms her. Completely exhausted, she wants to sink into the comforting earth and sleep until her body stops aching. The two dogs creep forward, nudging her with their noses.

"All right, all right. I get it. Not done yet." Releasing her dog-like form, it takes a little effort for Siren to twist free a couple of unsecured batons and flatten the fence enough for the dogs to send the herd skittering gratefully into the empty paddock.

"Good boys. Now stay here and guard while I see if anyone's home." The two dogs cock their heads as if trying to decide if they should listen to her now that she's no longer the alpha.

"I'll keep them company." Heaving himself over the resurrected fence, Warnner returns to his grounded sprawl. "I honestly don't think I could move, even if I wanted to."

"Good boy." She gives him a grateful pat on the head. Pulling her hair back into a rough knot at her neck, Siren wipes some of the mud from her clothes. "I guess this will have to do."

She jogs, half crouched, towards a wide gravel road snaking its way past the paddock and around stands of native bush. Tucked into the crook of each bend, unlit homes stand silently.

"Where is everyone?" After the third empty home, Siren is on the verge of leaving, hoping the owners will keep the horses safe until she can return for them, when she catches the distant sound of a guitar. Leaving the road, she cuts through a patch of rimu, their needle-like leaves scratching along her cheeks, and emerges at the edge of a wide lawn. In a rough car park is a single vehicle with its bonnet raised.

At the far end of the car park a simple archway, a waharoa, lined with a bench seat on either side, that forms the ceremonial entrance to the marae. A short distance from the arch are two larger buildings; the *wharenui*, or meeting house, stands proud, both challenging and welcoming, while the *wharekai*, or kitchen, peeks from behind. On the steps leading up to the wharenui, a single porch light illuminates a solo musician strumming *Ten Guitars*.

Siren walks towards the archway, twisting her bare feet into the gravel road, hoping the unnatural noise will alert the musician to her presence.

"Kia ora. It's a little late, but visitors are always welcome." The strumming continues, but the tune is lost to inattention. "Tell me how I can help, e hoa."

"I came to see Matua Panui." The smoke has roughened her voice, making her sound older. "I want to ask him a favour."

"He's not here. Gone North. With the whole bloody marae 'cept me. Poor Taihoa: always waiting." Taihoa comes closer, swinging the guitar onto her back with a practised twist. "You're lucky I'm here. My ride's been held up by the fire cordon on the main road. Is there something I can help you with?"

"I'm not sure. I'm not even supposed to be here." Siren takes a step back, hoping the musician has poor eyesight in the dark.

"Well, you're here now, so it won't hurt to ask. I can always say no."

Taihoa is dressed entirely in black, her short wiry hair shot through with grey and her hands covered in distorted, inky patterns. She walks unsteadily, the way large people often do, rocking from side to side. When she reaches the archway, she unslings her guitar, resting it against the uprights of the arch, and takes a seat on one of the long benches. The woman unzips a bag belted around her ample waist and rolls herself a ciggy. Only after she lights and inhales does she offer Siren a puff.

Siren shakes her head. “No thanks. I don’t smoke.”

“Good on ya, girl.” Taihoa returns the ciggy to her own lips. “These things are a waste of money and a waste of life. So, are you going to ask your favour or not?”

“I should’ve asked first, but I’ve put some horses in a paddock. Near the river.” Still wary, Siren sits tentatively on the edge of the opposite bench. “It’s a large herd. They really need someone to keep an eye on them as they’ve had quite a scare. I’d stay and help if I could, but I have to get back.”

“Okay.”

“Okay what?” The quick response catches Siren off guard; she was expecting to have to argue a bit.

“Let’s go take a look at them, and you can tell me what you need me to do.” Taking up the guitar and slipping it over her shoulder, Taihoa flicks the dying cigarette stub to the ground and crushes it with the toe of her boot. She levers herself up, and motions Siren to lead the way.

“You smell terrible, girl. Did you run through the fire to get here?” She wrinkles her nose.

“No. Not really, but it was getting close by the time we crossed the river.” Siren can’t think of how to hide where she’s come from. She hadn’t planned beyond speaking with Matua Panui.

“Thought that was probably where you were from. Heard about your lot. Been there a long time, haven’t you? Some sort of cult?" There are laugh lines around Taihoa's eyes.

"Yes. I mean no. We just like to keep to ourselves."

"Must be a bit lonely, though." Despite Taihoa's slow pace, they've returned to the paddock quicker than Siren expected. "How did you manage to get this lot here all by yourself?"

"Oh, I didn't do it alone. I had Warnner and the dogs." At the mention of his name Warnner drags himself to his feet, still battling with gravity as he stumbles closer.

"You're another strange looking fella. You know, I've heard other stories about you guys—taniwha and patupaiarehe. Perhaps they aren't the myths and legends they seemed."

"Matua Panui…" Siren sputters, darting a warning glance to Warnner.

"You don't have to worry about me." Taihoa laughs and pats Siren affectionately on the back. "Not sure about the rest of the whanau, but they're not here now, are they? I'll take care of your horses. Doesn't look like my ride is going to make it here any time soon, anyway." She reaches around for her guitar, thumbing the strings in a warm-up rhythm. "But it might be safer if you stayed, too. That fire doesn't look like it's going to burn out any time soon."

"We can't. I'll come back for them as soon as I can. But we have to get back. My parents don't know I'm here. They think I'm helping to hide the young ones." Siren clamps a hand over her own mouth. She's spoken too freely.

"You mean your people haven't evacuated?" The horses stop their munching, as Taihoa hits a sour chord.

"We can't risk being seen." Siren's words are almost inaudible.

"Bring them here." Taihoa pats the guitar. "They'd be welcome."

"They wouldn't come. Everyone is staying…to burn our own homes if necessary." She feels guilty about being so honest, but she's unable to lie to this good neighbour

"What about the children? Surely your way of life is not worth their lives?" Taihoa picks at the strings, the sound jarring.

"No, of course not. They're safe underground until the fire's gone." Even Siren can hear her doubt, her voice quavering over the word *safe*.

"And afterwards? When your homes are destroyed?" Taihoa asks tentatively.

"Maybe I'll have to ask for another favour."

"Well then, I think I'll be able to help you with that, too."

CHAPTER TWENTY

The cave is larger than the one Slate visited with his Grandfather. In fact, it's larger than any he visited with his parents—and warmer, too, with heat emanating from an underground thermal source beneath its floor. But it's still a cave. A short walk from the entrance, it opens into the largest section, its domed ceiling blinking with green constellations of glow worms.

Beneath Slate and Blue's watchful gaze, the floor space is being rapidly transformed into a cooking area, the deep fire pit in the middle already sending out an inviting aroma for empty bellies. Along the outer walls someone has hung lines of fairy lights leading into a number of smaller caves, set up as sleeping accommodation and storage. The lights are an unnecessary use of the portable generator, but they put the smaller children in a playful mood. Cries of delight bounce off walls and ceilings as the children race from room to room, checking out each area. Older siblings and guardians cast out warnings and admonitions like fishermen with hookless lines, before giving up and turning their attention to their own tasks. They're equally keen to be distracted from what could be unfolding beyond the cave walls.

After a brief negotiation with the triplets, who have taken charge of resettlement, Slate and Blue are assigned to the foremost sleeping area near the mouth of the cave. When they'd arrived, overloaded with personal belongings but not much else, they'd been relieved to discover that someone else was in charge of the babies. They handed over Rose's little boy, then found themselves with idle hands.

"Slate?"

"Yeah, Blue?" Slate makes no move to unpack, falling back into old habits of resisting getting too comfortable. Instead, he sprawls atop their combined luggage.

"I want to see my sister." Even more resistant to making herself at home, Blue has spent their short time in the cave checking the entrance, a narrow tunnel slanting gently towards the surface. They'd been the last to arrive through the tunnel, and Slate had suffered a bout of panic as he crawled on knees and elbows, pushing the bags before him into the dark unknown.

"What?" Slate mumbles, not bothering to move his mud-caked arm from over his face.

"We can't stop the fire, right?" Blue crouches beside him, keeping her voice to a whisper.

"Right," he replies, rolling on his side, careful with his still delicate head, like an old man with a hangover.

"And we can't stop people from coming to fight it." She continues rocking back on her heels as he sits a little straighter.

"So?" he asks again. Avoiding her pained expression, he uses the tips of his fingers to massage his forehead, still tender but beginning to heal.

"So, the last time I saw Malice, I wanted to kill her." Blue's voice catches in a half sob. "I don't want that to be her last memory of me."

"We're going to get through this." Slate stops his massaging and catches hold of her hands. Her head narrowly misses hitting the cave wall with her wild rocking.

"Are we?" Blue squeezes his hands, then lets go. "They've set the whole bloody mountain on fire just to get us."

"They won't find us here." He gestures to the entrance. "Siren said they'd never find the caves and I can see why. Who'd be brave enough to crawl through a hole in the ground unless they knew what they'd find on the other side? Other than the white rabbit and us, of course."

"How can we be sure they don't know? You're not the only one who was tortured." Blue doesn't need to remind him how her father had returned, or that they are not the only ones who'd been at the church. "I want to believe they didn't say anything, but even if they didn't, with the forest burnt to the ground, what's left to hide us?"

"I was hoping for a better ending than crispy critter."

"Who's a crispy critter?" Standing just outside their sleeping area, Stella's question reminds them that they're not alone.

"You will be if you don't mind your own business," Blue growls, baring her sharpened teeth.

"Fine. Keep your secrets." Never far behind, Nova drags her sister back into a game of shadows with some of the older youths, including Rip and Fade.

"You can stay, but I'm going." Blue pulls her hoodie over her head, wincing as the sleeves squeeze her bandaged wrists.

"Oh, I'm going. It's not like they need either of us here." Slate grabs his jacket, brushes the dirt from the knees of his jeans and prepares to follow her back through the tunnel.

No one tries to stop them leaving, but then no one has noticed, too busy with their own distractions. The crawl back up the tunnel, unencumbered by bags and babies, is shorter than the crawl down. Once outside, they discover that, while time inside the cave slows, the fire has not. All around them thick smoke swirls, bringing with it a flurry of dancing sparks too weak to have flown from far away. They both react with a start to the loud boom of a tree exploding, overwhelmed by the raging fire. Slate briefly debates the benefit of keeping covered against the rising heat, but he follows Blue's lead, zipping up his jacket and pulling his t-shirt over his nose and mouth, keeping his breathing shallow and regular against the ash and his rising panic.

"Sorry. I don't think I can go in." The mouth of the cave is wider than he remembers, but last time he hadn't been thinking about where he was heading, only about how he would apologise for his behaviour.

"Are you sure?" Blue hesitates, casting a glance towards the roaring fire.

He nods, no more eager to stay behind than he is to follow.

"I'll be as quick as I can," says Blue. "I don't want to be stuck here either."

The entrance splits into a maze of tunnels, wide and high, giving her ample room to run. It has been years since she'd crept into the home of the Lost on the heels of Grandmother, her curiosity overcoming her fear. She remembers the way, just as she remembers any place she's travelled before; and just as she remembers Grandmother transforming into a creature so fierce that in that moment Blue had realised the line between any of them and the Lost was just an uncontrolled outburst of anger away. In a way, it surprises her more that Malice is here, and not her.

"Blue?"

Her sister is wedged into the corner of her cell, the dirt floor showing signs of a recent scuffle or an inept attempt at digging an escape. Malice would have resisted her confinement until it was undeniable; Blue would have done the same.

"Who else?" Blue leans into the bars of her sister's cage, squeezing her cheeks between the cool steel. "They really did stick you in here."

"I didn't give them much of a choice." Malice stands up, wiping the dust from her clothes She takes a hesitant step forward, then pauses shamefully as Blue responds with a step back. "What's wrong? What's going on? Why are you here?" The questions tumble. The other Lost, roused by the sisters' reunion, stir fretfully. "You smell burnt."

"The Hill is on fire. We think..." This isn't what she's come to talk about, but now that she's here, Blue is glad to talk about something other than her feelings.

"Slate's mum," Malice calculates, slumping back to the ground. "I really messed up, didn't I?"

"Yeah, you did." Blue follows her sister's lead and sits cross-legged on the floor, her hands resting on her knees.

"Smart woman. Always knew that Leo would never fall in love with someone because of their looks." Malice bangs her head against the bars; the curved metal leaves parallel lines of red from chin to cheek to forehead. "Exposure to the world... We'd never be safe again." She runs her hands up and down the bars, her muscles pushing up ridges of spikes along her forearms. "You have to let me out. I can help."

"There's nothing you can do. The fire is almost here. We may not even have enough time to make it back to where the children are hiding." Blue curls her fingers into a fist, releases them and repeats the calming actions.

"I didn't mean I would come with you." Malice pulls herself up and begins to pace behind the bars.

"What, then?" Blue watches her sister. Her hair needs re-braiding, and the pinched look to her face hints that it's been a long while since she's eaten.

"No one else has come, but I'm here. I can hide this secret at least." The creature in the next cage throws himself against the bars, shedding a few flattened feathers as he claws the empty air.

"You want to protect these guys? No. I can't let you out... I just can't trust you." Blue shuffles back to greater safety.

She avoids looking at any of the Lost too closely, in case there's a shadow of someone she has forgotten behind their eyes.

"Then go before you're trapped here, too." Malice picks up one of the broken feathers and strokes it along her cheek, but she doesn't turn around.

"I'll come back. When this is all over. There's more I want to say."

"What are you doing here?" Nearing the entrance, Blue sees Slate grappling with a dishevelled youngling.

"Nova…" Stella is covered in ash, and she cradles her singed tail around her middle, exposing a line of reddened, burnt flesh.

"They followed us but got separated in the smoke," Slate explains. Stella twists away from his grip, but he easily re-traps her, one arm wrapped firmly around her shoulders.

"You silly girls. Why didn't you just stay where you were told?" Blue gingerly checks the younger girl's tail.

"We don't like being left behind." Stella repositions her tail, letting it hang limply over one arm.

"Nova might have thought we were heading back to the clearing," Slate suggests, changing his grip to a comforting, one-armed hug. "I know the way. I can check and meet you both back at the cave."

"No. I'm not going back. Take Stella with you, she needs that burn looked at." Blue waves them away, her fingers drawing clear lines in the thickening smoke. "I have to stay here. I can't leave my sister behind, and someone needs to protect this place from being discovered."

No longer is their journey through the forest a race to keep ahead of the ash and smoke, but an obstacle course around pockets of burning punga and fallen trees, the fire jumping from one fuel source to another. Slate half drags, half carries Stella forward. She chokes and stumbles, her eyes watering from the sting of the acrid smoke. Ash clings to her fur. Slate marvels at the lack of effect the rising heat has on his own internal mechanisms. He's never been affected by weather extremes that left his parents crippled in air-conditioned hotel rooms, gulping iced drinks through the night. But he's also never experienced temperatures so high as to blister skin and singe hair. Still breathing through the neck of his t-shirt, his eyes pierce the smoky haze and navigate the worst of the fire spots.

They burst from the forest and into the clearing.

"There she is," Stella cries. Slate lets her go, pushes back his hoodie, and pulls his t-shirt from his face.

"Mum?" Blinking, unbelieving, Slate stops in his tracks. On one side of the clearing groups of people are laying water-soaked cloths across the roofs of their homes. Steam hisses as the water transforms from liquid to gas before rising and mingling with the smoke. Another group furiously digs a fire-break between their homes and the forest's edge. Using spades and hoes, they scrape back the earth, exposing its heavy clay to the air, while others cut back the forest with axes and even their bare hands, ripping the earth clean. Desperate to save their homes, none of them have noticed Slate's mother struggling up the front steps of the abandoned lodge. With one arm clasped around Nova's middle and the other entangled in a handful of Stella's hair, she slams the door closed behind them.

"Mum?" Slate bounds up the steps. Shoving hard against the door, he ploughs through a bookcase, knocked over to block his way. His mother drags her captives towards the end of the room. The lodge had been the first to be cleared, along with the children. Upturned tables and wooden boxes are the only signs left of how hastily the room had been emptied, prized possessions safely stowed in the underground caves.

He finds his voice. “What are you doing here, Mum? Let the girls go.”

His mother pushes the girls through the door of a smaller storage room and jams a fallen chair under the handle. The girls bang against the door, their cries for help muffled but their panic clear. The handle twists as if it is being turned by a malevolent spirt, but the chair holds.

“Mum, it’s not safe here. We need to leave. Let Stella and Nova go.” The air is surprisingly clear; the well-sealed lodge keeping the smoke at bay, but it is distorted by tiny waves of heat rolling off the outer walls and dissipating near the cooler centre. He presses a hand against the wall. The wooden planks shrink under his touch, their moisture escaping inward, leaving the outer layer cracking under the attack.

“I’m looking for my son. I tried to save him, but they stole him from me—again.” Affected by the heat, his mother pulls away from the walls, seeking the coolest part of the room, but staying between Slate and his objective. She tugs at the collar of her shirt, revealing a ring of ash-free skin, like a noose around her neck.

“Mum, you’re not well. Why don’t you come with me and we’ll get some help?” He holds up his hands and takes a step forward.

“Get away from me. I don’t need your help.” She picks up an abandoned broom from the floor, stabbing at him with the bristles. “They didn’t believe me at first. I had to prove it. How tricky the monsters are. But they believe me now.”

“You mean that man and that woman, Mum? The ones who hurt my friends?” It’s hard for him not to run a hand over the stumps of his horns.

“Stop calling me by that name, demon. You wear his face

but you are not my son." The broom becomes a flailing limb, sweeping across the ceiling.

Taking shelter behind one of the central poles carved in honour of ancestors, Slate glimpses faces at the window. He darts a glance towards the back, where the twins have redoubled their efforts to break through the door. Thankfully, the faces duck out of sight before his mother notices.

"If you haven't come back for me, then why are you here?" Slate blocks the window with his body, the heat searing across his back, seeking to set his clothes alight. His mother continues her frantic pacing. She doesn't notice that the door handle is no longer twisting.

"I… I…" She seems disorientated by his question, she drops the broom. It clatters to the floor, distracting her long enough for Warnner to sneak off a nod, as he's joined at the window by the worried faces of Siren and her sisters.

"You came to find me, didn't you? You wanted to save me from the fire." Slate ignores the urgent tap on the window, for a moment winded by a wave of heat. It sends a chill across his skin, and it feels wonderful. But his mother is struggling, her eyes blinking away streams of sweat from her eyelashes.

"We don't have a lot of time," Slate says.

"Yes, the fire. I needed to burn the Hill to save my son." She pulls back her sleeves, exposing the scars running white up her arms. "See? I saved him before from the fire and I can do it again."

"Mum…" His voice cracks. He runs his fingers over her burns. The skin is smooth and shiny. "I remember. You had a choice. It was Dad or me. Dad was knocked out, but I couldn't undo my seatbelt. You looked at him, but you chose me. You saved me, Mum. But you don't have to save me now. I'm all right."

"No, no, no. I don't believe you. You're trying to trick

me." She rips her hands from his grip and shoves him hard, sending him sprawling across the floor.

"Ahhh." Instinctively, he wrestles with the leg attached to the boot heel that grinds into the back of his hand with bone-breaking force.

"Trapp. What are you doing here?" Slate's mother stumbles over her words as she fidgets with her clothes and pats her frizzy hair. "You should be in hospital."

Slate grimaces at the pain in his hand.

"A third-degree burn, in the shape of a hand?" Trapp presses a thickly bandaged arm to his chest and makes a low bow, his head lowering to meet Slate's own while his heel twists a little harder. "Now why would the threat of amputation keep me from the hunt?"

Slate sees the fist descending in slow motion and braces for the pain as his lip splits.

"The hunt is over, Trapp. The fire is here." Responding to her words, the outer wall bursts into flames. "But we need to leave now or we'll be burned, too."

"Not without collecting my payment." Trapp grabs Slate by the hand and slices the blade of his short knife across the base of his fingers.

"No, not him." She knocks the chair away and jerks open the door she's been so zealously guarding. "Let him go. You can have these two."

"Are they invisible?" Even with the room beginning to fill with smoke and flames, the only sign of the girls' recent occupation is a stack of wooden boxes leading up to a high, broken window.

"No. I..." She swings her gaze from the empty room to Slate, his mouth caught in a silent scream as he tries to stem the flow of blood by pressing the stumps of two missing fingers against his chest.

"It's him *and* that green bitch." Trapp laughs as he kicks away Slates fingers. They sizzle as they cook in the encroaching flames. "My fee has just doubled."

"Let him go and I'll show you. I'll show you where they'll have hidden chi… smaller ones. I've been there before."

Trapp lifts his foot.

Freed, Slate rolls to his feet. Taking advantage of his movement his mother steps in front of him, her head barely coming up to his chin.

"No. Mother. You can't. You can't." Slate's voice is raw with pain and fear.

The room is suddenly silent, as if all the air has been sucked out to prevent sound moving from source to audience. And then it explodes, sending them spinning away from each other, the room splintering into fiery shrapnel.

CHAPTER TWENTY-ONE

At daybreak, the fire is only a scattering of slow-burning embers. Grey clouds of dust settle over the Hill, a shroud pinpricked by the first rays of sun. The bush is edged by blackened stumps and smoking earth, a wasteland of shattered shelters, memories coated in ash.

Above the dawn chorus, Siren calls Slate's name.

"Siren, you should let the others look for him. He wouldn't like you to see… if he's …"

Side by side, Warnner and Siren bend to pick up and toss aside the burnt timber framing that had once been the heart of their community.

"No, Warnner. I know he's fine. He can't *not* be. It was my job to look after him." She wipes away tears with the back of her hand, drawing lines of soot across her cheeks. The fine dust cloaks their clothes—ghosts among the ashes. "I should have stayed."

They're not the only ones casting their eyes from side to side, hunting for some familiar item to rescue from the wreckage of their homes. But all that remains is broken, bent, and burned beyond salvage. The emergency crews have been brutal in their determination to gain control over the fire. Throughout the night, the water-filled bellies of plane after plane opened over their target. The ground crews were manned by locals, many from the nearby marae, who were quick to shield outsiders from the truth as the community allowed the confusion to hide their true nature. There's no sign that the fire-starters had any other plan than to send the inhabitants of the Hill scurrying into their burrows for safety like frightened animals.

The breeze picks up, creating tiny tornadoes of dust across the rubble and lifting the smell of blackened flesh towards them.

"Noooo!" Siren drops to her knees and claws frantically at the ruins of the lodge, shoving aside the crumbling remains of boxes and beams with unbelievable strength.

Beside her Warnner redoubles his effort, tossing the larger pieces into a semicircle behind them.

"He's here, he's here." Siren's cry catches in her throat as she uncovers a bare foot, unblemished by the fire.

"How? What?" Seizing on her discovery, Warnner pushes her to one side. "Let me do this. He shouldn't be alive, but he is and he won't be happy you saw him naked."

"Hey. How are you feeling?" Siren stands awkwardly, splitting the light from the tent flap in two as she picks at the skin around her thumb nail. She still can't believe he survived. In the end, it hadn't been his mother's sacrifice—covering his body with her own. Instead, it had been his father's genetic gift that let the fire blister his skin, but not burn his flesh to the bone.

"Good. Like someone dropped a house on me and then set it on fire." A healing burn on the left side of his face puckers and pulls at the corner of his mouth.

"Oh well then, why are you still lying around in bed?" Siren's not without her own injuries, lucky not to have lost her sight along with her eyebrows and eyelashes, as she fought her way back from the other side of the river. She tucks her shortened hair behind an ear with a trembling hand. "You should see outside. The carnival is back."

"I'm just waiting for your boyfriend. He's my right hand until these babies grow back." Slate waves a heavily bandaged fist like a club. "My fingers itch like crazy."

"Sorry I'm late." Warnner brushes past Siren, still hovering in the doorway, stopping briefly to drop a quick kiss on her cheek. "Everyone seems to need me today."

"I just wanted to tell you how sorry I am, Slate." Siren ducks her head to hide her tears. "About your mum. I should've been there…" She reaches for Slate's good hand, squeezing it tightly to telegraph all she can't say.

"I'm glad you weren't. Mum didn't need to save me when I was a child, and yet she never forgave herself." Slate lets Warnner help him sit up. "I don't need a protector, Siren. I never did. What I always needed was a place to call home."

EPILOGUE

From the steps of the newly rebuilt lodge, Slate watches Siren and Warnner emerge from the regenerating bushline. He smiles as they laugh, Warnner giving Siren a playful push and Siren gleefully swinging her pack and narrowly missing his head. In response, Warnner turns his stumble into a roll and flips to his feet in mock pursuit. Siren squeals and runs to hide behind Slate, who makes no attempt to defend her.

"Getting those tumbling skills down." Slate offers Warnner a fist bump in greeting, the stumps of his fingers shiny with new growth. They itch less now, though in the moments of quiet he can almost hear them growing.

"I finally listened to him, though I'm still not sure he's right," Warnner says.

He hooks Siren's bag and tosses it to one of the triplets, who passes it along until it's packed away with the rest of their gear in their caravan. All around the edge of the clearing, other restored caravans are being loaded up in readiness to leave. Many of the vehicles are new; too many had been beyond salvation, their burnt-out husks reassembled into metallic sculptures of remembrance around the edges of the clearing. Slate had designed a few of them, including smaller ones now welded like medals of valour to the bonnets of every travelling home.

"Listen to who?" Slate asks.

Siren wrestles Warnner's bag free and throws it over her head to find its own place among their baggage.

"My councillor, Noel Ledger, back at Hearth-Thorn Centre," Warnner says, catching Siren around the waist and pulling her close. "He told me I needed something to channel my anger—so I wouldn't feel the need to destroy the world. He even suggested it'd be through the performing arts." Releasing Siren from his grip, Warnner bends and turns a backflip into a tuck, his up-flung hands an invitation to the triplets to pull him onto the roof-rack of the truck.

"I think I like him better when I can't see him clearly." Siren cuts away her adoring gaze, her smile inexpertly hidden behind fanned fingers.

"So, you're leaving?" Slate says, threading his fingers through hers.

"So, you're staying," Siren says, squeezing his hand in return.

"Well, with you and what's-his-name going on the road, Gramps needs me." He guides her to the truck where the others wait.

"His name is Warnner, and Grandfather's name is Barnabas." Siren gives him a stern gaze.

Less interested in their farewells, Nova and Stella dance around them like a pair of performing monkeys, before peeling off to be swallowed by the forest, leaving behind only the echoes of their laughter.

"I'll miss you."

"I'll see you in July for the Welcoming. Someone still needs their arse Marked." Siren cups the side of his face, pressing their noses together and breathing deeply in and out.

"Oh, so that's where they'll put it? On his arse?" Warnner re-joins them, slapping Slate on the back and shaking his hand in congratulations. "Good choice."

"Come on, guys. The carnival waits for neither beast nor

beauty." Blue pulls herself into the driver's seat, patting the door encouragingly for Siren and Warnner to join her. "Time to move your money-maker."

"I'll be fine, Siren." Slate gives her a sad smile. "It's summer, and I'm home."

GLOSSARY

Aotearoa: the Māori name for New Zealand
Cutty grass: New Zealand slang for pampas grass
Haere ra: goodbye
Hoa: friend
Kereru: native New Zealand wood pigeon
Kia ora, Matua. Kei te pei he koe: Hello, elder. How are you?
Māori: indigenous New Zealanders
Marae: a group of buildings in a Maori community
Matariki: the beginning of the Maori new year
Matua: (important) male adult / teacher
Patupaiarehe: fairies
Ponga: trunk of a New Zealand tree fern
Pohutukawa: a New Zealand tree with red flowers
Puriri tree: a New Zealand tree
Rimu: a New Zealand tree
Taniwha: a powerful creature / guardian
Tapu: sacred / prohibited / forbidden / protected
Togs: a swimming suit
Tōtara: a New Zealand tree
Waharoa: a main entranceway
Waimaunganui: water-mountain-big
Whanau: family
Wharekai: kitchen building
Wharenui: meeting house